SHIMMER

ERIC BARNES

SHIMMER

UNBRIDLED BOOKS

Unbridled Books

Copyright © 2009 by Eric Barnes

First paperback edition, 2010
Unbridled Books trade paperback ISBN 978-1-936071-59-3

Library of Congress Cataloging-in-Publication Data

Barnes, Eric.
Shimmer / by Eric Barnes.
p. cm.
ISBN 978-1-932961-67-6 (hardcover)
ISBN 978-1-936071-59-3 (paperback)
1. Chief executive officers—Fiction.   2. High technology industries—
Corrupt practices—Fiction.   I. Title.
PS3602.A8338S54 2010
813'.6—dc22
2009053801

1 3 5 7 9 10 8 6 4 2

Book Design by SH • CV

First Printing

For Elizabeth, Reed, Mackenzie, Andrew and Lucy.
We are our own party.

'd started having dreams where I could fly. Not dreams where I took firm, superhero steps that catapulted me up and into the sky. Not dreams where I soared at high speed over rivers, mountains and streams. Instead they were only dreams where I brought my right knee to my chest, in another moment lifted my left knee from the ground, my tightly curled body now hovering a few feet in the air.

"If you were a food, what food would you be?"

It was Julie who responded to Whitley's question, not hesitating for a second, speaking as if this alone were her reason for working at this company. Julie said flatly, "Cream."

One hour into my Monday morning staff meeting, and the sensation of flight from my previous night's dream still hung lightly around my thoughts, a distant and comforting feeling made more real with every digression we took.

"A chef's salad," said our CFO, Cliff Rees.

Whitley nodded in appreciation. Julie's soft jaw shifted left as she mouthed Cliff's words. Leonard paused for a moment, heavy eyes leaving the pages of the network overview in his hands. Cliff himself tapped buttons on his calculator, then squinted carefully at the results.

"No, wait," Cliff said, lifting a hand from his calculator, interrupting Leonard before he could answer. "Sorry. I meant a cobb salad."

It was six in the morning. We had been here since five. We had already approved $200 million in monthly expenses, agreed to acquire eight suppliers in Taiwan and Korea, authorized the opening of three new field offices in England and Ireland. Monday, and the day had just begun. Monday, and all of us had spent the whole weekend in this building. Monday, and we would not go home till sometime late that night.

This was Core Communications, a $20 billion company linking mainframe computers worldwide via a high-speed network of low-altitude satellites, fiber-optic cable and dedicated connections to the Internet backbone.

"Mousse," Leonard said thickly, gold and broken light crossing his warm and round and biggest of faces, the sun rising to his left, the light somehow caught, then scattered by the high windows of the conference room. "Because all my life," he said, "people have thought of me as pudding."

Leonard, our head of technical development, was the smartest person I'd ever known.

"Would you be chocolaty rich?" Julie asked him, her small hands lifting from the surface of the table, her short fingers spreading as they met at her chin, her hands and arms and face all streaked in yellow and shadow.

"Would you have a texture so velvety," Cliff asked slowly, smile growing, "pearly thick and buttery sweet?"

Cliff and Julie shared an unspoken fascination with TV commercials, every Monday ready to mimic the coded rhythms and grammatically senseless phrases each had heard as a child.

Julie nodded. "That and more."

"I would be a filet," Whitley was saying, absently dragging two knuckles across the steel and wood conference table, the smoothness of her wrists scraping lightly across a hundred flaws and ridges, as always lowering her eyes behind her black hair as she thought, never hiding, never shy, just pulling in on herself for a moment to think. "A filet cooked well with only pepper and salt."

As I listened, I couldn't stop myself from floating toward the high windows, my dream now taking me out into the twentieth-story air, flying in my way above the streets and cars and people of TriBeca, drifting toward the streaks of sunlight now reflecting off the shore of New Jersey.

"I want to write a novel that will be billed as a *sexcapade*," I heard Julie saying.

"Why are you so preoccupied by sex?" Cliff asked.

"I'm not preoccupied by sex," Julie said, the edges of her teeth just showing as she turned her head, smiled. "I'm preoccupied by sexual innuendo."

Core was a company marked by the barely restrained sounds of a just-tempered joy. Five thousand employees so overly devoted to this place and each other. All so focused on the clients we served, all so happy in the work we did. Three years ago there had been just thirty people. Now the five thousand all took direction from us.

"The French are on board for the marketing campaign in Europe," Whitley was saying, the group easily moving into the next topic, the conversation shifting in steady, rolling waves.

"The EU has approved a renegotiation of the Scottish buyout," Julie said.

"The banks have signed off on the Asian joint venture," Cliff said.

I faded out, I tuned back in, not bored, not uninterested. Just unable to put aside my flying, floating dream.

"You can't say *stroke* in a meeting," Whitley was saying to Leonard, taking on the friendly tone of a lifeless HR manager leading a sexual harassment seminar, carefully articulating selected words of selected sentences. "*Stroke* has been deemed *inappropriate*."

"You can't say *vagina*," Julie was saying to no one in particular, she too highlighting selected words as she spoke, "but you can say *vaginal delivery.*"

"You can't say *penis,*" Cliff was saying as he cleaned off the screen of his small calculator, "but you can say *penal colony.*"

"You can't say *insert,*" Julie was saying as she passed out reports to everyone, "but you can say *insertion.*"

"No," Whitley said, voice returning to its normal tone. "You can say insert."

Julie shook her head. "Not around me."

Our stock price was up. Sales had quadrupled. We'd just bought this building. I now owned this view. These were the days after electronic commerce, after e-business and the dot-com layoffs, after the double burst in the market's bubble. The days when the market, the business press, day traders and the most level-headed of investors all looked at Core and saw a real company, a real product, real sales, real profits.

Ours was the bulletproof stock, they all said. Ours was the company without real competition or strategic threats.

That few of these outsiders actually understood what we did—this was unimportant.

"Planning for the next annual meeting has already begun," Julie was saying. "There will be insightful 3D bar charts. We have prepared color bullet points. Leonard will conduct a tour of the redesigned Web site."

Four of the brightest people, thirty to forty years old, all sitting around me, leaning heavily on the metal conference table or pushed back from the group, teetering effortlessly on the rear legs of their chairs. All caught in the spreading sunrise, each cast against a simple background of steel and glass and birch and sisal.

And all of them tired. Each silently carrying the accumulated exhaustion of the three years spent building this company. Seventy-hour weeks, separation from their families, stress beyond boundaries none of them could find time to see.

I'd slept just two hours before arriving in this office. I'd gotten e-mails from all of them at two in the morning, or three.

"Cliff, you'll play the role of cost-conscious CFO," Julie was saying, "sprinkling your glowing financial projections with penny-pinching jokes about the excessive use of tape."

Cliff nodded quickly. "Check."

"Whitley, you'll play the role of the demanding yet creative COO," Julie said, "the strategic spirit for us all who humbly portrays herself as nothing short of the life and mind behind our ongoing expansion and evolution."

Whitley blinked twice in affirmation. "Prepare yourselves for a generous overuse of the word *interactive*."

Julie nodded quickly. "Check."

I spoke for the first time in fifteen minutes. "And I assume," I started to say, words seeming to flow as slowly as my intermittent journey over the rooftops nearby, "that I will play the role of the vaguely mysterious, elusively appealing, yet charmingly effervescent CEO?"

Julie cocked her head, squinting her eyes, smiling with a warmth so artificial as she said, "As long as you keep using words like *elusive* and *effervescent*."

Soothing, calming, steady. Aimless but important banter at the start of a week. Deceptively meaningless. Functionally critical. Our Monday meetings were a microcosm of the disjointed culture rampant in the company around us, our detailed assessment of current operations always balanced against a constant array of offhand asides. The company's most productive meetings were inevitably filled with half-wrought reviews of movies seen that weekend, with musical interludes marked by an almost karaoke-like fervor, with vague but enticing insights into each other's personal lives. For us, on a Monday, this was what settled the senior staff into its shared rhythms, it was what we relied on to set the tone, to get us ready, to prepare us for another week of this life.

And it was a phenomenon that would be repeated all morning in departments and groups companywide.

"Sioux City confirms they are six months ahead of schedule," Leonard was saying.

"Omaha sees no hurdles to the pending acquisition," Cliff was saying.

"Cincinnati is ready for an internal expansion," Whitley was saying.

"Bellingham is poised to start its Asian production," Julie was saying.

I nodded. I agreed. I rejected. I deferred. *Yes,* I said. *Good,* I said. *Absolutely not,* I whispered. *Please, tell me,* I asked carefully, *tell me this is not for real.*

The three years had passed at a frightening speed, forming a connection among us all that seemed to have been built over a decade or more.

"We use St. Louis to shift cash into Omaha, right?" I asked.

"Clearly," Whitley said. "Like Chicago to Cleveland. It's the same."

"Whose group is watching for another false start on the lock boxes?" I asked, starting to point at Cliff, and Julie was already nodding.

"Cliff's," she answered. "But the real concern is the last-minute changeover of outdated networking."

"Yet when it's done you'll write your sexcapade," Cliff said.

Julie leaned toward Cliff. She smiled wide. She said quietly, "Fiction to be read with one hand. An underappreciated genre."

Cliff shook his head seriously. "You can't say *genre* in a meeting."

Cliff really did seem like some sort of salad. Leonard really was pudding on the verge of becoming mousse. Julie was unquestionably the smoothest, purest cream. Whitley was nothing if not well-done beef.

What food am I?

I floated toward the high, dim ceiling. The sunrise was spreading from the sky to the shore to our windows and walls. Like always, the sun seemed to offer the only light in the building.

"He's disarming and confident," Whitley said.

"He's focused and sure," Cliff said.

They were talking about me. It's not that they'd realized I had floated away—the senior staff had long enjoyed addressing me as if I were not there, once again deflating the unreal aura surrounding me inside and outside the company.

"He's energized and engaged," Julie said.

"Our confidence in his leadership grows every minute," Cliff said.

"He's salmon cooked rare over an open fire," Whitley said, and the rest paused. Pictured it. Then all began to nod.

I smiled. I thanked them. After a moment, I stood to leave.

Once more I remembered that I would bankrupt them all. Cliff with his six kids. Julie with her newborn. Whitley, who'd just turned down top jobs at the largest software and telecom companies in the world. Leonard, whose father had been with my father, back when the company had employed just thirty people. All four of them with their homes and families and futures leveraged completely against their share of the company's stock. Like hundreds of people throughout the company, these four would be left with nothing.

And although I'd never wanted it to be this way, I was set to walk away with millions.

CHAPTER 1

At some point it would become clear that I was not well. The people who would see it first, they saw it and had no reason to care. The people who should have seen it next, they were in no state to notice. Yet somewhere, at some point, I would see it myself. Probably I could have seen it all along. But then, back then, I was not seeing anything very clearly at all.

I was Robbie Case, the thirty-five-year-old CEO and largest single shareholder of Core Communications, a new world company that had, in just thirty-six months, become the de facto highway for the nation's critical financial information. Two-thirds of U.S. mortgage lenders, half of the insurance companies and three-quarters of the nation's pension-processing centers passed information over the Core network. Aerospace, automotive, defense industries—all used our network to transfer their most important information.

And, as our salespeople were trained to say at this point in their pitch—pausing carefully, smiling slightly, leaning forward in their chairs as they lowered their voices just a bit—"Keep in mind that the statistics I've just given you are, already, a few hours old."

Maybe, looking back, it was our offhand arrogance that I regret most.

We were not techies. We employed no geeks. Instead we were the work-obsessed.

Work has meaning. The money is secondary. Being here I find a kind of personal joy.

At least that's what it felt like at Core. Because by the year 2007, Core had turned the tediously complex, the horribly mundane, the deathly boring into something so technically cutting-edge and so financially lucrative that potential new employees had to enter a lottery to be considered for a job. The press of all shapes and sizes had to wait—for months at a time—before they had the chance to do an "insider" story on us. And investors and banks undercut each other in the most inappropriate ways for a chance to place ever larger amounts of money with Core.

"We could announce the creation of electricity," Whitley had once said to me, "and the investors would line up to hand us their cash."

My father had founded this company as the Mainframe Supply Center Inc. in 1970. Operating from a small office in Northern California, he soon built it into a $26 million reseller of hardware supplies for mainframe computer users. "This company," he had said to me when I was in my twenties, "is a small but highly profitable, third-party distributor of metal widgets and plastic doohickeys for a niche market of the computing industry."

I mouthed the word *doohickeys*. I pictured the word *widgets*. Rarely had I heard my father use a silly word. And never had he used one in conjunction with his company.

He smiled and nodded back, mouthing *doohickeys* in sync with me. "It is no more or less than that," he said.

Then, in 2004, just a few months after my father died and left the company to me, I bought into an invention. A system, really, of hardware and software and satellite uplinks and data protocols that allowed mainframe computers around the world to transfer information to other mainframes, or any other kind of computer, at heretofore unimaginable speeds. Our product, known simply as a Blue Box, did something that had previously existed only as theory and speculation— by pulling information from the mainframes at unthinkable speeds, the Blue Box freed up the mainframes to do, quite simply, even more work. It meant that companies faced with spending millions of dollars on mainframes and related servers could instead free up existing machines by spending just hundreds of thousands on Blue Boxes. The financial benefits were obvious, the productivity gains tremendous.

And, just as appealing to the freakishly obstinate tech people who inevitably had to agree to the use of our system, the Blue Box represented the impossible fulfillment of a long-standing, seemingly unattainable goal. Since the 1970s, companies, universities, independent entrepreneurs—all had been trying to do what we'd done. All had sought to pull information from mainframes at the speeds we'd attained. And all of them had failed.

The process had become known as drawing blood from a mainframe.

Once we introduced our system, I immediately refocused our handful of employees onto developing and marketing Blue Boxes worldwide. We began to sign up our first clients. New customers called us before we could call them. We increased our prices. Investors began to knock on the door of our New York office. We began to buy up those mainframe networking companies that we did not put out of business. We could not hire employees fast enough to support the people signing up for our service. We went public in a blur of upbeat newspaper articles and extended cable news features. We increased our customer base by a factor of ten. Then twenty.

Then thirty.

Then forty.

We did it all in three years.

And now, on that same Monday morning when I'd been floating out my office window, skimming across the rooftops of the cold Manhattan buildings around me, now Core was just ten weeks from hitting a record $21 billion in sales. We were four weeks from acquiring our one hundredth company. We were two days from hiring our five thousandth employee.

It seemed to every observer that we could not be stopped.

When he'd started the company, my father hadn't ever set a goal of becoming rich. He had become quite wealthy nonetheless, and for him that had been a very nice benefit of doing good work, of satisfying his clients, of building a valued reputation in his industry.

At some point, though, the desire to make money for its own sake did overtake Core.

Except that, three years later, I still wasn't sure if it was money that had ultimately driven my decisions. Because I'd spent almost none of the money I'd made. A near billionaire without second homes, sports teams, not even a car.

And so maybe it was something else that overtook me. A desire to grow, or face challenges, or find prominence.

Maybe.

There were two spreadsheets capturing the future of this company. One was a financial model showing a near unlimited growth in revenue, a moderate rise in overhead and expenses, a steadily increasing profit margin. Three hundred and ninety-two pages in length, it was the model I'd given to the first group of investors three years earlier. And it was the blueprint that still guided our daily operations and massive growth.

The other spreadsheet I kept hidden, buried deep in a private folder on the hard drive of my computer. It was password protected. It was key encrypted. It was filled with forty pages of fairly meaningless numbers— some personal expenses, a handful of stock investments. But this same file held a hidden, eight-hundred-page spreadsheet. And in those eight hundred pages were the details of the collapse I'd set in motion. There were the descriptions of secret networking, the records of borrowed satellite time, connections between shadow companies funneling money among offshore accounts, locations of hundreds of mainframes and servers hidden quite publicly in buildings and warehouses worldwide. There were procedures showing how no one's job was what it seemed to be, each employee helping with the spreading of secrets—and each employee unaware of what he or she was really doing. System administrators performing a routine installation on a client's mainframe in Tulsa were in fact connecting the client to secret mainframes in Budapest or Malaysia. Accountants approving the budgets of a newly acquired production facility were in fact hiding the costs of leased satellite time. Marketing assistants hyping the effectiveness of the great Core Blue Boxes were in fact distracting everyone—the clients, the shareholders, the stock analysts, and the employees themselves—from the true failings of our product.

Maybe most important of all, in laying out the details of a hidden operation only I understood, the spreadsheet also showed how the original model used to launch Core Communications had not just been incorrect, it hadn't simply been a grand and complicated mistake. Instead the hidden document showed how the original spreadsheet and the company it described had, from the beginning, formed an extremely intricate, carefully crafted lie.

The system would fail. I'd known it from the beginning.

I didn't know when it would happen. And so all I could do, every day, every night, was work to keep the company alive.

Monday at nine, and the office was in motion. Chairs being rolled into conference rooms for overcrowded staff meetings, voices calling out across walkways and workstation walls, people running down open stairways as the white light from windows all around us shifted from floor to wall to desk to door.

And I was moving too. From the senior staff meeting that had started my day, to the list of e-mails building up on my computer, to a financial overview meeting in a conference room on the nineteenth floor. Walking now with Cliff beside me, from the finance meeting back to my office, crossing through Accounting, and my movement seemed to slow amid the long steel rows of low black file cabinets.

Cliff held three checks totaling over $8 million. In his other hand, he held a large donut covered in an unnaturally blue frosting.

I nodded toward the checks. "Don't we have proper procedures for handling checks such as those?" I asked him.

"Actually," he said, smiling as he delicately shook loose frosting from the donut, quietly leading to a punch line we both knew he'd deliver, "this is the proper procedure."

I tapped on a file cabinet. We turned down another aisle.

Core operated from a building that had long been used by a series of quasi-legal sweatshops. The ceilings were high, the walls were filled with tall, multipaned windows, black ceiling fans and silver air-conditioning ducts hung high over everyone's heads. Every floor and room was lit by a mix of floor lamps, desk lamps, and track lights hanging among the exposed ducts and spinning fans. All of it combined with the light from the multipaned windows to cast shadows and streaks of white across the desks, workstations, open meeting spaces and wide walkways covering every floor of the building, the light itself frequently caught in the steel and glass partitions separating rooms and work areas, so that now, as I walked with Cliff, even the stoic and conservative white-shirted CPAs spread around us in Accounting were cast in an almost brooding, anxious light.

It was all I could do to not start floating again.

"And maybe," Cliff started to say, pausing to swallow the last bite of his donut, stopping in a hallway before turning away from me toward his office. "Maybe," he said slowly, his lips tinged blackish blue from the donut's smooth frosting, "what I really meant was a Caesar salad."

Cliff was a man of TV trivia and detailed balance sheets, the forty-year-old arts major with a gift for numbers and finance. Even for me, this fed into the uncertainty over which food Cliff really was. Because Cliff was without question the salad among us, but exactly what kind of salad might never be determined.

To my office and the two hundred e-mails waiting from the morning. Sixteen voice mails. Ten handwritten messages taken by my assistant. The messages in all their forms came from bankers, lawyers, outside sales representatives who'd found their way up to me, analysts from six large mutual funds in Boston and New York, employees from all departments and levels of the company, my life insurance agent, my dry cleaner, a man trying to sell me long distance for my home. It was a twisting kaleidoscope of requests, comments, complaints and chatter.

Twenty minutes and I'd responded to or deleted half of the messages. Quick conversations and short e-mails.

Yes.

Today.

Let me find out.

Talk to Julie, but sounds fine to me.

Unfortunately, no. Which I hate to say. But that's my only conclusion.

Thanks, but no.

Thanks, but no.

It's a tax issue.

He's got it wrong.

Great news.

Yes.

If you think so, then yes.

Unreal.

No.

No.

Thanks, but no.

Nine-thirty, and I was passing through meetings between teams from R&D, Strategic Planning, Technical Development, Production, Operations, Customer Service and Tech Support. Most Mondays I made brief, unannounced appearances at a handful of staff meetings. I nodded and smiled at group VPs, section managers, entry-level employees still learning to use their voice mail. I shook hands. I dispensed *Hello*s. I asked for the names of the many people I had never met. I told them to go about their business as usual, leaning against a high window or a green glass wall, sometimes sitting down in a corner next to a group of latecomers to the meeting, knowing I needed to sit silent, motionless, fading from the minds of the attendees around me, and hopefully they'd begin to sit back in their chairs or stand up to talk as if I weren't there, some of them flicking bits of paper at their neighbors, others doodling in their planners or swearing at the person writing too small on the whiteboard, and I watched as the group followed a sometimes well-designed, sometimes undefined path toward decision, compromise, acquiescence and assent.

"If the Germans can come through, then yes," said a financial analyst in one meeting.

"Not that I'm skeptical, but can we see it on a Pert chart?" said a programmer in another.

"Ergo, I give to you six months of research," said a marketing assistant.

"Beneath my clothing, I, like you, am naked," said a trainer from Tech Support.

This was not a normal company.

By eleven A.M., two business reporters were following me across the sixteenth floor. It was a puff-piece interview arranged by our Public Relations department, which had spent the last three years pitting the business papers against TV, cable against the networks and the networks against the newsmagazines in order to keep the name of Core Communications and Robbie Case, its poster-boy CEO, in every possible media outlet.

"This kind of growth is what we always said we wanted," I told one of the reporters as we walked down a hall toward Strategic Planning, where I would pass them back to our PR group. "Still, anyone who tells you they're ready for this is, I think, lying."

It was one of my standard lines.

"By your saying that," one reporter asked, "couldn't you drive your stock price down three, four, even five dollars?"

I shrugged. I smiled slightly at him. "But I've got other things to tell you that will drive it up by ten."

Who is this person I have become?

Passing through the home of one of the main marketing groups, the reporters scribbling eagerly as they heard hip-hop music rolling across the tops of workstation walls. These were the product development people, ad-agency refugees now creating taglines and branding campaigns not just for our famed Blue Boxes but also for a wide range of new products and services unrelated to Blue Boxes. Whitley in black in the center of a group of eight, for a moment dancing with her hands toward the ceiling, silver bracelet on each wrist caught for a second in the light, her black suit coat unbuttoned, her still face now smiling as her sharp hair fell to the sides, the group around her laughing in sudden surprise, clapping for the boss who in that motion had revealed herself as a onetime club kid turned Chief Operating Officer.

"Stop that dancing," I said loudly, standing back from the group, the appropriately benign comments of the passing CEO, a scene tailored on the fly to the trailing business press.

"No rock and roll," Whitley yelled back. "No swear words. No long hair. No smoking. No laughing. No thinking. No fun."

Leaving the reporters with one of Whitley's press people.

Walking again, usually with a group, rarely alone—informal meetings made faster if we did not sit down. Walking and discussing any range of issues as we passed through the divisions of the company, the meeting participants sometimes scheduling their walks with me ahead of time, sometimes intercepting me in stairways or elevators or tracking me down on my cell phone, and all of it was okay if we did not stop, if we kept walking, talking fast, never bogging down in one issue, all of this time—my time of walking and meeting—all of it scheduled, in advance and down to the minute, by my assistant on twenty.

Always in my life as CEO of Core Communications, there was merely the appearance of spontaneity.

Picking up Julie for a discussion of production issues at two European facilities.

Passing people in suits, people in jeans, people in shirts that crossed the line from earth-tone casual to weekend camouflage.

Seeing bright computer monitors reflecting off glass walls and young faces.

Glancing into a makeshift bunkhouse in the middle of fifteen, a onetime conference room now lined with small beds and padded cots, all used for late-day naps or overnight stays.

Reading a list of the animal names we gave to our computers, the tree names we used for our servers, the former republics, capitals and other landmarks of the Soviet empire that we gave to our many conference rooms.

There was an overriding if obscure logic to our company, one formed so chaotically out of the disparate rhythms of so many different people.

One hundred new e-mails by noon.

Four women entering a conference room named Turkmenistan, and all of them wearing green.

Walking again, now talking with Cliff as we passed through a new, still uninhabited area, one of the building's recently built-out sections that were collectively known as the Unoccupied Territories. Turning a corner and expecting to find people but only seeing more empty desks, empty chairs, the clean delineation of steel and glass partitions. All of it untouched, all of it quiet, all of it ready for the next wave of workers. Most Unoccupied Territories sat unused for just a few weeks. But sometimes, if we misjudged the scope or type of the next big staffing need, the areas remained unassigned for as much as two or three months, months when the spaces would be used as wrestling death pits for high-strung programmers, as sleeping quarters for accountants trying to close the quarterly financials, as extra workspace for squatters from all areas of the company, all of them needing more room.

Into a scheduled lunch meeting where I reviewed reports on the roll-out of a wide range of new products and services, each meant to broaden our product lines, expand our revenue base and diminish our dependence on sales of Blue Boxes. Already we sold over a hundred products and services in addition to the Blue Boxes. Together they accounted for less than two percent of company sales. Certainly not enough revenue to support the current operations and growth of Core Communications. Barely enough to cover the R&D money we continued to put into other new ideas.

And nowhere near enough money to head off the bankruptcy I had forecast on the spreadsheet model hidden on my computer.

But I kept putting money into new products. New services. Anything that helped keep the company afloat.

Because always it was there, the need to find a way.

Somehow, Robbie. Somehow. Keep the company alive.

Whitley called me on my cell phone as I crossed fifteen with two VPs from Japan. "Come up to seventeen," she said rapidly, her voice bursting with the poorly restrained exuberance of an overachieving child. "Security's about to bust a rogue section in Marketing."

I made my way to seventeen just in time, finding Whitley standing at the edge of a workgroup of almost twenty desks, workstations and shared meeting spaces. The two of us were semihidden from the group, standing behind a steel partition with a manager from Corporate Security. Everything in the group seemed normal—the noise of keyboards, phones and talking coworkers rising and falling beneath the lights all around us. There did not appear to be a security problem, let alone a security action in progress. But then I noticed the odd number of white-shirted messengers and office services assistants who were wandering along various walkways near and within the group.

Plainclothes security officers, each moving into position, preparing to break up what we called a rogue section.

What made a group a rogue section was a careful if unexpected mix of creativity, subversion and pointlessness. They were discovered from time to time. The group in front of us, Whitley whispered to me, had spent four months generating elaborate—albeit fake—project plans detailing the creation and marketing of a new translation of the Old Testament. Complete with detailed biblical justifications, historical timelines, annotated budgets, slide shows and legal documentation, the entire group had been working late into the night, week after week.

It was not at all clear why.

I'd never seen a rogue section get broken up before. It was a little like watching a shoplifter being arrested. An increasing number of plainclothes store personnel nonchalantly moved into aisle nine of the supermarket, working their way down the stacks of canned soup, seeming to study the relative merit of one brand over another, all the while closing in on a young man with two beers shoved into his pants.

Except, in this case, the computers of four marketing coordinators near the west side of the group suddenly went dark as the ten or more messengers and office services assistants hovering nearby all pulled security badges from their pockets, quickly moving in on the four workers, asking them to stand, asking them to please cooperate with this investigation.

"There's definitely a very Gestapo-like quality to this," I said to Whitley, watching as security officers escorted the employees away while a specially trained team of tech support reps began to go through desks, file cabinets and the now reactivated computers of the rogue section.

"Which," Whitley said, "secretly increases the thrill for me."

Whitley was the day-to-day manager of the entire company, the trusted adviser to me and all the senior staff, the implementer of each phase of our expansion. But she was also someone who found an only poorly suppressed pleasure in tracking the activities of our rogue sections. Whitley oversaw the task force investigating the rogue sections and—more importantly—other far more serious security threats from industry spies and outside hackers. It was a task force comprised of fifteen security officers, twelve system administrators, two reformed hackers, three industrial psychologists, four financial auditors, three lawyers, four members of the R&D department, a former FBI investigator and Leonard, the head of the company's Technical Development Group. They shadowed suspect e-mails, tapped problem phone calls, reviewed inexplicable documents and project plans and—when necessary—attempted to infiltrate a rogue section.

The group was officially named the Subversives & Intrusions Task Force. However, they were known to most everyone as the Core SWAT team.

"SWAT was a compromise name," Whitley always liked to recall. "Some members wanted to be known as Army Rangers, others wanted the Coast Guard. Personally, I lobbied hard for calling us the Royal Canadian Mounted Police."

Responsibility for something like the SWAT team—and the rogue sections—was something I would have given only to Whitley. I'd hired Whitley when the company had hit sixty employees, all of whom were madly chasing the plan I'd laid out—domination of the high-speed mainframe networking industry through a fanatical commitment to drawing blood from mainframes around the country and the world. However, as devoted and well-intentioned as we tried to be, as revolutionary as our Blue Boxes were, none of us had a clue how to work together effectively. Departments didn't communicate, managers didn't coordinate, and so despite the best efforts of the best people, we were making only very slow progress.

Whitley made us communicate.

Whitley made us coordinate.

Whitley made us make progress.

She was one of those people who, in everyone she touched, instilled a sense of benevolent fear. She smiled, she was kind, she understood. And she made people fear any possibility of not doing their best.

"You'll get it done," she would say, nodding, hard shoulders drop-ping just slightly as she spoke. "I don't know how, but you will."

And so, throughout the company, in any department, any division, Whitley was the only person who ever really told me *no*. Julie, Cliff and Leonard sometimes laughed off my suggestions, vice presidents shifted uncomfortably in their seats as I relayed an idea, the board of directors periodically moved to put one of my initiatives under "ex-tended review."

But only Whitley told me *no*.

In the past three years Whitley and her SWAT team had, without realizing it, come closer and closer to various parts of my lie. Rogue sections, outside hackers, industry spies—all had caused security prob-lems for the company. Each incident had led to an even deeper inves-tigation of Core's operations, a greater expansion of Whitley's SWAT team, new security measures for Leonard and his technical staff. And all of that made my lie more difficult to sustain. SWAT pressing closer to the hidden satellites, the secret servers, the increasing flow of un-tracked money.

My own secret police, unintentionally hunting me down.

On bad days I pictured myself walking into my office to find Whit-ley and her SWAT team at my computer, studying the secrets of my spreadsheet model.

And what they could find was almost unimaginable. My lie, grown terribly large and impossibly complex in the three years since it had begun. A high-tech fraud made up of a thousand interdependent deceptions. The people who worked here, the companies we acquired, the stock we sold—all of it was an unseen disease. A cancer, really, spread silently through this company and still, every day, infecting and reinfecting each department, each system, each person who was here.

When it did finally kill us, it would do so suddenly. Completely. The computers would stop working. The mainframes would shut down. The satellites might as well fall from the sky. And no one—not SWAT, not Whitley—would be able to decipher what exactly had happened.

———

Paper sorted, paper printed, paper copied, paper piled, paper flowing toward destinations unseen and unknown, paper sitting untouched in tall piles on bright tables, sitting dusty and still on high shelves along the wall. Paper bound, paper clipped, paper stapled and stacked and filed and sent and all of it reflecting white as it shot quietly from copiers and printers, or landing heavily as it was moved from desk to file, from file to binder, from binder to conference room. Paper was the breath, it seemed, the air we inhaled, then released.

"Core Communications," I heard someone behind me say, "owns approximately two thousand six hundred and twenty-eight whiteboards."

Walking with the head of Human Resources, finding myself in the middle of an afternoon basketball game in the wide walkways on fourteen, the Lady Gunslingers of PR favored by ten over the Warlords of Admin. It was one of multiple events in an endless and informal buildingwide Olympics—Nerf basketball, laser tag, yo-yo face-offs, darts, pool, air hockey, marbles, video games of all sorts and kinds, poker, chess, D&D, cubicle badminton, Wiffle-bat baseball, chair races, Yahtzee!, Scrabble, checkers, elevator bingo, untold betting pools devoted to elections, births, sports and office romances, periodic foot races around the auditorium on two, broom-and-tape-roll shuffleboard, Frisbee, full-contact rollerball, Magic: The Gathering, tag-team wrestling, Sumo wrestling, paper-airplane competitions based on an arcane Italian formula gauging distance, speed and altitude, and six separate putt-putt courses, each with a rating of novice, pro or addict, that were spread through offices, workspaces, hallways and conference rooms to form a total of one hundred and eight holes of golf.

"Foul!" someone yelled, throwing their hands in the air.

As with every other group in Core Communications, the people playing basketball were not only some of the most productive people in the company, they were also the most productive workers in their professions. Outsiders never believed it. Even the board found it hard to understand. But despite the games and jokes and constant digres-

sions, Core was one of the most productive and efficient companies in
the world.

I played five minutes of basketball with the Warlords of Admin. I
managed to contribute two assists and a foul shot but had three jump
shots blocked by a fanatical Bulgarian intern—a lightning-quick woman
with a twelve-inch vertical leap and no idea I was the owner of the
company, the building and the court she so freely dominated.

It was, for me, an unlikely but welcome moment of anonymity and
untainted employee contact, even as other people stood around us,
watching their CEO run the court.

Walking with two financial analysts, each updating me on fluctua-
tions in various European stock markets, the meeting soon carrying us
from the eighteenth to the eleventh floor, Worldwide Network Operations, where sci-fi marathons met the complete works of Nietzsche,
where junior programmers in tuxedo T-shirts worked alongside engineering PhDs and tired dropouts from Cal Tech.

Picking up Julie, the two of us walking across thirteen, a floor with
a particularly large number of windows, the rooms cast in shadows
from the windows around us, rooms sometimes angular, sometimes
round, sometimes softened into shapelessness as the light reflected
off the steel and the glass and the ducts in the ceiling.

"I've got a meeting with the blind," Julie was saying, "then a review
of new day care policies on the Korean peninsula."

Julie was our goodness. Our corporate soul. It was her staff that
led tours of inner-city schoolkids through the office, her staff that
cost-justified employee day care worldwide, her staff that spearheaded
blood drives, canned food collections, volunteer teams for neighborhood soup kitchens. She did this while overseeing the production of
all Blue Boxes and hardware in over fifty facilities around the globe.
Did this quietly, without once asking for praise or recognition. Did
this without seeming soft or maternal. In another age, men in gray
suits would have called her a kind den mother. Cliff once jokingly re-
ferred to her as *dear* and she turned to him and hit him, hard, in the
arm. He could not rotate his shoulder for more than a week.

Yet even more than her strength and temper, what probably most prevented the senior staff from calling her *dear* or *maternal* was Julie's endless appetite for discussions about sex.

"The head of production from that Korean company we just bought reminds me of an aging leopard," she said to me now. "A sleepy, languid man who rises only to breed."

I nodded. Waiting. Sure something more would come.

"He's taking early retirement tomorrow," she said. "He agreed with my suggestion today."

She nodded. She turned and was gone.

One hundred and fifty e-mails by three. Suggestions from staff members. Requests from board members. Favors to be returned. Thanks to be given.

Another group of four, all in green, this time near the elevators. Already today I'd seen an oddly large number of people in green.

People saying *Hello* to me as they moved out of the way of another of my walking meetings, some people even whispering, a few even pointing, sometimes a group slowly spreading apart, graciously and with unintended formality, making way for their CEO.

"I'm not royalty," I'd once said to Whitley.

"It's not your choice," she'd replied. "They've made of you what they want to believe. And they want to believe you are not like them."

The steady sound of the ventilation system, metallic and barely audible below and between the noise of so many people in motion.

Shadows in my office I'd never noticed before.

Six hours' sleep in the past three days.

A memory of Julie with her head on her desk after lunch, the five-minute nap of the exhausted executive vice president of worldwide production.

The spreadsheet, eight hundred pages, open on my screen. For a few minutes only. Updating the model. Incorporating new purchases of secret mainframes. Adding recent leases for yet more satellite time. Tying in the hidden cash I ran daily through acquired companies. Removing now defunct shell corporations through which I bought and sold equipment. Moving assets to newly formed shells based in Bermuda and the Caymans.

"Timeless," I heard a woman's voice say from outside my office, the words drifting to me through the noise on twenty, through the noise in my office, through the noise coming in from the city now caught in the windows around me. "Placeless," the voice said. "Godless. Sourceless."

Not till four that afternoon did I realize it was all the members of the company's Tech Support, Network Administration and Software Development groups who were wearing green.

"I like your shirt," I now told Leonard, the head of those groups.

"Thanks," he said with a pleasant nod, but offering no explanation as to why his shirt matched his pants, his pants matched his sneakers, his sneakers matched his socks. "As expected," he said, "the equipment will total two hundred twenty-nine million dollars over a three-year period."

Somehow I hadn't noticed Leonard's green ensemble at our senior staff meeting that morning, or in any of our interactions earlier in the day. Maybe that's because Leonard was one of those big people, not fat or overweight, but big in a way that was startling every time I saw him, an unexpected amount of space suddenly occupied anytime he entered the room. Big hands, big eyes, big features, big motions. He had the largest fingers I had ever seen. His size tended to overwhelm whatever it was that he wore.

But now I saw that he was all in green. I wondered if maybe he'd changed clothes at some point, inexplicably donning a costume for the fading light of the afternoon.

Unlikely.

Cliff, sitting next to me now, nodding and taking notes, hadn't seemed to notice the green. Or maybe he didn't care. With numbers in front of him, calculator at his fingers, Cliff became a living computer, a machine purely focused on absorbing, processing and refining the information presented to him. In those moments he had no ability to register anything else.

All day, though, I'd been seeing the tech people in green—a gangly system administrator typing frantically on a marketing executive's locked-up computer, a near teenaged girl changing toner in a brightly glowing copier, three Chinese programmers in a heated debate as they reported to Whitley about security threats from Indonesia. Some were in olive-green pants, some were in forest-green shirts or light-green shoes, one was in a dark-green hat.

There were no secret handshakes as they passed each other, no furtive hand signals, not even a shared smile. They simply all wore green.

"Leonard," I said, "you're wearing all green."

He glanced up, nodded, said, "NT, XP, 2000, UNIX." It was as if he'd launched into some high-tech haiku. In fact he was listing a range of computer systems in use at a number of our newly acquired companies. "Multiple flavors on the UNIX side," he said. "Irix, Linux, lots of Solaris. And of course that's in addition to every mainframe platform known to this planet." He sighed heavily. "So many platforms, so many skills."

Cliff nodded carefully. I nodded knowingly. Leonard turned a page.

Located on the ninth through twelfth floors, the tech group formed four floors of highly rambunctious but remarkably good-natured individuals. They hacked into each other's computers, they organized floorwide competitions in various Web-based role-playing games, they logged into the computers that operated the building's air-conditioning system in order to raise the temperature in rival programming groups by ten, then twenty degrees.

As I watched Leonard's thick fingers trace absently along the sharp edges of the papers in his lap, I wondered for a moment if any of the industry spies or bored college students trying to hack into our systems were themselves sitting at their computers dressed entirely in green.

"Green," I said, to no one in particular it seemed. "All green."

"Collabra, Marimba, Domino, Exchange," Leonard said, turning a page, then continuing. "Java, C, VB, Korn. So many skills . . ." he said, and let the sentence trail off.

Cliff looked up. "The real cost is personnel, yes?"

Leonard nodded quickly. "The real cost is personnel, but there's a notch up in training."

Cliff tapped on his calculator. I nodded knowingly. Leonard turned a page.

And really, I did know. I knew exactly what Leonard meant. I understood everything he and Cliff were saying. In Technical Development, in Strategic Planning, in Sales and R&D, everywhere I knew the workflows, I knew the org charts, I knew the software tools, I knew the strategies for the best communication and support. I knew what markets we were in, what markets we wanted. I knew the product lines and the version changes and the roll-out schedules and the launches.

In the night, when I did sleep, these were the things that drifted through my dreams.

I leaned back in my chair, absently touching the thin, straight edge of Leonard's desk. Everything in Leonard's office was set at right angles to the walls. As always, this had a calming effect on me. His four computers, his five monitors, his multiple stacks of status reports, software documentation, heavy reference books, even the requisite collection of sci-fi trading cards—not only was each item squared to the desk or table on which it rested, but Leonard had clearly gone so far as to bar the public display of any rounded items in his office. Leonard's office—Leonard himself—gave me a sense of order and uniformity, not just among the physical objects within my reach but within the very structure of the universe around us.

"Corel, Claris, even Quattro, even Symphony," Leonard said, sighing again. "In this there will be no diversity. We go to the one place. We go to the big boy."

Cliff nodded quickly. I nodded again. I said once more, "Leonard, you're wearing all green."

He looked up from his notes. In a moment, he nodded, flat tongue wetting his wide lower lip, his whole presence seeming to prepare itself for an extended response. "Yes," Leonard said, "I am."

He nodded again, Cliff asked for costs, Leonard gave him answers, I glanced toward New Jersey and smiled. Leonard's sincerity, the pure earnestness he brought to his work, to this life, it could make him impenetrable.

"Forty-four K, thirty-two K, an even hundred," Leonard said.

"Was there a memo?" I asked. "Or an e-mail?"

"What's that?" Leonard asked.

"How did everyone know to wear green?"

He paused, letting his head fall to the side, confused. Then he nodded. "Right. Yes. I see. Green. No. It's the first of the month. On the first of the month, we've all decided to wear green."

Cliff asked for supporting detail. Leonard handed us articles, budgets and comparative charts. It was thirty seconds before I had to smile again, looking out the window once more, realizing that Leonard still hadn't really told me why they were wearing green.

"Spread the main software over three months," Leonard was saying now. "Schedule the attached hardware over five."

Cliff nodded. I nodded. Leonard picked up another report.

I could see that even his watch band was green.

A joke that just couldn't be shared with the CEO. Or, more likely, a decision that Leonard—a young man completely lacking in even the most basic awareness of irony—simply could not find a way to explain.

"Impact, Freehand, Composer, Paint," Leonard said.

"We go to the big boy?" Cliff asked.

Leonard and I both shook our heads. "We change," I said, answering the question. "But it's not to the big boy."

Leonard nodded quickly, flipped me a thumbs-up. He placed the completed reports at right angles to his desktop.

In his first year as head of technology for Core, Leonard told me he'd taken business cards to his high school reunion and passed them out to all the people he had never known.

And now he was starting onto another list, Leonard with his deep, almost mystical ability to bend, shape, start and even stop the world of Core Communications. And so I sat taking in everything he said. Just as I'd absorbed every report, every plan, every budget and forecast I'd seen in the past three years. Every cost for every department. Every idea from each meeting. Sometimes even every responsibility and goal for each person in a room.

I took everything in. I remembered it all.

Because really this company was my whole life.

Nearing the end of the day. Holding an impromptu meeting with Julie in the mailroom. Staffed by eager, always well-meaning recent immigrants to the city, the mailroom was centered around a series of six huge copiers—six remarkably complex machines with smoothly harmonic noises, rapidly blinking indicator lights, brightly mirrored interior surfaces.

The paper so crisp, the sound an unwavering heartbeat of order and routine.

For years I'd used the mail room for meetings with Julie. Like me, she felt a deep and inexplicable comfort in being in the presence of the highly synchronized noise, light and human movement. This time, as always, the two of us left our meeting rejuvenated and ready, our ears still echoing with the densely orchestrated motions and sound.

Moving across ten with my assistant now, who took a moment to point at one of the oversized workspaces the company built for supervisors and managers. "Another owner-financed double-wide," he said.

I squinted. Not understanding.

"You know," he said with something like surprise. "The joke goes, 'Did you hear about Sara? She got that promotion to section manager—

and, best of all, she done got herself an owner-financed double-wide!'"

I made a mental note. We moved to eleven. My assistant continued with a list of Whitley's plans to conduct security reviews of all backup systems in our Asian offices.

My lie, ever present, brought to the surface for a moment, once more my mind searching for ways to dodge the constant reviews and investigations that Whitley and her SWAT team were conducting.

Walking with Cliff, his thumbs twitching rapidly as we discussed the turnover rates of our German accounts receivable. We turned a corner, and a man bearing the telltale distant stare of a sleepless programmer came up to me, cutting off Cliff as he looked me in the eyes and said, "Here's a question you can answer—if I reinstall the service pack on the Japanese Maple in Nicaragua, will I lose all config changes to my ODBC connections?"

I stared back at his heavy, glassy eyes. Clearly he'd confused me with someone else. But I started to speak.

He raised a hand. "Never mind," he said quickly. "Obviously, I've just answered my own question."

And he was gone.

And I would never see him again.

And actually I had known the answer.

Walking with Whitley once more, finding her on seventeen, Public Relations, bright-faced young professionals and darkly clothed cynics all breaking plans into parts, offering a simple spin to define the chaos, trying in all things to spread the word, the good doings and best efforts, of Core Communications.

Three hundred e-mails.

Thirty more reports waiting on my desk for review.

Four holes of putt-putt with two novice players from Finance.

The ventilation system turning on, purring above us, Whitley and I hearing it for the second time that day, when usually it blew silently above the swirling noise of people, computers, phones and copiers.

Collabra, Marimba, Domino, Exchange. Software. Satellites. A marketing push into Asia.

Nineteen, and I was alone, passing through another of the Unoccupied Territories. And this time stopping. Standing still for a moment. Seeing the walls freshly painted, feeling my feet pressing easily into the untouched carpet, looking at the desk chairs still wrapped in paper and plastic. Standing alone in this area, untouched and pristine. In some deepest way pure. And all of it waiting. Waiting for more.

Every day there was more.

My ears seemed to ring. I felt short of breath. I could see the whole day, blinking once, it was there and gone and somehow with me forever, each part disconnected, the all of it forming a solid, bright whole.

It was eight o'clock.

And at two in the morning, she came into my office. Like many nights, though not all. A short e-mail sent at one. A brief call back to me at two.

A woman in a black suit walked into the room.

She followed me upstairs to my apartment on the twenty-first floor.

A black suit, black hair. The edge of her smooth white bra just visible as she stepped close.

All my life I hadn't slept much, even when I was a child. I can remember whole nights when I was six or five or even four and I lay in my bed, staring up at the ceiling, unable to sleep. Now, at thirty-five, instead of lying awake, I spent my nights in my office, there from nine till two, spreadsheet open on my computer, feeding more information into my secret model.

Now I was here, though. In my apartment. Six tall rooms cast in the gray light and dark shadows of lamps placed two or three or four to a room. A kitchen I didn't use, a bed I could not find sleep in, wide windows onto the city, in every room, those windows. It seems now that I lived in those windows, raised from the wooden floors, suspended in the glass between building and city.

This black suit in front of me. The black hair long and a face beautiful and indistinct, only dark eyes, a mouth, chin, the neck and shoulders and arms and legs. The edge of that bra. The two-color silhouette of a woman in front of me.

Always somehow they were the same. Darkly perfect, quietly fit, seemingly kind, seemingly happy. This woman with the dark hair, thick, pulled lightly into a tie at the base of her neck, standing in front of me in a fine wool suit, low and simple shoes, as if she'd been pulled from a board meeting or presentation. But really she was a total stranger to me. Even the women I'd seen five or ten times in the last two years, all were strangers even if they'd been sent to me before. Because there was no banter, there were no questions, no anxious answers.

A few instructions maybe. Sometimes a guiding word.

But really I preferred no talking at all.

I did not do drugs. I did not gamble, did not even spend the money I was paid. This was my vice, dark music and gin, a woman escorted to me by my bodyguard.

There were no dim fantasies, no perversions or abuse. There was only nameless sex, steady closeness, the just quiet sounds of clothes coming off. Her participation imagined or faked, I didn't know and didn't care, because in all this there was acting, some play in the dark with shadows and silence, an agreed-upon game with simple rules and clear roles, much of it no different than the circling rhythms of Monday meetings or hallway games, all of us playing, all of us paid, everyone trying to leave behind each moment and role at the end of the day.

I came inside her.

Three offices to open in England and Ireland. Eight acquisitions in Taiwan and Korea. Cash soon shifting from Chicago to Omaha.

Five thousand, two thousand, six million, seven.

Collabra, Marimba, Domino, Exchange.

Messages, rogue sections, another meeting, another floor.

Every day was the same. For three years, I'd spent each day keeping the company on track toward its demise, adding pressure by the hour, all the while trying to find a way out of the trap I'd created.

This is what it meant to live a lie.

I came inside her again.

They do not have any kind of disease. They are not criminals. They are not forced into what they do. They were simply delivered to an anonymous apartment.

In New York, with enough money, you can buy anything.

These things were important to me. Because this was about the absence of any risks or possibilities or needs or cautions. This was only about the touching, the sounds and sex.

No cash exchange. No late-night cigarette as she or I broke the spell. No shared insights into her childhood or upbringing, no sharing of my weaknesses, wants and faults. It was over and she would leave and then I would finally sleep.

Masturbation on a credit card in a penthouse apartment.

And so at four in the morning on this Monday night, I did sleep. Lying on the sofa back in my office, the best place I'd found. The glow of the city, the distant glare from the waterfront over in New Jersey, all reflecting in on my high ceiling and I would sleep a few hours, till the sun came up, my mind moving through meetings and plans and expenses, finding details, concepts, tasks big and small.

In two months revenue would cross $21 billion a year.

At some point, any point, we'd be bankrupt and done.

I'd managed to keep us alive another day.

And I would sleep in that state, listing and racing and listing more, and maybe once, maybe not, would I think about the woman who'd visited me that night, maybe picturing her face, more likely her hair or clothes, some remnant memory of pleasure and silence, some memory just marked by a disconnected guilt, and now I'd be awake, never sure how much I had really slept, now only staring out the window at the morning turning gold and white and a deep, deep blue, Tuesday, and I was floating, legs quietly pulled up to my chest, so silly, so obvious, but floating, flying, out the window, and toward the sky.

He rides home, nighttime, with the numbers still moving. There in the cab, riding home as he sits among the tightly stacked papers and clearly labeled files. Calculator still pressed between his narrow hands. CFO, still. Nine o'clock. Maybe ten now. The numbers of a hundred reports and a hundred budgets and a hundred campaigns and a hundred launches, all those numbers moving across the screen of the calculator in Cliff's hands.

But, really, moving across his eyes. Because the calculator is more habit than need. Pressing the buttons only absently. Barely glancing at the results, results he already knows. Results he can do in his head.

In fifth grade he learns geometry. In seventh he learns calculus. By tenth he is on to college.

There aren't any numbers Cliff can't do on his own.

The taxi bottoms out, hitting hard on a steel plate, then lifting for a second, just a second, and his papers slide in place and two files start their slow, slow fall to the floor and he's lifted with the cab and his stomach's fluttering and high in his chest and he smiles that kid's smile of riding in the car with his mom, a kid, in the backseat, with mom in the front, and he's thinking now, What night is it? What street are we on? What time did I leave home this morning? What time did my kids go to bed?

And there's only guilt when he thinks about that. Because why is he doing this? To himself and to his wife and to his kids. My kids. Six kids. None more than ten years old. Home asleep now. Most nights, asleep. Weekends he sees them. When he's home for a few hours. Weekends they all smile with him.

No one makes him do this. He can make money somewhere else.

He will get home and slide into bed and he'll want to sleep and already he knows he'll be out of bed by twelve, roaming the house, trying to empty himself of the numbers still moving through his mind, and finally he will give in, sit down, turn the TV on and stare. Stare for hours. Two hours or three. Bright infomercials and lost sitcoms and sad, heart-felt commercials. He likes the commercials best of all. And over time his mind will stop working. Finally it will let go. Emptied, dumbed down, left tired and somehow cold.

Then he'll sleep.

This is his ride home. Guilty and tired and the numbers moving. Once more folding the results, turning them over, seeing them again.

And of course, like always now, just as it's been for the past year, the numbers don't work for him. The numbers aren't right.

He's never seen a number he doesn't understand.

But he doesn't understand these numbers. The company's numbers.

And he thinks something's wrong with him. He thinks that, finally, the company has moved past him. He thinks that, finally, he's not able to understand. Finally the company needs someone else. Someone older. Someone more experienced.

Someone smarter.

He doesn't understand. The numbers are balanced. They're checked. The auditors sign off. His staff okays them. The bankers smile happily. Wall Street nods and nods.

But he can't touch something inside the numbers. Can't see some part of them.

And he thinks that Robbie always knows. Always, he's sure. Always, he understands.

But there's something, somewhere, that Cliff does not understand.

He doesn't know how to change this. He doesn't know who to ask for help.

How does Robbie see it?

The car hits another plate, lifting and even turning so slightly to the left now, stomach emptied and that glimpse of his mom and for some long second he even thinks that this will be his moment, his epiphany, the second when it comes to him and he sees and, finally, he can touch the very bottom, the very edge of the numbers he doesn't understand.

And of course it is not that moment. You don't see when your epiphanies come. They just come.

And so still, like every night, something, somewhere, does not make sense.

I wonder if I could maybe wake up the kids for a little while.

CHAPTER 2

A longtime regional sales manager was reluctantly confiding to me that easy listening music was, in fact, not very good. "Your average person," he was saying as we sat together in a conference room during one of the prearranged, informal Tuesday get-togethers I periodically held with managers from the field offices, "your *nonaficionado,*" he continued, "he talks about jazz and he's thinking about easy listening. In his mind, easy listening is really the top of the top."

He leaned his face close to mine. His breath smelled of mouthwash. His skin smelled of shaving cream.

"Well, Mr. Case," he said, "let me tell you a secret, a secret from a humble insider: *It's not true.*"

I smiled. I nodded. I cocked my head to the side. Noncommittal gestures somehow positive yet restrained. "Call me Robbie," I said to him.

Frequently in my work life, it was the most formulaic of responses that served me best.

The sales manager smiled wide. He slid his bulk forward to the edge of the couch. He settled his heavy fingers on the soft, springy cartilage at my knee.

For the briefest of moments, it was all I could do not to reflexively kick him in the shins.

"And call me Bill," he said.

The employees of this company all wanted to connect with me. To talk to me. To please me with their performance. To share thoughts about their role, the company's growth, the future we shared.

And, more and more, they wanted to touch me.

They would touch my arm in the hallways, pat my shoulder in an elevator. In meetings they had me trapped, patting my wrist as it lay on a conference table, squeezing my shoulder as they stood to leave the room for a moment, squeezing again as they returned to their seat. Sometimes a particularly bold, usually older, usually male VP would go so far as to stand behind my chair, hands resting heavily on my shoulders. In a break room I once even felt a young woman with the highly tailored appearance of a marketing assistant slowly, carefully, ever so lightly press her shoulder against mine.

This was not an outcome I'd sought when I took over the company. This was not something that made me feel proud. Moreover, all my life, I have never liked to be touched.

I'd spent thirty-five years avoiding unnecessary physical contact.

I didn't let people know I felt this way. Only in the last six months had I shared this with my senior staff—a momentary lapse in personal judgment that had resulted in each of them, every week, creating an opportunity to touch me on the hand, the shoulder, the arm or leg.

Each except Leonard, of course, who lacked even the most basic recognition of irony.

I leaned to the left on the couch now, casually shifting away from the sales manager as I repositioned a security document I'd set on the couch. It was another security review.

Five more investigations under way by Whitley's SWAT team.

Ten more steps I had to take to avoid them.

In my office now, I'd managed to move a safe distance from the sales manager as he started a discussion about the intermingled history of soft rock and modern jazz. But then I realized that Trevor Case, Core's executive vice president for all product sales, had walked into the conference room. Tall, with dark hair and a suit. As always, a suit and shirt and tie and all of it speaking to his complete disregard for everything around him. He was not moving now, still and quiet. Thin eyes staring past the two of us sitting down. The sales manager still hadn't realized Trevor was here.

In all the company—in all of our industry—there was no one more feared than Trevor Case.

Seeing him now, I almost had to stand.

I hadn't known Trevor was in New York, let alone in the building. Working entirely on the road, Trevor was a kind of omnipotent ghost, a powerful yet unseen specter rarely sighted in person but who continually made himself present in the lives of the people around him. He used airport pay phones to hold conference calls with his sales managers worldwide, used poorly lit cybercafés to outline his revenue goals for each region, used waves of overnight deliveries to fire whole teams of underperforming sales reps.

Trevor was also my thirty-six-year-old cousin, one year older than I, and since we were kids he'd been something of a brother to me. A very difficult half-brother, really, who came in and out of my life at uneven intervals, each time inevitably leading me into trouble.

"Consider New Age music," the sales manager was continuing, leaning back comfortably on the sofa. He still hadn't noticed Trevor. "The average guy, he thinks New Age is folk. Well, Robbie," he said, shifting in place, his weight resettling from left to right, "it just isn't true."

He winked knowingly. He nodded conclusively. He reached for my knee another time.

"How are sales?" I asked him, shifting in my seat again, really only trying to make conversation in the midst of Trevor's almost unprecedented daylight appearance. With Trevor I always had a sense of waiting. Waiting on him to speak or act. Waiting until he took control of the moment.

Even Whitley had no influence over Trevor. "Trevor," she would say, "is yours."

"I put people on the street, I sell product," the sales manager was saying. "I put people on the phone, I sell product." He shrugged heavily. He draped one arm across the back of the sofa. He held his glass of water like a highball, even tinkling the ice cubes before bringing the fluid so carefully to his lips, then grimacing mightily as he swallowed. "Whatever we do," he said, "I sell product."

"That's wonderful," I said, talking only to fill the space.

He shook his head. "No, sir," he said, pausing, leaning forward again, and I leaned back easily, crossing my legs, carefully taking myself out of his reach, "if I may, I'd like to say that the word is *extraordinary*."

I nodded again. I glanced out the window. The sunlight shone brightly, evenly, on the Jersey shore. It was eight A.M.

Trevor's voice entered the pause, a sound so fluid filling all space in the room. "But why are you successful?" he asked the sales manager.

The manager had been tinkling the ice in his glass again, but turned now and saw Trevor. The manager's face went red, then pale. He took his arm from the back of the couch. He slid forward on the sofa.

"You've been with this company since the '80s, correct?" Trevor asked, moving now, carefully, in a suit that was blue or black, staring at us with eyes that were thin or small. "Worked for Robbie's father, yes?"

The sales manager spoke quietly. "Yes."

"And before that, you sold what?" Trevor asked, stepping carefully around the corner of the couch, settling down between the sales manager and me. "Long distance, cable TV? You sold shoes, magazines, aluminum siding?"

The manager nodded. He put his glass on the table. He put his hands on his knees.

"In all your years selling," Trevor said, sitting now on the very edge of the couch, touching as little of it as possible, "selling hobby magazines and cookware, selling anything. In all your years has anything, ever, come this easily?"

The sales manager put his hands on his knees, then rubbed them together slowly, then put them palm down on the couch. He spoke very quietly. "No."

"And late at night," Trevor said, "after you've cashed your commission check, after you've called your broker, after you've talked to your insurance agent and set up your golf game for the weekend, after all that don't you lie in bed, staring at the ceiling, and don't you wonder?"

The sales manager was looking down at the floor.

"Don't you wonder?" Trevor repeated, voice getting quiet, and he'd crossed his hands in his lap, the strongest hands I'd ever known, since we were kids his hands had been no bigger or longer or wider than anyone else's but they'd always been the strongest, holding him up in a game, knocking others down in a fight, clutching so easily to a tree or a wall or a windowsill as we climbed, two kids running wild through the neighborhood in summer.

The sales manager glanced toward the window. He was carefully gnawing on the inside of his lip. He turned to me, hoping I would break in. But then he turned back to Trevor. He started to speak, stopped, then finally spoke quietly. "I'm sorry. To you and Mr. Case. Mr. Case," he said, turning to me, "Mr. Case, I am sorry."

"There is something unexplainable happening," Trevor said, leaning forward even more, more than seemed possible, lowering his head just slightly as he stared at the sales manager.

The sales manager nodded. "I'm sorry. I really am."

Trevor touched the manager's knee. Trevor held it hard. "And so," he said, "late at night, you wonder, don't you? Tell me. What do you wonder?"

The manager nodded, again looking out the window. Finally he turned back to Trevor. When he spoke his voice was rough, quiet, not a whisper but a kind of uneasy breath. "I wonder when it will end."

Trevor was pressing harder on the man's knee. "Don't talk about how easy it is," he said.

"I won't."

"Don't talk about how great it is."

"I won't."

"You get comfortable and I will fire you," Trevor said.

The sales manager nodded.

"You start to believe the bullshit Robbie here gives you, and I'll come see you at home," Trevor said.

The sales manager closed his eyes.

"You get comfortable and I'll come to your house and I'll repossess your car and sell off your clothes and I'll take your kids out of private school and I'll burn down your fucking home while you sit on the curb, crying into your hands, because if you let up for one second, if you let up in your thoughts, if you even have a dream that this is easy, then I will be there, instantly, putting you and your family on the street."

"Have you ever thought—" I started to say to Trevor, the two of us back in my office.

He interrupted me. "Have I ever thought that we might be better off if I were a soothing and supportive executive in charge of sales?" he asked. "No, I have not."

"I'm saying you're an asshole."

"Because I keep that sales manager motivated and focused, that makes me an asshole?" he asked me, smiling, moving now, easily and almost quickly, steadily pacing from window to door in my office.

"You keep him afraid," I said, feeling thin and light in my clothes, and as always I felt like I was shorter than Trevor, an inch or two smaller, even though I knew we were the same height.

"I keep him selling," Trevor said, stopping for a moment, his hands in the front pockets of his suit coat.

"I really don't like you, Trevor," I said.

"And yet, at the same time, you can't help but find me lovable and endearing," he said, smiling, and he was pacing again.

"Why do you do those things to your people?" I asked.

"Sales are up, the expansion continues," he said.

I shook my head. Couldn't answer. "Why are you in town?"

"Omaha," Trevor said, a hand in his dark hair, moving it, slowly, from his eyes. "The acquisition. There are a few assets I do not want us to buy."

Carefully I sat down in my chair, then turned away from him. I stared out my window. I knew what Trevor meant. It was what Trevor always meant. "Their sales team," I said.

"Correct."

"You want them fired."

"Yes."

"We talked," I said. "You and I talked. We agreed you would keep them. I have told them they will stay."

"Yes," Trevor said, "but I was lying."

"How many people?" I asked.

"A group of fifty, I think. Plus support staff. Call it an even sixty."

When we were kids, Trevor wasn't the bully who beat up other boys at school or soccer practice. He wasn't the kid who shot dogs with pellet guns. What Trevor did was taunt. Quietly, fluidly, relentlessly. He charmed girls until they smiled, showing their braces, which Trevor then made fun of. He befriended heavy kids on the walk home, buying them donuts and grape soda, asking them what they liked to do, what games they were good at and what things they collected, until finally he started to ask why they had no friends, why they ate so much food, why they were so stupid, why they collected baseball cards, why they were so fat. *Why are you so fat?* Still asking as he followed them along the street, across yards, down an alley, all the way to their porch steps.

Trevor had been an awful person. Really, he still was.

I was staring out the window. "I'll call Omaha," I said. "I'll do the firing."

"You know I'll do it," he said.

"I don't want you calling them," I said. "I'll call."

"Make Whitley do it," he said. "Distract her from SWAT for the day."

"I'll do it," I said, and realized I could see Trevor's sharp and smiling face reflected in the glass. "No one calls Omaha but me."

"You do love me, Robbie. Don't you?"

"I really don't like you, Trevor. I wish you weren't here. And never had been here."

"But you love me?"

"I want something bad to happen to you, Trevor. I want you to feel pain."

He was still staring at me in the glass. Still with his hands in his suit-coat pockets. And smiling, tongue at his lip, teeth just hidden, a face so sharp and hard and still.

Inside, I'd known all along that Trevor would appear in my office a few days before we closed the Omaha deal. I'd known he would never hire those salespeople. I'd known he'd been lying to me from the start. I always knew these things about Trevor. And yet always I tried to believe that this time would be different. That this time he would surprise me.

He never had.

And so I would have to fire these people. Each one. I would fly to Omaha, I would stand in a room, I would tell them they were done.

The regional sales manager I'd been meeting with was, in almost every way, completely unlike Trevor's other salespeople. That manager had worked for my father, and even for Trevor, this made him essentially untouchable as long as he produced. The salespeople Trevor hired were more like assassins—calculating, mean and focused solely on ways in which their employer, Core Communications, could further their own personal success. They were sports fiends and sex freaks, they were women who called each other cunts, they were men who threw punches at each other during their separate Christmas party. Because of this, Trevor himself was required to report to me personally whenever he came to headquarters, a corporate restraining order on my own sales executive.

"I'll be in town for a few days," Trevor said to me now.

"Do you ever wish we had other family?" I asked him, staring out the window, looking through his reflection. "Do you wish there was more to the family than just us?"

"I'll come by again," he said, not answering my question. Because Trevor never answered questions about our dead parents.

"Do you think any of these fired employees will ever try to hurt you?" I asked.

"It'd be like some TV miniseries," he said, and I didn't even have to look at him to see him, to know the tip of his tongue was centered in his smile, his dark eyes turned upward in the pleasure of his joke. "Open Season," he said, his voice rising as it emphasized each word. "The Omaha Office Massacre."

"It could happen," I said. Although I didn't believe it. Knew I was only talking to talk.

"In my mind," Trevor said, "the only person who might hurt me is you."

"Really?" I asked, slowly turning around to face him, almost smiling as I spoke. "Are you afraid of me, Trevor?"

"No," he said. "But you still might try to hurt me."

"Even though, as you say, I love you so much?"

"Yes," he said, grinning now, so happy, so satisfied, Trevor's reactions like those of a child, so complete and so pure. "Yes," he said, "even though you love me so much."

Trevor could sell anything. He was charming and deft, so tremendously intelligent and quick. His salespeople, all of them, they were the same. A cult ruled by fear, worshippers of money, ready at any moment to destroy everything and everyone within their reach. And yet they were, as a group, some of the smartest, most highly skilled people I had ever met.

It was Trevor and his sales team who had made me rich.

And it was Trevor alone who knew my secret—that Core Communications was hurtling toward collapse. He'd bought in completely. In fact, he'd known from the very beginning.

Jaywalking had set all of this in motion—Core's growth, Trevor's sales, our grand journey toward collapse. It had been a jaywalking computer engineer named Frederick Fadowsky, actually, who'd retired in 1977 after a twenty-five-year career in technology research for the Defense Department. In the months after his retirement, working day and night in a poorly lit basement in a uniformly pristine subdivision in northern New Jersey, Fadowsky developed a mathematical algorithm. It was a formula, really. One that would change the world. Because, with what was called the Fadowsky Formula, the speed at which mainframe computers could transfer information suddenly increased by a factor of forty.

"The revolution has begun," Fadowsky wrote in his journal just hours after his discovery. "The rate of transfer I've now made possible, the level of compression I have obtained, is the overture to an orchestra of speed and efficiency."

Mainframe programmers have never been known for their humility.

And mainframe computing isn't known for its allure to the outside world.

Yet within the small, cloistered universe of mainframe programming, Fadowsky was hailed as a brilliant, groundbreaking thinker, a man whose work would someday be compared to the achievements of Franklin, Edison and the Wright brothers. Fadowsky gave all-day seminars to standing-room-only gatherings of spellbound engineers. He gave lectures at colleges throughout the Western world. His journals were published, in annotated and unannotated editions, through an alliance of six university presses.

Meanwhile, Fadowsky had partnered with his brother-in-law, a retired electronics salesman, to market and sell his formula. Together the two of them sold the Fadowsky Box, a TV-sized machine featuring heavy knobs, sharp edges and thick cords that plugged directly into a company's mainframe. Fadowsky and his brother-in-law traveled the country in a dark-green sedan, pitching large corporations and government agencies on the benefits of this incredible machine.

Almost immediately, they were selling Fadowsky Boxes faster than the machines could be produced.

"My vision is a world made smaller, not larger, through the proliferation of these tools," Frederick wrote in his journal in a roadside motel outside St. Louis. "It is a vision that we have, today, begun to fulfill."

I was in preschool at the time, a quiet but active boy most concerned with drawing an ever-larger cityscape on a sketchpad in my bedroom.

And Trevor was off taunting some neighborhood girl, years away from introducing this story to me.

Much like standard computer modems, it took two Fadowsky Boxes—one at each end of a phone line—to transfer information. But unlike standard modems, the Fadowsky Boxes required a massive amount of mainframe processing in order to operate, so much so that companies immediately found themselves needing to double the capacity of their mainframes in order to use the Fadowsky machines. It was almost like having to buy a second PC simply to send an e-mail. Still, for the large corporations and huge government agencies that wanted to send information quickly and easily among multiple locations, the Fadowsky Boxes were worth the price.

"The value of my system," Fadowsky wrote, "its importance to the world, will, over time, be measured not in dollars, not in gold, but in knowledge and enlightenment."

And then, less than a year after the first Fadowsky Box was installed, Fadowsky died. Hit by a garbage truck while jaywalking across an intersection in northern New Jersey.

And then Fadowsky's brother-in-law realized that Frederick had never told him where to find the complete mathematical algorithm. Understandably, Fadowsky had not published the formula with his journals, nor had he kept the formula in a public place. Finally the brother-in-law concluded that Frederick had kept the algorithm in his head, fearful that it would be stolen by competing inventors or large companies.

There was actually some speculation that, in fact, Frederick had had no idea how his discovery worked. That he'd stumbled onto an invention he did not understand. That he'd gone on to stage his death in order to withdraw into seclusion, hiding from the inevitable demands to document his formula. In the three years since Core had introduced its Blue Boxes, stories like this had surfaced every few months, spread on Web sites populated by mainframe programmers. Just as frequent were rumors of a lost journal, a notebook that clearly documented the Fadowsky Formula and that had, finally, been discovered. None of the rumors had ever proven true.

Despite not knowing how the central technology in the Fadowsky Boxes worked, the brother-in-law continued to sell the machines at an incredible pace. Car manufacturers, airlines, insurance companies, the Social Security administration, the Department of Defense—they were companies and organizations with thousands of mainframes in use. And by 1980, virtually all of them had purchased Fadowsky Boxes from the brother-in-law or one of his salespeople. Even by 2004, no one had found a better, faster way to pull information from a mainframe.

And no one had deciphered the Fadowsky Formula—a kind of Fermat's Last Theorem for the computer industry.

And so, when Trevor came to my small office in New York in 2004 and slowly sat down in front of my desk, leaning forward very carefully as he whispered the words *Frederick Fadowsky*, I certainly knew who he was talking about. But in my fifteen years working for networking companies in Silicon Valley, Fadowsky had never been anything but the writer of some books I'd read, the name on a machine I had seen many times but not thought much about.

Trevor continued to stare at me. He leaned even closer. He whispered even lower. "Picture a man in thick black glasses," Trevor said. "Picture a pair of unnaturally crisp, chemically stiff brown trousers."

I had just taken over my father's company, having immediately moved the headquarters of what was then still called the Mainframe Supply Center Inc. from Redding, California, to New York City with vague but ambitious plans for expansion—doubling, maybe tripling, the number of employees from the thirty we then had as we moved away from merely selling third-party mainframe supplies. My father had died that summer, leaving me eighty percent ownership. Trevor, my only cousin and only living family, had been given the remaining twenty percent.

Trevor had come to my office to tell me that he'd bought a piece of software that was not only capable of deciphering the Fadowsky Formula but could increase the boxes' transfer rate by another factor of forty.

"It's a cash cow," Trevor told me. "A no-brainer add-on for companies with billions of dollars to spend."

"Why would someone sell this system to you?" I asked. "Why not market it themselves?"

"Because the woman who wrote the code is dead," he said. "She was from China. Her family just wants a royalty."

He told me her story. And I nodded. And I said, *Okay.*

And, as always, I believed him.

We sketched out a business plan. Trevor—a gifted programmer who'd long ago dropped out of college and who, until now, had shown no interest in my father's company—became salesman and product manager.

I managed the traditional mainframe supply company while laying the groundwork for expanded production, marketing and tech support. Trevor, who was still living in California, coordinated between the Chinese programmer's family and a series of outside software firms that were helping Trevor create the first pair of Blue Boxes. The two of us spoke daily, Trevor giving me updates on the progress of the programmers, until finally, nine months and more than $4 million later, two crates arrived in the New York office. Inside were the first Blue Boxes. Heavy, two feet tall, perfectly square except for the corners and edges just curved by the designers, the boxes looked like the newest minimalist creation of a long-cloistered German design team. They were covered in dark-blue plastic, had just a few connection points near the base and a few indicator lights on the front.

The boxes stood in the center of my office, and people came by, sometimes more than once, all looking at the machines, a few even asking to touch them.

Trevor arrived from California a few hours later, pulling two small silver crates that held a set of mobile satellite dishes. "The best news," he said, taking a bottle of vodka from his luggage, pouring himself a drink as he stared at the machines sitting between us, "the best news is the delay."

I stared silently at Trevor.

"The programmers," he said brightly. "They implemented the system with only a two-hour delay in the delivery of information from one Blue Box to the next."

I shook my head slowly. "You're saying," I managed to get out, "that people who use these boxes will have to wait two hours to receive their information?"

He sipped from his glass. He nodded toward me. "Yes."

"Trevor," I said carefully, "that's a huge problem."

"No, no, Robbie," he said, smiling and sipping again. "We call that a bonus feature."

The greatest value of the Core Blue Boxes was not really speed, Trevor explained to me, already falling into a well-honed—but as yet undelivered—sales pitch. The value of our Blue Boxes was that they freed up a client's mainframes from the time spent feeding information to the Fadowsky Boxes.

"Our clients free up their mainframes for the valuable work they need done," Trevor said to me. "And what some might call a delay," he added, shrugging, smiling wide, addressing—then deflating—a potential buyer's concerns, "well, be assured that our clients will never notice the delay. Because now, given all the mainframes they'll be freeing up, now they'll be able to send their information at least two hours *earlier* than before."

It was an extremely appealing yet highly circular concept that, even for me, seemed to slip away just as I'd digested it. But when Trevor purred *clients,* when he smiled that easy smile and shrugged so confidently, any concern I had drifted away.

And I had already learned that as powerful as Fadowsky's Formula was, Fadowsky's boxes did suffer from one severe weakness—companies had long ago realized that they had to double their mainframe's capacity with every eight pairs of Fadowsky Boxes they installed. As one company executive said, "Fadowsky marked the beginning of our addiction to speed."

With the Core Blue Boxes, however, the addiction could finally be broken. The extra mainframe capacity would be unnecessary. The cost savings would be huge.

A few days after Trevor arrived in New York, we made our first demonstration. Trevor had hooked the first company he'd called, an international auto parts supplier outside Detroit. We flew to Michigan the next day on four overextended credit cards and the last of our frequent-flyer miles. We met with the financial controller and the head of information technology, leading them through the demonstration. First Trevor told them about the many benefits of our Blue Boxes, described the development effort we'd put into them, and pushed the long and successful history of my father's company. Meanwhile, I connected a Blue Box to the Fadowsky Box on a mainframe in the company's headquarters, then drove with one of the company's IT people to a field office sixty miles away. There I connected the second Blue Box to a second mainframe. For the next twenty minutes, a series of small lights blinked on the Blue Box at the headquarters as the company's information was sent to our network.

"What is about to happen," Trevor told them, "is that, over the next twenty minutes, we will pull forty times more information from your mainframe than normal. And your mainframe will be ready for other uses."

The controller nodded warily. The head of IT frowned dismissively. Trevor smiled again, nodding in agreement with his own presentation, even casually offering both men a mint.

An hour later, Trevor arrived at the field office with the controller and the head of IT. At four P.M., on schedule, the information from the headquarters arrived at the field office, hitting our mobile satellite dish after spending two hours in our network. Once more Trevor emphasized that the delay had in fact created an opportunity. "Look at the many mainframes you have in operation, add up the total time now spent sending information from those mainframes, consider the speed at which data can now be sent not just to mainframes but to any type of computer, and you'll see what a series of Core Blue Boxes can do for you."

The head of IT checked the accuracy of the information that had been sent. The controller wrote numbers on a notepad. The two of them left the room. Trevor and I sat in silence, as if by speaking we might break some spell being cast around us.

When the two of them returned half an hour later, the head of IT sat down quietly. After a moment, he said only, "Interesting."

The controller nodded carefully, sitting down slowly, absently tapping his pencil on his notepad. "Yes," he said. "Interesting."

"We like to think so," Trevor said, smiling, leaning back in his chair, and I realized I was leaning back as well, legs crossed just as Trevor's were, hands in my lap just as his were.

The controller sat forward. "How much?"

I winced slightly. Throughout the development cycle, Trevor and I had argued back and forth about pricing for the Blue Boxes, Trevor pushing for a higher price, me pushing for a lower one, the two of us finally settling on $40,000 per box, which were always sold in pairs. Now even that price seemed embarrassingly high.

Trevor glanced down at his lap. He nodded slowly and seriously, his voice seeming to echo even before he spoke. "Eighty thousand per box," Trevor said, "with an annual service fee of twenty thousand."

The head of IT sat back, eyes getting wider. The controller very slowly licked the end of the pencil in his hand.

Meanwhile, I had lost the ability to breathe. My stomach had gone stiff. All light in the room was turning bright yellow. Never in my life have I had to urinate so badly. If I'd had a way to reach Trevor without standing, I would have shoved his head into the conference table.

If I'd had a way to speak, I would have dropped the price immediately.

"Well," I heard the controller say, his voice drifting toward me through the swirling, fading vortex into which I had sunk, "at that price we'll only be able to take delivery of ten boxes this year. But I think we can budget for another twenty in July."

And so it began.

The pricing was set. The boxes were in production. The expansion was in motion. Over the next three weeks, Trevor and I pitched another ten companies, each time running the same demonstration. Six of the companies said yes on the spot, two took just a few days to respond, and the other two—a California-based insurance company and a Boston-based pension-processing center that each bought thirty Blue Boxes—wrote us down-payment checks before we left the building.

"Certainly this will get you to the front of the line," Trevor said, shaking the hands of everyone in the room, thanking each person individually, making a joke tailored to some line or bit that each person had revealed during the meeting, ultimately leaving not as a salesman but as a revered ambassador sent to help that company.

He was brilliant. And I was in awe.

I remember flying back to New York after that tenth meeting, the two of us sitting in first class, a previously unheard-of luxury that, this time, Trevor had insisted on. I remember each of us replaying the day's presentation. I remember Trevor running his long fingers across the two down-payment checks—$300,000 sitting on the tray in front of him. I remember talking about plans for hiring a whole new staff of sales and customer service reps, network administrators, programmers, a marketing department and more. We would have to find larger office space. We would have to consult with bankers, lawyers, a new accounting firm. I remember Trevor making a toast to Fadowsky, who had made it all possible. I remember us smiling, the two of us laughing, these young men in fine suits so happy with the world.

I remember Trevor saying we would want to take the company public as soon as we possibly could.

And I also remember the blue and white fabric covering the seat in front of me. Remember the flight attendant passing by, remember each line and turn of her round face, the tray she held in her thin hands, remember the sound of the woman behind me clearing her throat, remember Trevor's eyes so black and wet and bright, remember the lights above us flickering for a second as I heard Trevor say that we would definitely need the money from an IPO. We would definitely need as much money as we could possibly get.

"Because now," I heard him saying, "now you've got to figure out how to make these Blue Boxes work."

I turned to him.

He smiled wide.

I said to him quietly, "You told me they worked."

He was still smiling. He nodded slowly but eagerly. "Yes," he said slowly, "but I lied."

I felt myself breathing carefully, speaking but not sure I was making sound. "About how much?"

"All of it, Robbie," he said quietly. "All of it is a lie."

"The demonstrations," I heard myself say. "How?"

"The information was sent to a couple of mainframes," he said. "In India, as a matter of fact. They processed the information, then sent it on to the destination."

I managed to put down my drink rather than spilling it in my lap. "Other mainframes," I said emptily.

"Yes."

"There was no Chinese programmer," I said. "No family that sold you this system."

"No."

"You had an idea. You needed my help."

"Yes."

"The Blue Boxes do nothing," I said slowly, empty, even emptier.

"Actually," he said, "I did have quite a bit of code written just to pull the information from the mainframes correctly. And I did come up with a way to pull information faster than ever before. It's just that the information can't be received without, well, without a lot of work."

I started to say it but stopped, knowing what Trevor would say next. Knowing exactly what words he would use.

"I mean, Robbie, why else would I need this bizarre two-hour delay?"

And I could only close my eyes.

Later I would tell myself it had all happened too fast for me to respond any other way. I would tell myself I had to fulfill the promises we'd made to these first companies. I would tell myself Core's reputation, my reputation, my father's, all had been put on the line.

But none of that is true.

There'd been time to stop this.

There had been plenty of time.

Instead I made a decision, made it in the first moment after Trevor told me the truth. I made a decision when I did not, immediately, say no to Trevor. When I didn't reject what he had done. When I didn't call him what he was—a fraud, a liar, a high-tech con man. The awful, sick feeling that spread through my chest as I rode on that airplane, the anger and disgust, the deepest disgust pushing down on me already—all of it was real. But even then I was thinking about something else. Already my thoughts had, at the lowest level in my mind, turned to something else entirely.

How to make this work.

And I can't say I was trying to protect my reputation or Trevor's. Not the company's. Not even my father's.

And I can't say I was doing this for the money—the $28 million in sales Trevor had closed in those first three weeks. The hundreds of millions we could raise in venture capital and an IPO.

And I can't say it was fear. Fear of being caught, of being embarrassed by the exposure of the lie. Fear of being arrested for the fraud we had already committed.

I thought about those things. All of them. But it was something else that drove me to push forward despite the lie. Something in myself. Something I was already repeating as I sat on that plane.

I can make this work.

All my life, I have worked. As a boy I went to my father's office on the weekends and during the summer and often after school, trailing him around the company he ran, happily doing whatever work he would give me. I took out the trash, I sorted papers, I typed nonsense on computers with fingers that couldn't spell my own name. I did anything he would let me do. Because that was my world. There was a comfort in that place, a warmth in the sounds of people talking and the sounds of computers and the sounds of the programmers and salespeople who all worked for my father. Over the years I would work hard in school, would take after-school jobs doing landscaping, construction, tech support. College, then graduate school, jobs during school and after, working sixty then seventy then eighty hours a week, programming, managing, coordinating the growth and development of new products, new applications, working till I was breathless and spent, and never once during that time did I question why I was doing it. All of it was work, and I enjoyed every moment. All I had ever wanted was to finish the task in front of me, then pick up the next, then another, then look around for more.

Faced with the lie Trevor had laid out in front me, my response was the same one I'd always had. Work. Work harder. Work until the problem went away. From the moment he told me the truth on that plane, my thought was to move forward, to do the best work I could. And if I did that, then soon, soon, I was sure, I would overcome Trevor's lie.

And so I set us out to grow. Adding staff, adding office space, adding computers and networking and servers and satellite connections, adding departments and managers and production capacity and adding clients and vendors and suppliers and partners.

And from that first day, adding pieces to a hidden series of mainframes and satellites and servers. Creating, almost immediately, a shadow network that made the Blue Boxes work.

Or, really, that made the boxes appear to work.

As Trevor had said, his Blue Boxes did do one thing as promised. Trevor had come up with a way to pull information from a mainframe forty times faster than a Fadowsky Box. The problem was that the information could not be sent to its destination—another mainframe or server—without a massive amount of processing.

What this meant was that for every minute of processing time we saved a client, we created five minutes of processing time for ourselves. And it was processing that could only be done by a mainframe. Many mainframes. Given the number of Blue Boxes Trevor sold in just the first few weeks, and given the huge amount of information being passed by the clients we were signing up, I could see that I would immediately be forced to set up a series of farms of dedicated mainframes. Soon the math became very simple. For every pair of Blue Boxes Trevor sold, Core was $100,000 in the hole.

In the first weeks after the demonstration, I spelled this out to Trevor. He only shrugged.

"Trevor," I said, "it will only take us a few months to spend what this first group of clients has paid."

He smiled. "Then I guess I'll have to bring in more money."

And that was something Trevor could do. He was on the road seven days a week, traveling across the country, across borders, across time zones and oceans. Calling me from cell phones and pay phones and hotel phones to report his sales for the day, the week or month. He sold Blue Boxes to banks, government agencies, defense contractors and insurance companies. He began to hire a sales staff that, by the end of the first year, numbered three hundred, all of them working from the road. No office, no desk at headquarters, they were trained by Trevor in hotel rooms worldwide, then given a corporate credit card, a stack of business cards and two rolling silver cases holding demo Blue Boxes and satellite dishes.

Soon they too were reporting sales to the New York headquarters. Within a year sales reached $50 million a week.

And soon we were deep into a course that was part shell game, part Ponzi scheme as I took money from new clients to pay for the processing of the old, secretly buying services from vendors around the world, rapidly buying our own mainframes to covertly process the clients' information. It was a race, really, that we could lead, for now, by adding new clients, by finding outside investors and by taking the company public. And we did all that. In a flurry of glowing press coverage, singularly positive word of mouth, and the flawless analysis of the Wall Street brokerage houses.

Within six months of the first demonstration, Core was a phenomenon. First we were pictured on the covers of some twenty niche computer magazines. Then we started finding our way onto the front pages of major newspapers and the covers of national magazines. Trevor and I were hailed as groundbreaking and tenacious entrepreneurs, farsighted capitalists who'd outlast the faddish dot-coms, new-thinking visionaries climbing to the forefront of the newest of the new economies.

Meanwhile, the incoming money meant that, in the first year, I'd been able to build a massive secret network of satellites and mainframe computers. Stretching from Oregon to Ireland to Indonesia, at first the secret systems lived within the cracks of our normal operations. They were funded without the knowledge of our internal and external auditors, hundreds of millions of dollars shuttling between field offices, subsidiaries, foreign bank accounts and, increasingly, a series of shell corporations owned by me personally.

This was the shadow network, and, in the first months of our growth, I accessed it through the main control center for all of Core's systems. Comprised of ten huge status boards and four long, dense rows of computers and monitors, the control center was staffed twenty-four hours a day by thirty technicians—a kind of small-scale Johnson Space Center in the heart of lower Manhattan.

Soon, though, I realized I couldn't manage the shadow network through the control center. Too many people had access to those systems. Too many people might see what I was really doing. And so I'd led Leonard and his tech team in the creation of a single server that would control the flow of all information through the company. It was located off to the side of the control center, behind a heavy door leading to a small, temperature-controlled room only I could access. No one but me could log onto the machine. No one but me could even touch it.

The machine was called Shimmer.

To all the employees, to the observers from the outside world, Shimmer was Core's ultimate corporate secret. By managing the movement of information among all our Blue Boxes, Shimmer was the key to having solved the problem of the Fadowsky Formula.

But in truth Shimmer was much more than anyone realized—more, even, than what the programmers themselves realized. Shimmer was an interface between the company and what soon became the thousands of pieces of the shadow network.

And so, late at night, I stared at Shimmer, Shimmer representing all the information in full motion, data transformed into images and color, curling shapes and ever-turning lines. Shimmer was omniscient, the infinitely powerful reflection of the secrets it tracked. And, of course, this was yet another reason I was the only person who had access to Shimmer. Because Shimmer simplified everything it controlled. With Shimmer, the shadow network could be displayed in the simplest of images, made clear to every manager in the company, to every analyst on the outside, and to Whitley and her SWAT team.

Imagine a dream, a dream with clarity and precision, a dream that can't be explained or deciphered, but a dream so real you believe it, you touch it, you remember it completely because every idea in that dream, every person, every notion and decision, every part of it makes sense. That was Shimmer.

And so it was Shimmer that kept Core Communications alive. Because without it, without the simplified images and controls Shimmer gave to me, I would never have been able to manage the shadow network, its breadth, its changes and constant growth.

By the year 2007, Shimmer controlled a shadow network made up of almost two hundred locations inside and outside the company. Shimmer made sense of the elaborate mix of technology, finance and deception that drove the shadow network. Faced with handling an ever-increasing amount of information from the new clients we brought on, Shimmer could easily decide which part and place of the shadow network would be used to sustain the company. Shimmer might instantly decide to use one of Core's own satellites to bounce information to a strategic partner in Mexico, who in turn might send the information to a set of mainframes housed in a building managed by Tech Now, LLC, in San Antonio, Texas, one of the faceless locations that made up the shadow network. Essentially an air-conditioned warehouse feeding uninterruptible power to twenty-four mainframes and a satellite dish, Tech Now was housed in a building owned by an Arizona-based real estate development company of which I, personally, was sole shareholder. The mainframes in the warehouse were owned by a Washington-based networking supply company, which in turn was owned by Red Tree Limited, a holding company operated out of the Cayman Islands and funded entirely by me. The dish on the warehouse roof pointed to a satellite leased from an Austin-based company that resold the services of Global Satellite Security, one of fourteen wholly owned satellite subsidiaries of Core Communications. The few system administrators needed to operate the mainframes in San Antonio had been hired by yet another company, this one based in Germany and funded by a series of my personal foreign bank accounts. These admins came from a local Texas employment agency, were paid high wages by the hour, and were given only the lowest-level access to the machines.

(Probably, given the usually disjointed, even paranoid state of mind so frequently exhibited by contract technical help, most of the admins thought—or at least wanted to think—that they were working for some secret outpost of the CIA.)

And what made possible the use of the San Antonio mainframes in the first place was that, months earlier, the mainframes and satellite uplink had been configured by a team of friendly customer service and tech support representatives from the world's leading provider of high-capacity mainframe networking solutions, Core Communications. A Core team had been hired to install twenty-four Blue Boxes. They'd gone through a test upload and download of information and billed the then Portland-based owner of the mainframes for the work. Once the invoice had been paid, Core had never heard from the Portland-based company again.

What this all meant was that, in a period of three months, I'd used one of my personal bank accounts in the Cayman Islands to push money through a short-lived Portland limited liability company in order to pay Core—whose stock I'd sold in order to deposit the money in the Caymans in the first place—to connect the computers to Core's real network. Once the bill was paid, a Seattle attorney working at the behest of an anonymous client had closed the Portland company, ended the contracts of the three workers and sold the company's assets, which consisted entirely of twenty-four new mainframes. The assets were bought by a recently formed company in Washington, D.C., whose attorney hired two local temporary employees to fly to San Antonio and install a relatively small piece of software on twenty-four mainframes sitting—untouched but operable—in a warehouse near the airport.

It was that final small piece of software that told Shimmer these mainframes were part of the shadow network.

These were the trails and connections that I tracked in my spreadsheet and that flowed through Shimmer. Even more, these were the threads and connections wrapped around all my thoughts and all my dreams. The shadow network was, for me, a mass of places, people, machines, work and decisions. Bright and shifting and shimmering as it grew. And it did, always, grow.

And none of it—none of this growth—was questioned or doubted inside or outside the company. Because as long as we were acquiring new businesses every few weeks, as long as sales continued to exceed our best projections, as long as the press continued to treat Core— and me—as a darling of the business world, then the board of directors, the investment bankers, the brokers and financial analysts, no one would look past the surface of what I did.

From the beginning I'd feared every sale Trevor made, each addition putting pressure on the shadow network. But from the beginning, I'd known that in truth Trevor and his salespeople were the key to keeping the lie alive.

But not even Trevor knew all the details of the system I'd built. He'd never seen Shimmer. He didn't know about the spreadsheet I used to track the pieces of the shadow network. And really, Trevor didn't care. For him, Core was only about today's sales. From the beginning Trevor was sure I would figure out how to support the commitments he made every day, each sale adding pressure to the shadow system I was frantically attempting to build, each sale sinking us further into our fraud, lies and secrets. But Trevor had never worried about the collapse. Not only because he was soon worth half a billion dollars but also because Trevor found easy justifications for what we were doing.

"Core works today," Trevor would say to me. "If it crashes tomorrow, we'll cash our last checks, drop our bankruptcy papers at the courthouse and move back to beautiful California."

Early on I'd found myself repeating Trevor's logic. I'd told myself it was an end no different—to the outside world at least—than the unintended failures of so many tech companies.

Except that we were lying. And we'd been lying from the very beginning. Except that we were violating untold laws and regulations just to stay afloat. Except that when Core collapsed, Trevor and I would go to jail if someone managed to figure out what we'd been doing.

And except that, for me, the commitments I was making to people every day—to clients, investors, the board and, especially, to the new employees I had asked to join what soon became a high-tech crusade—all that ultimately outweighed Trevor's prearranged justifications for the collapse. These people were giving their time. They were leveraging their futures. And they were doing it all for Core Communications.

And so the only exit possible was to keep building the company. To try to outrun the collapse.

That, at least, is what I told myself each morning. Each night.

Make it work.

Once Shimmer had been completed and I was able to rely on it to manage the growth of the systems, I realized that as long as sales continued to explode, as long as cash from investors continued to pour in, it would not be a lack of money that ultimately caused our collapse. What would bring about the end was the very size of the system I was building. The shadow network would collapse at the exact moment when the amount of information passed by our growing number of clients finally and very suddenly outstripped the capacity of the network. And when that moment came, the system would simply stop working. The shadow network, Shimmer, the real operations—all of it would suddenly go dead.

That is what Shimmer told me.

The only thing it couldn't tell me was when the collapse would happen.

Again and again throughout those first years, Shimmer showed me ways to extend the company's life. I'd stare at Shimmer, watching on my screen as Shimmer ran through scenarios, possibilities, options, answers. And each time I'd see it, in the images and notions and numbers of Shimmer, I'd see another way to keep the company alive a little longer.

It had been three years. Three impossibly long years of anxious, exhausting work by thousands of people.

And when it did collapse, I would be rich. Because every dollar I spent building up the shadow network, every shell company I established, every outside asset I purchased, all of this meant I was moving my money away from the collapse of the company. Moving it to safety. Hundreds of millions already were safe.

None of this had been set up by Trevor. None of this had been his thought or suggestion. From that first moment on the airplane when he'd told me the truth about his lie, from then on, Trevor—the evil cousin who'd haunted me since we'd been children and who I wanted, more than anything, to blame all of this on—from then on Trevor had been completely uninvolved in making the Blue Boxes work or in creating a shadow network to support us.

From that moment on, all of it had come from me.

It's in the morning that he sees it. Having been here all night. In the dark of a test center on eleven, he feels it in his eyes. Feels suddenly that it is morning. Knowing it before he even looks at the clock. And it is, of course. Morning again. And Leonard makes his way to nineteen, to an old storeroom with a window that still opens, and he lifts it, looking out toward the sunrise with the air pouring in, and he wishes he could describe it. Wishes he could draw it on paper. Put it into words.

What Leonard sees is the company. All of it. Each building and each office and each server and each keyboard and screen. And, even more, what he sees is each connection. The machines and the lines and the information, each tiny bit of information on and between each building and office. He sees it. There. Frozen but moving. Captured and described in his vision. There is no part that he does not see. Does not know.

And he smiles.

He feels the morning light growing warm on his face, the morning air clean, blowing in on his neck and eyes. Clean like California air,

*clean like San Francisco. And now, for a moment, this is not New York.
This is somewhere else.*

He wishes he were somewhere else.

Not a different company. Not a different job.

But a different city.

I hate this city. I hate it, every day.

For this morning, though, there are the connections. And in the sunlight they feel real and full and within his reach, and he loves these mornings, when he can see it all. Seeing something more, something like all the lines between everything around him. Not just in the company. Not just in the systems. But connections everywhere. There have to be connections.

How could there not be?

How could it not, in the end, be made sense of?

He tells himself he doesn't believe in God. But he knows he does. Because there has to be an architect. Of everything Leonard knows and sees and especially everything he feels, now, in the sunlight, in this window. There is good and bad.

I hate this city.

Maybe it could be different, though. Maybe, if he knew more people. Knew some people from here. From New York. Even from work.

Just some people. Friends.

And he knows he can't really see all the connections in the company. Knows that Robbie's kept him from seeing so many parts of the company. There are secrets only Robbie can see.

Leonard knows that.

I know.

But he doesn't like it. Because it's not safe. Not right. He should be able to see it all, see the whole of the company. It's the safest thing. The best thing.

I only want the best thing.

But he knows, also, that he wants to see it. Wants to see Shimmer. Again. Wants to see the system he built, then lost. The server at the heart of all the connections, the ones he can see and the ones he can't. Robbie's server now.

How much more he could see with Shimmer. So much more.

He smiles. Because he misses Shimmer. And it's a silly thing to miss.

And he smiles because he thinks that, with Shimmer, he'd see as much as Fadowsky.

Almost. Because no one saw as much as Fadowsky.

But he thinks that maybe, with Shimmer, he'd see all the parts of the Fadowsky Formula. He thinks that maybe, with Shimmer, he could write his own solution to the Fadowsky Formula. A solution like the ones he hears about almost every week, these rumors of lost journals, a lost Fadowsky journal that finally solves the formula. That finally gives everyone like him an answer.

How did Fadowsky do it?

How did Robbie do it?

He hears someone walking across the floor above him. Knows the motion of the building will soon begin. Knows he should head to his office. Pull clean clothes from a drawer there. Wash up in the bathroom. Start his day.

But he's not quite ready.

Not quite.

There is an architect. There has to be.

And there is good and bad.

And there is this sunlight. And there are these mornings. And there are these times, like now, when he feels so tired, feels so far past exhausted, when it's as if he's never slept and will never sleep, and in those moments he feels something wonderful.

He feels good.

Someday, maybe, I'll tell someone about this.

He'd like to hear what they might say.

CHAPTER 3

I 'd entered a day of half-finished projects. Wednesday afternoon, and my notes on draft reports were ending on page two or three. Partially completed e-mails waited in my outbox for another revision. Files with titles like *InvestorOverview— DRAFT1* and *PerformanceAnalysis—UNFINISHED* littered the desktop of my computer.

I knew it had been caused by Trevor's appearance the day before. And by the firing I would have to do in Omaha. One more sales team. Sixty people.

I would have to leave for Omaha this afternoon.

You take away a part of someone's self when you fire them. You tell them they are not as good a person as they thought they were.

I sat at my desk, unable to finish anything. I clicked aimlessly on my mouse. I restacked the papers in front of me. I stared at the ceiling, then floor.

I'm sorry, but I have to let you go.

I closed my eyes. I saw their faces.

I have to tell you that you aren't what you wanted to be.

There was nothing I hated more.

And so the answer, as always, was to visit Perry.

"So much of my life was being conducted from the sitting position," Perry was telling me now, as I sat in his office. "Even when I stood it seemed to be in preparation to sit down again. And so I decided that, during working hours, I would forgo lateral movement of almost any kind."

I was sitting in a child's wooden school chair in Perry's very dimly lit office on the eighth floor. There were no windows, no lamps, only the glow from four computer screens. Five more small chairs like the one I sat in were positioned around a very low butcher-block table that served as a conference table. Perry himself was in a full-sized desk chair with arms, but one positioned low to the floor, like both his desks.

"And sitting's been made so much better," Perry said now, voice taking the tone of a late-night infomercial announcer, an unprecedented performance made more disjointed by the fact that he was speaking directly into his screen, "because of the addition of this wonderful children's furniture."

I shook my head slowly. Maybe, I thought, this is what it's like to be a parent, looking at these people I've brought into the company, that I've enjoyed and spent so much time with, but who continually make me wonder what I've done to cause them to turn out this way.

The children's furniture was a new addition to Perry's office. However, an office without light had been Perry's normal environment since he'd started our R&D department two and a half years earlier. "All successful R&D," he'd told me then, "must be conducted in the absence of light."

In truth, the darkness was just one more sign of Perry's deeply scarred state of mind. Perry, who had joined Core just weeks after Trevor and I sold our first Blue Box, was an almost mystical figure within the company. Having worked in, started or run virtually every department in the company—Technical Development, Strategic Planning, Network Support, Human Resources, Accounting—Perry was now an enlightened burnout hiding quite publicly from the pressures of the company, an internal savant resting quietly in a darkness he'd created for himself. Longtime employees sought out his advice on the most vexing of problems. New employees were told stories of how, when we started the expansion of the company, Perry went weeks without leaving the office, how he wrote and tested software, generated press releases, created marketing campaigns, hired and trained new staff.

When Core went public, Perry knew I was ready to give him any job he wanted. Instead, he'd told me he would have to quit. "I've left something behind," he whispered to me as he lay on the floor of my office, his thin frame looking gray and light and fragile after three days without eating, six days without sleep and two weeks without leaving the building. "And whatever I've left behind," he whispered, "I don't think it will come back."

I immediately sent him to the Virgin Islands for a two-week stay. I bought him a new co-op on the upper West Side. I sent him to a therapist with the best of reputations. In total, it was enough to keep him working at Core. But he refused my offer of a position on the senior staff, finally saying he thought a comfortable job in R&D would suit him best. He'd been hoping for a quiet, almost clerical position. "I want my job to follow a linear path," he told me then. "I do A, which combines with B to form C. I do it over and over, every day. No uncertainty, no anxiety."

Instead I made him senior vice president of the entire R&D department, where Technical Development, Production, Marketing and Operations all converged in an unclean mix of competing priorities and constantly shifting goals.

He didn't speak to me for two months. But he didn't quit.

"I can go five hours, sometimes six," Perry was saying now, "and still not have to stand."

"Are you alone all this time?" I asked.

"They just come to me," he said, his fingers moving fast on the keyboard, hand moving the mouse in slight, fluid bursts, yet the rest of his body somehow absent of motion. "They bring questions, they bring reports, someone orders me food, others bring me coffee. There is always coffee."

Perry's thin legs were stretched out easily below his low desk, his bare feet crossed near a small bank of plugs, his toes wrapped absently around two black network cables.

I'd heard women say that Perry was the best-looking man in the office. It was a realization each had come to not immediately but only after years of seeing him walk quietly through the office, tall and thin and boyish in the simplicity of his dark features and uncombed hair.

"And so what do you do while you're here?" I asked.

"I answer questions. I dispel rumors. I offer context to various employees' apprehensions. I'm like some kind of priest, really, ministering to a wayward band of directionless youths."

"Powerful."

"Surprisingly so."

"And everyone who comes here," I asked, crossing my legs now, eyes fully adjusted to the dim light, the pale glow of the screens, "everyone sits happily in these tiny chairs?"

"Absolutely," Perry said. "There's something therapeutic about those chairs. A return to innocence and simplicity."

"My elementary school normally kept the lights on," I said, tilting back just a bit, front chair legs lifted from the dense carpet.

"So it's a mixed ambience," Perry said, shrugging easily, eyes so bright and white as he blinked, blinked from one screen to the next, blinking slowly, easily, the fluid, simple shifts of Perry. "And actually, I'd like to mix it up even more, adding blacklights, mirrors, maybe one of those smoke machines. There's talk of raising my office a foot or two, then building an outer office where the people wait before entering my chamber."

I found myself tilting my head to the side. I picked up a paper clip, a shining silver line just a foot from my low seat. "Your description of this suggests it is more than a joke."

He shrugged again, a slow and easy motion paired with another blink, another shift of screens, another pass at the mouse, another rapid, silent flurry across his keyboard. "The Facilities people are actually considering the request much more seriously than I'd anticipated. They sent up an engineer. Two men measured my desks. I'm told I'll have draft plans for review by the end of next week."

"Will you please join the senior staff?" I asked, a question I posed to him so frequently that it had become a kind of incidental segue in our communication, an empty filler phrase like *let's see* or *so anyway*.

He waved me off, turning to face another screen. "Please. We've discussed. We've decided. It's not for me."

I nodded slowly. I glanced out the door. Young men peered toward us from the openings of their workstations. Young women walked slowly along the aisles near Perry's office. All had clearly manufactured a reason to look in on us as we talked.

"You're a rock star," Perry said, although he seemed not to have looked out his office door or even to have noticed that I was looking out at the people. Actually, he'd yet to turn and look at me.

"They try to touch me," I said. "In the hallways. In meetings."

"Relish it," he said.

"I hate to be touched."

"Seek therapy," he said. "I've got a good person in mind."

"No time."

"You could give up whatever sleep you're managing to get."

"Join the senior staff," I said.

"But then they'll start to touch me too."

"No, they won't. No one touches Cliff. No one touches Whitley. No one touches Leonard or Julie."

He waved me off. He turned to another screen. He tilted the monitor toward me, his finger tracing a long line of numbers and accounting codes. He said quietly, almost to himself, "Do you see how payroll is growing faster in Advertising versus the PR group?"

I scanned the numbers. "Isn't that because we're adding people faster in Advertising?"

He shook his head. He clicked a mouse. A color chart appeared. "It's not people," Perry said. "It's raises. Apparently the ad people are lobbying harder and, most notably, more effectively for raises."

"Surprising," I said, nodding as I studied the numbers. Then I turned to look at him, raising my voice slightly. "Are you supposed to have access to this information?" I asked him.

"Me?" he said, still staring into the screen. "Absolutely not. It's some kind of loophole from the old days, when I ran Accounting, Advertising and PR. No one's ever taken me or my password out of this system."

"Get the hell out of there," I said, voice rising.

He waved me off, turning to another screen. "Whitley and her SWAT team are so worried about rogue sections and outside intrusions, they'll never find me."

"I'm not worried about them finding you," I said. "You're not allowed in there, so you shouldn't be in there."

He nodded slowly, once more looking at the payroll information as he built a color graph on the screen in front of him. "So it's an ethical issue," he said carefully.

"Right and wrong."

"Basic principles."

"Fundamental questions."

"By the way," he said, "I want a raise."

"Don't you have to pee?" I asked suddenly.

"Now?" he responded.

"While you're here in your office. Five or six hours without standing. That's what you said. But don't you have to get up to pee?"

He shook his head. "I've trained myself not to be distracted by the needs of the outside world."

"Freak."

"Okay, so I sneak out sometimes," he said, thin shoulders rising easily, falling in a slow and thoughtless shrug. "But only when I'm sure no one's looking."

"As long as the spell isn't broken," I said.

"Exactly," he said.

"There are some things I'm worried about," I said. Leaning back in my chair again. Carefully placing the silver paper clip back on the floor.

"Such as?" I heard Perry say.

"Join the senior staff," I said.

"If you're saying that joining the senior staff means sharing in your worries, then you're a worse salesman than I already thought."

"I am definitely a worse salesman than you already think."

"How is Trevor?" he asked.

"He's in town."

"I thought I saw him. I often think I see him, actually. Turning a corner into a conference room, stepping into an elevator as the doors close, disappearing down a hallway leading to Unoccupied Territory. He's a phantom."

"Trevor likes you," I said.

He paused, finger poised above his mouse. I thought he might even turn to me. "That makes me worry," Perry said, then carefully swiveled his chair to another screen. "I don't want Trevor doing anything for me. No special treatment. No favors."

"Pact with the devil," I said.

"Pact with the devil," he said.

A young man entered the office, trying to hand a number of papers to Perry. I glanced out the door and caught five heads leaning out of nearby workstations, saw another five people standing near a printer, all staring into Perry's office.

"A critical delivery," Perry said to the young man, smiling slightly, taking the papers without looking at them. "Documents that could not wait. That had to be given to me in person, right now."

The young man nodded awkwardly. "Well," he started, pausing, glancing at me. "Yes. I guess."

I slowly uncrossed, then recrossed my legs, carefully leaning to the left in my tiny chair, gradually removing myself from the young man's reach. I was sure I could see him hesitate, unprepared for my shift in position, quickly rethinking his previously planned effort to touch me. For a second I thought he might even pretend to stumble and fall.

And for that same second I envisioned myself moving out of the way as he hit the floor.

Fortunately, he left Perry's office without any sudden motions or feigned accidents.

I was suddenly very aware that I was sitting on the floor.

"I think Trevor might be evil," I said to Perry. "I think something might be wrong with him."

"You've said this for as long as I've known you," he said, his head tilting right as he followed the information on his screen. "Why are you saying it again now?"

I shrugged. "With every acquisition, he throws out another forty, fifty, even sixty salespeople."

"And so because of this you're worried about him?"

It was a moment before I found an answer. "I'm worried one of these people might hurt him," I said.

"No, you're not," Perry said, then tilted another monitor toward me. It showed a three-dimensional color graph floating in the center of the screen. "Watch the green bar," he said, and for now we wouldn't talk about Trevor.

Perry alone could do this to me. He took me out of my world. Although, maybe, with Perry alone did I let it happen.

Perry's eyes squinted eagerly as he spoke. "We're about to take an upload from a regional Medicare office in Tulsa. There'll be a massive spike in the DMZ," he said.

"DMZ?" I asked.

"The control center," Perry said, referring to the main control center for Core's entire network.

"Apparently," I said, part comment, part question as I reflected on this new bit of company lingo, "apparently *control center* was just too simple."

"Too clear."

"Too boring."

"Too obvious."·

"How do you know it's coming?" I asked quietly, absently, but staring at the screen, now beginning to study the multicolored bars.

Perry tapped a mouse. A second color graph appeared in a corner of the screen. "This program here," he said. "It tracks the historical patterns of our clients in order to create a predictive model for upcoming data transfers."

Again my voice was rising. "And why are you able to get in here?" I asked. "This is a new, highly classified system. You shouldn't have access to this."

He shrugged. "I know people in the DMZ," he said. "They'll do me favors."

"In return for . . . ?"

He shrugged again. "There are a lot of favors being exchanged in this company," he said. "In many ways, favors are a currency more valuable than purchase orders, budgets or signed supervisor memos."

"More powerful than me?" I asked, smiling slightly.

"Sometimes," he said, "favors are even more powerful than Whitley."

I turned back to the graph, had taken the mouse from Perry before I realized it, rotating the image to the left, then down, studying the patterns shown in the colors. "I can imagine you doing a lot for this kind of access," I said.

He shrugged again. "There are all kinds of favors. I've heard of high-end computers being delivered to a particular employee weeks ahead of schedule. I've heard of Swedish-designed desk lamps appearing, unannounced, on a programmer's desk. I've heard of extended oral sex in Unoccupied Territory. I've heard of fries and an orange soda brought in for dinner." He turned to me for the first time. "Sometimes it doesn't take much."

I was suddenly aware of how close we were, just a few inches apart.

One of those moments in an office, physical self-awareness in the fray of talking and thinking and things so removed from your body, your motions.

Perry was still turned to me. His eyes a violet from the light of the shining screens. I wondered for a moment if my eyes were white and shining too. "You're worried about something else," he said.

I shifted in my small chair. I crossed my legs. I realized I was extremely comfortable. In a moment, I nodded.

"No one's going to hurt Trevor," Perry said, sitting back easily in his chair.

"No."

"That's just a story for you, some quip about how a disgruntled former employee might go postal on Trevor, taking him hostage in a conference room."

"Right," I said.

"There's something else," he said.

"There's something else," I said.

I'd first met Perry that night three years ago. The night Trevor had told me the truth about the Blue Boxes. The night when, already, I was telling myself the decision to continue Trevor's lie was made for me, around me, a course set out for us before I even knew what had happened. Any number of people could have happened to call me that night, asking to join the company. But it was Perry I talked to. He called because he wanted to get in on what we were doing. He didn't care about salary, about perks or a title, about anything except the opportunity, the idea, the limitless potential of Core Communications.

There were so many people who'd shown that kind of commitment to this place, that kind of confidence in what we were trying to do. But Perry was the one who called first.

"I'd love to bring you on," I'd said to him on the phone, staring vaguely toward the wall behind my desk. "Because these Blue Boxes, it's amazing what they can do."

I looked at Perry now, seeing in him all the years of late nights, of new projects and expansion, seeing the memory of those longest six months when we'd first launched the company, and as I looked I saw in Perry some kind of real-life mirror, my tiredness, my worry and my success all sitting in a low chair in front of me.

I stood up now, moving slowly, staring for a second at the child's chair so far down on the floor. "Join the staff," I said to Perry.

He turned back to the first screen. He shook his head. He smiled and there was a look like he'd just been told the smallest of jokes. An easy, glad look.

I have had a lot of friends in my life. But at this point, Perry was my only close friend.

Although, in the last year and a half, I'd seen him outside work just once.

"It's amazing, Perry," I said, already stepping back toward the door, seeing the words I would say, knowing they would be nothing more than some partial truth, one more distraction from what I really wanted to tell him, what I wanted to tell everyone. "It's amazing," I said, "the things Trevor gets away with."

Perry turned to me again. Staring. Nodding. Still with that look, easy, the joke still funny, retelling it to himself. And for a moment it was as if he knew what I was thinking, as if he'd broken into one more system at Core, this time trading untold favors for complete access to my thoughts.

And for that moment, I just smiled.

I sat in my chair. Staring at the names.

It was Wednesday still, late morning. I'd left Perry's office wanting to track Trevor down, to try and force him not to fire the sales team in Omaha. I was ready with my arguments—performance histories for each salesperson, the potential legal ramifications of such a complete purge, the financial and morale risks a dismissal like that would entail.

Then I found a note from Trevor on the chair in my office. He'd left New York. And he'd called Omaha himself to fire the sales team over the telephone. *Open Season,* his note ended. *The Omaha Massacre.*

Sixty names.

I sat down in my chair. I stared at the names of each of the salespeople who'd been fired. And, after a minute, I put the names in a file. Put the file in a tray, where it would be taken away by my assistant. Feeling something like anger toward Trevor, feeling something like sadness for the people in Omaha. But, more than anything, feeling a sense of resignation. Resignation that, inevitably, Trevor always got his way. And resignation that, inevitably, I let it happen.

I stood up. Walking out of my office. Out into the noise and people and paper and meetings. Moving again. On my cell phone again. Asking Julie to meet me in the mailroom to discuss production goals among the motion and light of those huge copying machines. Wanting to lose myself once more to the rhythms of the company.

It was a few hours later that my phone clicked. A text message. I read the words. And I almost dropped the phone. Almost spoke out loud.

No.

The message was simple. An automated notice from a server in Budapest.

Server security scan begins.

It was an unscheduled security check. A check of the most detailed and severe kind. A check on a facility that housed machines not just for the real network but also for the shadow network.

Security scans had been done many times before. But today the scan would be different. Today Whitley had found another rogue section. And this one was in the DMZ, the most critical, most secure area of the company.

I called Leonard.

"So you're conducting some checks on the system," I said to him.

It was a moment before Leonard responded. "You heard about my rogue section," Leonard said slowly. "SWAT says they did no damage." He was quiet for a moment. "But Whitley wants me to run major checks on any systems that the rogue section recently touched."

It was the worst response he could have given me. This was a check that could quickly reveal whole parts of the shadow network.

"That's good," I said, trying to breathe easily, trying to keep my voice slow, normal—even as I turned toward the nearest staircase, making my way back to my office as quickly as possible. To my office and to Shimmer. "Good to be safe," I said.

I could see Whitley, across the floor, standing near an office doorway. Watching me as I all but ran toward the stairs.

I had to get back to my office and move all traces of the shadow network off the servers in Budapest. And I had only a few minutes to get it started.

Leonard was quiet, and I thought maybe he'd hung up. I almost ended the call, but in a moment he spoke.

"There's something you didn't ask me," he said. "About this rogue section."

I was slightly breathless as I came out of the stairwell onto the twentieth floor. "What do you mean?" I asked, moving past metal desks and glass conference rooms toward my office.

I knew Leonard was upset about this rogue section. A group of three working in the DMZ. Leonard's DMZ. We were calling them a rogue section. But they weren't. Because they hadn't been working on some fake project. Hadn't been playing some joke on each other or their boss.

These three had simply been doing nothing. For months.

These three had simply burned out. Completely.

"You haven't asked why they did it," Leonard said. "The rogue section. Why do I think they did it."

Into my office, past the couch and chairs and conference table, up a step and to my desk, near the window, almost pushed against that window.

Leonard wasn't going to respond to his own question. I pulled back my chair, starting my three monitors, asking him, "Why do you think they did it?"

"I know these people," Leonard said. "I hired them. Each of them."

I was launching Shimmer, already searching for an available facility. Some place that could immediately accept the work being done in Budapest.

"I realize that," I said to Leonard. "I do."

"I think they were afraid," Leonard said, and I paused for a moment. Stopped my search.

"I think they were afraid they were about to fail," he said.

And I knew I had to keep searching. Had to reroute data, had to destroy and erase the shadow network from Budapest. Now. But I needed to listen. Wanted to know. Wanted to hear Leonard.

Leonard was quiet. I thought maybe he wouldn't say more.

The colors of Shimmer spun, a fading mix of numbers and motion.

"Fail at what?" I finally asked.

"Fail," he said.

"Why would they fail?"

"They were part of the group," he said. "My group trying to come up with an alternate Blue Box."

In his first few months working for Core, I'd started to think Leonard might figure out how to make a Blue Box really work. That he might see a way around the shadow network. And so I'd given him that task, asking Leonard and Perry to create a group dedicated to building a better Blue Box. I'd framed it as an internal challenge to the assumptions behind our current system, an attempt to prevent us from becoming technically complacent, an effort to find new ways to work with the Fadowsky Formula.

The group they'd formed was made up of some twenty-five of the best programmers and network administrators in the world. They worked in the DMZ and in a private area on the eighth floor, not far from Perry. They were freed of distractions. They were highly paid. They had no limit on their resources or budget.

Two years later, they still had no idea how to create a Blue Box that worked.

Now I had Shimmer in front of me. But I had heard something in Leonard's voice. His own fear. Leonard's own fear of failure.

But I was moving again. I had to be moving. I pointed Shimmer at Eastern Europe. Then Asia. Then America. And saw it. Saw where to move the information from Budapest.

Shimmer. Always, it seemed, I came back to Shimmer.

I sent the command to begin the move, Shimmer immediately playing out the shift, this outpost of the shadow network in Budapest now a solid green sphere emptying itself from each axis. Each axis leading to another sphere far off in the distance. Each axis leading to another piece of the shadow network.

"Can't do it," Leonard said. "Can't find a way. Can't come close."

I didn't know how to respond. Felt myself only nodding as I listened.

Shimmer was still green, the sphere slowly emptying out. But now three red strands were crossing the bottom of the shape. Leonard's scan had reached my servers, the scan crossing the surface of the shadow network like the thin red tentacles of some microscopic disease.

Please, I thought. *Please don't find it.*

I heard myself say, "It's okay that you can't find an answer."

Shimmer was shining green, the sphere half empty, the tentacles multiplying, spreading over the surface, trying at every point to break into the globe.

And I wished suddenly that Perry were here. Beside me. Wished I were in his office.

"It is failure," Leonard said. "How could it be anything but failure?"

I didn't know how to respond. Wanted, for that moment, to tell

Leonard the truth. To tell them they weren't failing to make a Blue Box. Because it couldn't be done.

I heard myself say, "Maybe it can't be done."

"But they can't even repeat what you did with the Blue Boxes," he said. "Can't even understand that."

I blinked. I nodded.

Shimmer glowed red, the tentacles like a web now, covering the sphere, the spaces between each tentacle filling in, one by one.

An image of Whitley appeared in the corner of one of my screens. She wasn't able to see me, was instead making a call to my computer. Wanting me to switch on my camera and talk to her at her machine. I didn't. But still it was as if she were watching me, Whitley and her SWAT team spying on my efforts to salvage the shadow network, as if somehow she could see the model spread out across my screen, could see Shimmer reflecting the scan in Budapest.

Shimmer moved inside the sphere now. It was almost empty. All remnants of the shadow network almost completely removed from Budapest. The tentacles, Leonard's scan, beginning to enter the globe one at a time, dropping fast through the empty space, just missing as the shadow network poured out of the bottom of this world.

My assistant called from outside my office. "Whitley's looking for you," he said.

I covered my phone for a moment, leaning toward the door to my office. "Tell her I can't," I said. "Not now. Can't."

Leonard's tentacles kept falling, now seeming to fill the inside of the globe.

"It's failure," Leonard said. "There's nothing to call it but failure."

In a moment, Whitley's face left the camera, then the camera turned off. In another moment, I saw I had an e-mail from her.

I haven't told Leonard yet, her message read. *But, so you are aware, SWAT has seen some things in the past few weeks. Some odd movements. Some unexpected shifts at a host of overseas facilities. It could be that there are more rogue sections like the one we found today. We're concerned.*

"I don't think," I started to say to Leonard, but my voice stopped. I watched the screen. The last of the globe would not empty. I tapped on my desk. I pressed back against my chair.

And watched.

Watched as the tentacles fell, full speed, each one crashing toward the last pieces of the shadow network. Each one missing. Missing. Only just missing.

And then it ended. The globe went white.

The shadow network was gone. Removed from Budapest.

The tentacles had disappeared.

And I was fine. I'd made it.

I'd won.

I turned away from the screen. I stared toward New Jersey. Closed my eyes. Wanted to yell. Wanted to scream.

"It's not failure," I heard myself saying to Leonard, eyes closed tight, trying so carefully to breathe, breathe slower, *slow down, you won.* "Don't," I was saying, "don't ever let anyone believe they have failed."

But in another moment I realized that Leonard had already hung up.

Trevor was on the phone, breathless as he made his way through some unidentified airport, his voice rising above the noise, then fading into static. He'd called to report the week's sales. Calling me as he always did, every Friday for the past three years, this time as always each word and number blurring into the next.

It was three days since I'd spoken to him. Two days since he'd fired the sixty people in Omaha.

"Auto insurance for ten million," he was saying rapidly, speaking about the newest companies he'd signed up.

"A pension processor for four million," he said. "Spark plugs for a two-million-dollar trial. S&L for sixteen million over twenty-four months." As he spoke, I made one more check on the storage center in Budapest. Shimmer shining nicely, the globe itself now gone, the space it had taken reabsorbed into the real operations of the company. Shimmer now simply reflecting the smooth operation of a healthy facility within Core Communications, the world's most efficient networking corporation.

No anomalies. No shadow network.

No harm done.

"Securities for a million two over twelve," Trevor said, and I turned away from Shimmer, seeing the sunset growing across New Jersey. Warm and curving out, wide against the sky, and for a moment I pictured the bright white airport where Trevor must be.

"Credit cards for ten million," he said. "Some vaguely identified branch of the CIA for sixteen million over eight."

"So you're telling me," I said, a part of my mind unintentionally but automatically adding up the numbers he'd listed, "you're saying that you alone did fifty-eight million in sales this week? Twice your normal sales."

"I did the CIA meeting on no sleep," he said, not answering my question. "And my God, Robbie, I was beautiful. I was fluent and cohesive and I made clear, ringing, deeply lucid analogies. I called their internal systems a metropolis and our service the secret police, quietly bringing order to the neighborhood chaos and political upheaval. I went to the whiteboard and drew out this huge map of a city. Houses, offices, apartments and industry. I had red and green markers in one hand, blue and brown in the other, and I drew out the brown dirt and the fucking brown exhaust from the factories, Robbie. And then, real carefully, with lots of right angles and solid lines, all orderly and complete, I overlaid our system, Core, like the secret police introduced so quietly to the sprawling metropolis, which, before you say it, isn't even remotely true. We're not the secret police—if anything, we're the fucking garbage men, which is nothing to be ashamed of—but that whole secret-police analogy, oh, Robbie, their eyes went glassy and damp with excitement. They loved that shit, all these short-haired white men in white shirts, fucking CIA circa 1952, Robbie, it was a freak show, and I was in on it—white shirt, black shoes, a black tie, did I tell you I got my hair cut, can you fucking believe it?"

"Fifty-eight million," I said, and as I spoke I thought about Omaha. The firing that had led each of the senior staff to come to me in the last few days. Whitley standing in my doorway, hands at her lips, shaking her head, saying little, saying, *Omaha*, saying, *Trevor*. Julie stopping a copier as we stood in the mailroom, wanting silence as her shoulders pulled together so tight, torn between anger and sadness, saying, *Trevor. No more of this from Trevor.* Cliff so uncomfortable in the stillness of a conversation that didn't involve finance. Leonard reaching into territory wholly unrelated to his work but seeing a duty to make a comment to me.

Each saying in his or her way, *You can't let Trevor do this again. You can't let Trevor go on this way.*

None of the senior staff had ever liked Trevor. And none of them really interacted with him. To them, Trevor was my problem, an unmentionable bastard child out of step with the rest of the company.

Only through Trevor had I ever disappointed anyone.

"I haven't slept in three days," Trevor was saying, "and I'm playing golf with one of the top systems guys at an aeronautics supplier on Sunday and so, hey, you, hey—" he was yelling now, voice directed away from the phone, talking to someone, repeating the question, "hey, how do I get there from here? Seattle. How the hell do I get to Seattle, for Christ's sake?" He was yelling and I thought—worried, really—that maybe he was standing alone in an airport, yelling at strangers passing around him. "Hey, lady," he yelled, "do I look like I give a shit about your crying child? Get in your own line!"

I shook my head, closing my eyes. I said into the phone, "You're not wearing anything that identifies you as a Core employee, are you?"

There was no response.

Omaha.

And yet there was no way to lead a conversation with Trevor. It was barely possible to stay connected with his thoughts.

"Yeah, well, take it to your shop foreman, union lackey!" he was yelling, his voice growing louder even as his mouth seemed to be moving farther from the phone, the words sinking deeper into the echoing, humming noise of the airport. "I want two seats in first class, side by side, and fly me the long way because I need some sleep!"

"Where are you?" I asked, raising my voice, hearing the footsteps in the airport, the carts being rolled along a hard floor, hearing all that motion around Trevor, each sound framing his voice.

"Fucking-A right, Robbie," he said into the phone, his voice now eliminating the echoing airport noise, "just what kind of fucking place is this? Hang on, battery's dying."

The phone went quiet. I hung up. The silence of my office was sudden and complete, me alone in the quiet of the fading light. I had a vision of sixty people exiting an office building in Omaha. I pictured the threads of Leonard's server scan falling so close to my emptying remnant of the shadow network. I had a distant memory of floating. I wondered, for a moment, if I could close my eyes and sleep.

My phone rang and I picked it up.

"I feel like a fucking Navy Seal out here," Trevor said, "roaming from battle to battle with all this gear, loading new batteries into my phone like clips into an M-16." He paused, and all I could hear was the swirling sound of feet and voices. I thought maybe he'd passed out. "Jesus," he said in a moment, "I need to use that in a meeting next week."

"Will you just tell me what state you're in?" I asked again.

"Forty-nine million plus nine in options," he said. "So, yes, fifty-eight, loosely speaking."

"Leonard almost found the shadow network yesterday," I said, trying to get Trevor's attention. Trying to bring him into my conversation. "He almost found it in Budapest."

"But I really wanted to hit sixty," Trevor said, moving forward without me.

"And we had a rogue section in the DMZ," I said, knowing he heard nothing.

"What I'd like some day," he said, "is to hit sixty."

"And SWAT is seeing problems everywhere," I said, staring out the window. Feeling the cold air pressing against the window in front of me. "It's coming in from all sides," I said quietly.

"But," he said, "fifty-eight's not bad."

"I've got some things I'd like to talk about," I said, making an empty attempt to bring up Omaha.

"Every week," he said now, "someone offers to sell me a Fadowsky journal."

"Who does?" I asked, surprised. He'd never mentioned offers to buy a Fadowsky journal.

"Which reminds me," Trevor said, his voice clear and rapid, rising above the blurring noise of the airport around him. "We need to raise our prices across the board, five to ten percent, in my opinion, which I know we'll have to fight about, so let's wait till I'm in New York and I can argue for it in front of the full team, do a cost/benefit, whatever, but I'll go ahead and preview you on the outcome: I'll win because at some point this week—need to check my notes—I raised the prices for certain types of companies. Called it our 'Focal Service.' The masses love that shit. *Focal* Service. It came to me on the spot. Amazing. So, anyway, schedule a meeting and we'll talk about it. What was I saying? Oh. No. Right. Right, because the more people I sign up, the more who seem to want to be sold. These people are fucking sheep, Robbie, just following each other around."

"And you're the sheepherder," I said, thinking again that he wouldn't hear me.

"Yeah, and you're my three-legged little sheepdog, you lame piece of shit!" he yelled. "I'm not a fucking sheepherder! That's the stupidest fucking thing I've ever heard! Next time I'm in New York I'm going to shave your ass with a pair of sheep shears! Put me through to your assistant so I can schedule a fucking time to shave your ass bald!"

I started to laugh quietly, shaking my head. I closed my eyes, picturing this half-crazed salesman in a fine but wrinkled suit, screaming wildly into a cell phone as he marched toward Concourse B.

Mention Omaha.

Trevor was yelling away from the phone, "Keep moving, keep moving. It's an escalator. Stop acting like some sort of idiot savant."

"Please tell me you're not wearing a company shirt," I said, although I knew he wouldn't hear me. "A company hat. Tell me there's not a business card on your luggage."

"I'm in Kansas City," he said, "which is funny, really, because actually I have no idea what state I'm in. There were rumors of tornadoes in Cincinnati, so I ended up here. Have you ever heard of a fucking tornado in Cincinnati? It's some airline lie, I think. Fucking flight crew probably slept in."

"I think maybe you're being a little paranoid."

"Earthquakes, sure," he said, voice fading a bit, the noise around him invading the phone once more. "But a tornado?"

"You know," I said, and again I wasn't sure he would hear me, "all of this—all these sales—it completely ignores the fact that at some point we won't be able to deliver anymore."

"Well, fuck that, Robbie," he said, his voice clear, and I could almost see him focusing on the phone, could see his sharp face, his black, wet eyes, even his long hands all now focused on the one and only thing that mattered to him. "Just fuck it. We can deliver today, all right, and I don't give a shit about anything else."

"Wonderful."

"Fuck you. Don't get all superior with me. Computers fail. Software fails. The company will collapse and we'll announce that our system stopped working. Period. We'll call it overload. We'll crash and burn with some ugly articles in the papers. Bankruptcy. Hand everything to the attorneys. Auction off the assets and blame it all on some rogue section. Fuck it. Who cares? You're rich. I'm rich. I don't fucking care."

"It's not that simple, Trevor," I said, even though, as always, I couldn't help but find some truth in what he was saying. Something possible. Something attractive.

"You see that too, don't you?" he said, voice so close to the phone now, speaking to me as if he were in the room.

I stared out the window. "What about the lying, Trevor? We are lying."

"Okay, Robbie. I hear you. Really. You've made a point about the ethics of the situation. I hear you. But hear me out, all right? Because I mean what I'm about to say. Eff-you-see-kay-why-oh-you. Fuck you. All right? I don't care about lying. Everyone lies. Companies lie. Churches lie. Teachers lie. The fucking butcher lies."

"What the hell are you talking about, Trevor?"

"I'm hungry. I'm light-headed. Forget the thing about teachers and butchers. What I'm saying is it doesn't matter to me. It shouldn't matter to you. And I don't care about anyone, anyone else in the whole motherfucking world."

"Do you really care what happens to me?" I asked, standing, moving through my dim office, following the long windows. "Or do you just want me to stay on board so I'll keep this all afloat as long as possible?"

"Of course I fucking care. Besides these pissant, pantywaisted clients I suck up to on an hourly basis and the salespeople who are dependent upon me for their every thought and word, besides them, you, Robbie, are the only person in the entire fucking world who will speak to me. No one else will talk to me. No one else will even accept a phone call from me. People hate me, Robbie. They're disgusted by me. Christ, they're fucking *scared* of me. And here's the thing, Robbie. Here's what's worst of all. I like it. I enjoy this. I enjoy every waking moment of my life."

I was standing just a few inches from the window now, touching the glass with my hand. "I have to say, Trevor, that I'm scared of you too."

"And you should be. I'm a lying, self-serving, arrogant monster. I don't sleep. I drink too much. I want to have more money than anyone. Anyone, Robbie. And that alone could drive me to do anything."

I shook my head. There was nowhere to go with Trevor. No end to it. No point to our talking, no purpose in what was said beyond the goal he defined himself.

"So just when is all this going to crash, anyway?" Trevor asked.

I looked toward the darkened floor, blinking. "I still don't know for sure," I said.

"There's a fuckload more money to make before this goes under," he said.

"Will you stop using words like *fuckload*," I said, seeing a glimpse of myself in the light of the glass, tall and young and thinner, it seemed, than I'd remembered.

"Yeah, I know," he said, and for a second he paused, the whirling sound of the airport filling his silence. "It's silly, really," he said in a voice that had slowed just slightly. "It makes me feel good, though. Again I think about the Green Beret analogy. The lone soldier out on the battlefield."

"I think it was a Navy Seal," I said, smiling.

"Whatever," he said, voice slowing another step, the tailing roar of jet engines passing between his words. "My point," he said, "is that I find comfort in playing the role of the asshole."

The light was turning red and orange in front of me. My reflection dimming in the glass, the fading image of the CEO on twenty. "What if we only had one day left?" I asked suddenly, not sure why.

It was another moment before he spoke, and I wasn't sure he'd heard me. "I have to eat now, Robbie. I have to sleep. I'm playing golf on Sunday."

"You told me."

"Really?" he asked carefully. "Did I tell you about the CIA meeting?"

"We'll bring order to their metropolis," I said, and again I remembered Omaha.

Mention Omaha.

"Where am I, Robbie?" he asked slowly, seeming to pause and look around.

"Kansas City."

"And what did I do in sales?"

"Forty-nine plus nine in options."

"That's pretty good," he said, slower now, his voice fading again. "Isn't it?" he asked.

"Eat something," I said. "Sleep."

"I hate to golf."

"Sleep."

"One day left," he said, still quiet. "Did you just tell me that?"

"Maybe."

"And how close did Leonard get in Budapest?" he asked.

"Close," I said.

He was silent. Wandering, I imagined, though it was an image foreign to my thoughts of Trevor. But for that moment, I saw Trevor wandering.

"Rogue sections in the DMZ," I heard him say, voice drifting from the phone. "SWAT finding problems."

Wandering.

"One more day isn't enough, Robbie," he said

I was quiet.

"And Whitley," he said. "SWAT. They could find us. You're saying they could find us soon."

"Yes," I said.

"Forget the money, Robbie. For a second. Because really, I just don't want all this to end."

I touched the window again, pressing my fingers against the glass, watching the light on the horizon, shifting red to purple in just the last minute.

"Do you?" he asked.

I stared at those fingers. Saw the sky behind them. Waiting to answer. Trying to find an answer. "Do I what?" I asked, phone turned away from my mouth. Hoping Trevor would move on to something else.

"Do you care?" he asked, voice still quieting, still fading with every word. "Do you care if this ends?"

I took my hand from the glass. "Sometimes I'm not sure," I said.

"The last time I slept," Trevor said, not a whisper but halting, so quiet that I had to replay each phrase, repeating it in my mind to be sure of what he'd said, "the last time I slept, I had a dream about your dad."

I watched the sky change color. I saw beside me, above me, how the light was now gone from my office and I was standing in near darkness.

Talk to him about Omaha another time.

Next week, Omaha.

In a moment, I asked Trevor, "What was he doing?"

"Nothing," I heard Trevor say, and still I had to repeat his slowing words as he spoke. "Nothing. Just watching. The way I remember him. The thing I miss. He was just sitting there, in your chair, watching the two of us play on the floor."

It was only a few months after our IPO that, as I neared my office door, a man and woman broke into tears, the man rushing forward, throwing himself at my feet.

"Robbie!" he moaned loudly, his heavy face pinched in pain. "Robbie, it's your papa! It's your papa!"

My father had died years earlier. But as an adopted only son turned near billionaire, I'd found that this was a scene I would have to deal with regularly. People worldwide hoping they could get rich claiming to be my birth parents.

My assistant had stood up at his desk, covering his eyes as he slowly turned away from me. My driver—a man who most employees knew was actually my armed personal bodyguard—winced and rose from a chair near my assistant but only stared at the man now writhing on the floor.

"It's your papa!" the man moaned again, his wet mouth twisted with some uneven mix of joy and pain.

The strikingly short woman standing over him stared up at me, teary-eyed, unblinking, her wide mouth choking on words she found herself unable to form.

My assistant turned back to me. "I'm sorry, Robbie," he said quietly. "They had authorization. They showed proper ID. They were supposed to be with the local news."

When I was a child, my father had told me that my birth parents had died a few weeks after I was born. During the three years of mass publicity for this company, however, women and men kept calling me, writing me, running up to me in the lobby, all telling me I was their long-lost son.

Sometimes they even ran up to Trevor, having seen our pictures in the same article or feature and confusing him with me.

Single and fifty when he brought me into his California home, my father was neither a hardened, emotionally vacant businessman who'd groomed me to be a CEO nor a kind and gentle caregiver who'd always wanted the deeper warmth of raising a child.

All his life he'd lacked the time to get married. At fifty he'd found himself wanting to be a father. Because, as he told me when I was much older, over time he'd become jealous of the joy his friends had found in raising their children.

"Joy?" I'd asked him carefully, the two of us riding in a car near his office in Redding, California. I was twenty-five then. Living and working in Silicon Valley. Home for the weekend to see my father.

He nodded. He shrugged. "Not a word I use often," he said quietly. "But what they found, what I wanted, was joy."

My father was a gracious, settled man who I most easily remember sitting in his office, at work, his long hands in careful motion, moving simply and slowly as he talked about business. Even when I was very young, as I played in the corner of his office while he met with the people who worked for him, I could see how he was the person in control. Talking carefully, with a measure and weight, those strong hands moving slowly across the pages of a report or plan, fingers pulling gently at a paper clip or staple. He was the owner, the president, always leading and admired.

And since then, all my life, he'd been that whisper in my ear.

You know, Robbie. You know this is right. And you know that is wrong.

Yet only in this fourth year after he'd died did I realize that my conscience had been formed by the work he'd done. Not by anything he'd ever said aloud. He'd committed his life to his company, and to me, and nothing else. Work was our only religion, ever present. It was in the phone calls I heard my father place after he'd put me to bed. It was in the trips we took to visit clients—and theme parks—all over the country. It was in the talk from the investors who joined us for Wednesday dinner, each taking a break from their discussions with my father to spend some time with me on the floor, or at my table with the crayons, or in front of the basketball hoop outside.

Rarely did my father seem distracted by work. Rarely did the pressures enter our home or life together. And yet never was there a time when work was, really, gone.

Maybe it's like being a farmer's child, growing up in a world you never question, that permeates your existence, that you enjoy and see no reason to leave. It's what you know. What you want. What has always been.

It just is.

My father certainly saw in me the next generation of his company. But it wasn't that he pushed me to take over his business. Instead it was something I always wanted. He told me often that I did not have to do it. But I always said I did. Because always I'd expected it to happen.

My father's mistake wasn't pushing me too hard. It wasn't setting too high a standard for me. My father's mistake was not holding me back, just a bit, from the only life and pursuit and meaning I'd known.

In the self-pitying days of middle school, on a few first dates in high school and even college, I sometimes portrayed myself as an orphan child plucked from the gray and damp aisles of some Dickensian maternity ward. Whispering this darkest truth to the girl at my side, I could sometimes evoke from her a kind word, a muttered moan. Sometimes even a careful, soft but quite promising kiss.

But I had not been an orphan child. I hadn't been plucked from some dark maternity ward. Actually I'd been purchased, bid on through a private network of wealthy white families, a transaction brokered by a husband-and-wife team that, decades later, was shut down following an investigation by a national TV newsmagazine.

And by the time I'd reached my twenties, all this—the adoption, the purchase—struck me as absolutely irrelevant, adolescent angst I had long since accepted, incidental cocktail banter that did not haunt, curse or bother me. My life with my father had always been nice, often great, and never once truly bad. It was my father who had told me that my birth parents were both dead. He'd had no reason to lie to me. I have always been certain he never lied to me about anything.

Except that three years of constant calls, claims and inquiries from so many people had, at some level I could not control, made me wonder if maybe my birth parents actually were alive.

And except that Trevor had always liked to raise doubts about my father's story. Only because Trevor was mean. Only because Trevor forever seized on any possible weakness in the people around him.

"There was always talk," Trevor would say to me. "When we were kids. Anytime you left the room. Christmas, Thanksgiving, a Wednesday night in spring. Always there was talk."

"Talk of . . . ?" I would ask, sitting back, turning away, having learned early on that dealing with Trevor usually called for as much distance and disdain as possible.

"Bastard child," Trevor would say flatly. "Born of some tryst between your father and a Czechoslovakian maid."

"Actually," I would reply, "I prefer the term *illegitimate.*"

He'd shrug. He'd turn his hands to the sky. "I'm just telling you what was said. And what was said was *bastard child. Spawn of deceit. A one-nighter turned lifelong mistake.*"

Trevor was the only son of my father's brother, a top salesman for an international aerospace firm who spent most of his time roaming the great cities of Asia in search of new business. It was during these trips that Trevor lived with my father and me, a bad-boy cousin who bunked in my room. Staying in my room, not a guest room, because as a kid Trevor hated to sleep alone. Life with his father—a cold, distant and unavailable man—was a kind of transparent breeding ground for Trevor's growing anger. As a kid, I always felt bad for Trevor. Until he would spend three days calling me *bastard child*. And so through the accumulated confusion building up in me from those moments, and from the pain I could see Trevor so clearly feeling, I knew—knew in a kid's way, a way that isn't ever defined or spoken—that Trevor was something other than me or my father or any child or adult I'd ever seen. Scary, funny, mean and vibrant. The boy who drew kids to him no matter how cruel he would always become. The teenager who threw the best parties, who had the quickest access to beer or vodka, who quietly spread more fear among the kids our age than even the usual teenaged felons revolving in and out of juvenile hall.

After dropping out of college, Trevor moved to Bangkok, then Singapore, then London, then San Francisco. Always he worked in sales, selling computers, selling networking gear, selling consulting services, selling e-commerce deals, selling Internet ideas thought up by himself or others around him. Making money, so much money, in every job and on every deal and always, I think, always in that most transparent way, Trevor was trying to outsell and outperform and finally outdo his father.

Of all the problems Trevor liked to point out or create between the two of us, the one he never mentioned was the one that was most obvious—his had been the life of an afterthought son unattached to his distant dad, and I'd been the one living a peaceful, happy childhood with a good father. Only once did Trevor come close to saying this to me. It was his sixteenth birthday, and we'd gotten drunk on my father's roof. Trevor talked about how he hated his dad, how he missed him, how he wished he were around. How he wished his dad were more like my father. And Trevor began to cry. He cried for hours, finally falling asleep on my bedroom floor, and at breakfast in the morning he started a fight with me, one more transparent response to the anger inside him. He didn't talk about having cried the night before. In fact, he never has. Some much-deserved moment of pain and self-pity, but one for which he would never forgive himself. And for which, quite possibly, he will never forgive me. Which isn't true. Which is too simple. But by the time I was thirty-five, by the time I was three years down this path of lies with him, by then I was desperate for anything that could make sense of my life with Trevor.

Darkly beautiful. Always beautiful. Smiling and patient and perfect. Always perfect.

"You live here?" she asked.

If, somehow, I could have slept. Maybe then I would not have called.

A thick brown sweater. White blouse.

Probably, though. Probably I would have.

Heavy hair across her shoulders, bundled on her back in a loose cotton tie. Jeans and clogs. A college girl. Sent to me that way.

Yes. Yes, I would have.

Maybe you'd like a college girl?

Maybe.

A college girl.

A warm, light smell of familiar perfume. The faintest smell of gin. Gin on my breath. Gin on hers. Her low voice saying, "You don't talk?" and I just shook my head.

In the living room, now the bedroom, rooms all gray and black and white with shadows. It hardly felt like I lived here at all. It didn't seem like I'd found time to move in, this not a home but a place to wander alone, removed from the office by just one story of the building, pacing these near empty spaces, waiting to go back downstairs.

Darkly beautiful. Familiar beautiful. Like some model in the background. Not the cover girl, not the star. But one of the models who fills out the picture, who confirms that impossible space of beautiful homes, beautiful restaurants, beautiful streets and cars and drinks and people. Beautiful people.

Unbuttoning her sweater. Untucking a corner of her blouse. Enough to see her belly, to touch it lightly. To follow the curve, to touch her hip, her smooth, smooth hip.

"I'd like to touch you there," she said.

Nodding carefully. Trying to say in that nod, *Slowly, touch me slowly.*

Maybe you'd like a college girl?

A woman on the phone. The same woman every time. Suggesting thoughts to me. Forming images in my mind.

It was four days since I'd last called.

Jeans that button, now unbuttoning. Worn fabric, soft stitching. Metal buttons. White panties. Touching them only barely. The top edge. The coolness.

"Slower?"

Slower.

It's like watching a movie, maybe, or reading the slow, circling sex scene in a book. Somehow watching but involved, drawn closer, sinking into that moment, that motion. Filling in your own images, filling in the sounds, the smells, the light and feel. Watching but being there. Watching yourself. Watching both of you.

"Can I take off my pants?" I heard her say. Smiling, behind her dark hair, only her lips, her ear, showing themselves to me, turning below that hair, her whole body turning, touching, touching me just one bit faster.

Paper printed, paper sorted.

"Can I open my bra?" Smiling, touching, touching me even slower.

Whitley in silence, just a few hours earlier, as I told her I hadn't yet talked to Trevor about Omaha. Whitley only looking at me, saying nothing, all disappointment in her silence. In her eyes.

"Can I put my other hand there?" Smiling, touching, touching me just one bit slower.

Disappointed in me. Whitley, SWAT. Whitley, my coworker. Whitley, my friend.

Smiling, touching, muttering some word.

Spreadsheets that had to be updated, adjusted. Money that had to be shifted, then hidden.

Another day. Another. I'd gotten us through another day.

Touching, lying back, muttering some word.

The SWAT team searching so close to the shadow network. Budapest just some glimpse of what might happen. And what they might find.

Whitley watching. Everywhere, watching. As if, somehow, she could even see me now. Her face near mine, watching me here, seeing me from the edge of my bed.

Touching on top, below, slow movements, now wet, wet motion, still slow, still that hair, my eyes caught and lost in that hair.

Do you want this to end?

Maybe, somehow, there was a way to save this. A way I hadn't seen. Maybe, somehow. Maybe, somehow.

I came inside her.

It was Friday still. Seven hours after my conversation with Trevor. Seven hours only because I could see a clock now. Because otherwise I would not have been sure how long it had been. Without a calendar I wouln't have known for sure what day it was. This is what happens without sleep. Two years. In two years I hadn't slept for more than three hours at a time.

I touched her hair. I touched her chin and neck, her chest. She smiled and I watched. She touched me and nodded. "There," she said. "I see, there."

No cheap talk. No sassy lines. No heavy moans. No high-pitched voices. Only a quiet aching. Sex a release, temporary but complete. A release from everything bad. Everything wrong. Everything past.

Although, even in that moment, I knew there was something wrong with this too. Of course I did.

Do you want this to end?

The sweater near the bed. The worn jeans and clogs, the tie from her hair. Those panties. That bra. The clothes, a costume, a college girl.

Inside her again.

Nothing bad. Nothing wrong. No past. No future. No talk. No regret. No love.

I came inside her again.

She is, in so many ways, forgotten. She is the other one, the fourth. She is simply in charge of building the boxes. Manufacturing, production. She is the orchestrator. Every machine, every new product, every process behind them. All of it is built by Julie.

And somehow, all of what Julie does is forgotten. All of it taken for granted. All of it only barely noticed.

Julie's parenthetical life.

Which, for her, is absolutely fine. For her, that is absolutely right. Her work gets done. Her facilities deliver everything on time.

There are no questions.

No one has any doubts.

She wanders the basement now. Two floors below the street. Midday, weekday, and she walks among the boilers and brick hallways and hanging pipes and unmarked doors leading to unknown rooms. She likes it here, in these hallways with the thickly painted floors, shiny paint, all green and rubbery in their layers of color.

And she thinks that any normal person would want to leave this company.

And all she wants is to stay.

One more fight with her husband. The night before.

Leave, *he says.* Don't do this to yourself another day. Leave.

And there is a baby now, and she is older too, and her husband thinks maybe they should move out of the city, and she thinks she would like that too.

Maybe he's right. Take an offer. Leave the company. Leave as soon as you can.

Maybe it's time. Forget about money. About stock options waiting for you. About bonuses just a few months away.

Leave. Before you lose completely the ability to sleep. Before you begin to cry, alone, one more time.

Leave.

She tells her husband that she stays because of the security.

She tells her husband that she stays because of the money.

But what she doesn't say, what she can't say, what she can't make sense of to him or to anyone, is that she stays because once a week Robbie and she meet in the mailroom on the fourth floor. Talking through production problems, talking through expansion plans, talking but the point is to be sitting in the mailroom. There with the CEO of the company, both of them smiling quietly in the soothing sounds of the copiers and mail sorters and postage meters and printers. There and it's the rhythm of it, she thinks. The noise and motion. The timelessness of the place. The simplicity of the place.

Her boss has a secret interest in copy machines.

Her boss thinks postage meters are cool.

Her boss is known to blush when she makes another stupid joke about sex.

And, maybe best of all, her boss has never once asked her about the community work she does. The programs she leads here and in every office she can. He just nods, he says, Good, he gives her any support she needs. But he never brings it up. He never makes much of it. And she likes that.

She does it because it's the right thing. Not for any other reason.

She opens the door onto an empty room now. More concrete walls. More fluorescent tubes. A door on the far side of the room, leading somewhere she's never been. She walks to it. Thinking about facilities worldwide, about production steps being refined, about efficiencies her people search for and find every day.

And she thinks about the odd things. The overbuilt servers in European facilities. The extra satellite dishes in a manufacturing plant in Asia. And she wonders why Robbie set up the company this way. Wonders why it often seems like she is a step out of place. As if there's a number out of order, some step in the logic that she just can't quite follow.

Robbie has always had a vision. Maybe a vision grander than Fadowsky's own plan. And sometimes it's a vision she can't quite see.

I wish, for one moment, that I could see his plan.

But for now what she gets are the meetings in the mailroom. And, most often, that is more than enough.

She's not sure what other kind of work she would do.

She's not sure where exactly she would go.

But it's more. More than that.

She can't say it to her husband. She can barely say it to herself.

And now she finds a stairwell leading back up into the building. And she stops for a moment at the bottom step. And she closes her eyes and she breathes two breaths. And she lifts herself up and takes the stairs two at a time.

I'm not sure who I'd be without this job.

CHAPTER 4

I t was a discussion they fell into at least once a month, an interchange part dark confessional, part tentative celebration.

"I leased a new car," Leonard said.

"We're buying a pool table for the kids," Cliff said.

"We're converting an abandoned building into a home," Julie said.

"I'm eating out," Whitley said.

"When?" Leonard asked.

"For the rest of my natural life."

Core was a company of millionaires. All of the senior staff, the best salespeople, the top vice presidents and programmers in every division of the company, all had stock, stock options and a very high-paying bonus program that made some three hundred of them millionaires.

Millionaires on paper, that is. Or, more exactly, millionaires in waiting. Waiting for the chance to cash in their accumulating bonuses and stock options.

"My credit is pressed, though," Whitley said.

"My borrowing is high," Cliff said.

"Please," Julie said, smiling knowingly at the rest of them. "I'm so overextended I can't bear to open my mail."

And the laugh they shared—a nervously embarrassed, almost reflexive release—was possible only because of the stock and bonuses awaiting them.

"Grace," Julie said quietly, and the rest of them were quiet, nodding.

Grace was what people called the waiting period. It was the grace period, an unusually long one, between the IPO and the time when employees could sell their stock and receive their bonuses.

There was no specific date for the end of the grace period. Instead the end was defined by a series of revenue and profit targets. And so, every day, we moved closer to, or sometimes farther from, the target, from grace, moving at a pace that was mysterious to some people, elegant to others, and barely understood by most. It was because the calculations were so confusing that most people now called the date itself *grace*. Personified, ethereal, mythical.

By Cliff's calculation we were, on this day, four months from grace.

Cliff and all the senior staff held stock and options valued at nearly $100 million. And every employee, regardless of tenure, was offered options to own stock in Core.

But none of them were free to sell more than a fraction of that stock or to exercise any of the options or to receive the bulk of their bonuses until we reached grace.

It was because the date for grace had shifted so much—and had always moved closer—that many people had been borrowing against their stock packages for most of the past few years. Seeing grace within their reach, people had decided to secure quite uncommon loans from family, friends, even banks and finance corporations.

Even Cliff—the CPA and father of six known for the safest, most conservative decisions regarding the finances of this company—even he had overextended himself in the lead-up to grace. "Around here," he'd once said to me, "there is only the room or energy to go forward. You can't stop. You can't step back. You end each day excited and anxious and hopeful and tired," he'd said slowly, absently, drifting in his tiredness even as he spoke, our feverish CFO now finding an almost poetic place from which to speak. "Then you wake up. And you know there will only be more."

Some days, I wondered if we'd make it to grace.

But most days, I tried not to think about it.

And of course, the restrictions placed on the employees hadn't been placed on Trevor or me. We could—and did—sell our stock freely.

"Of growing concern," Julie was saying now, "is that I can't manage to get the basics done."

"Food for the dog," Cliff said.

"Milk in the fridge," Leonard said.

"There is no time," Whitley said.

"None," Leonard said.

"I know we've made a choice," Julie said.

"Yes," Leonard said.

"But still. Within that choice, there is no time," Cliff said.

"This isn't just me," Whitley said.

"Yes," Leonard said.

"It's my friends," Julie said.

"It's the people under me," Cliff said.

"If I could just get the basics done," Julie said again.

"My wipers have fallen off," Cliff said.

"I still haven't paid last month's bills," Leonard said.

"The food in my refrigerator has all congealed," Whitley said.

"My dogs have been waiting at the vet for days," Julie said.

"My home phone's not working."

"The car's making a noise."

"I'm wearing dirty underwear."

"I haven't worn any in weeks."

This was the day someone tried to blackmail me.

A man called, speaking distantly about threats and concerns, and at first I wasn't sure why I kept listening to him.

"There's talk," he kept saying.

"I don't follow," I said.

"There are rumors," he said.

It was Friday.

"Rumors about?" I said into the phone, leaning forward toward Shimmer on my screen, hardly listening to the voice.

Alone in my office. Ordering data to be moved. Satellites repositioned. Connections rerouted. I hired six outside consultants. I severed two contracts with lawyers. I sold my own stock in Core to cover more purchases. Sixteen million dollars in purchases. Another sixteen million of my money into hiding.

Another sixteen that was, inadvertently, protected from the collapse. Selling my stock in the company as I built up the shadow network.

"Longtime rumors," the man was saying, "that have now resurfaced."

"I think I'm going to hang up," I said, phone against my shoulder, typing.

"Rumors aren't important to you?" the voice said.

"You aren't important to me," I said absently.

I wasn't sure why I continued to listen. Why I didn't hang up like I'd threatened. Maybe it was the offhand confidence in his voice. Maybe it was something beyond the calculated confusion, the distracting crossways conversation he wanted with me. Something real. Something authentic.

And something familiar.

"Talk means little to you," he said. "Am I right?"

"Right," I said.

"Except when talk becomes rumors and rumors become not even a reality but a possibility," the man said. "Do you know when something moves from rumor to possibility? Can you see that point in time? Can you, Robbie?"

"I suppose so," I said.

"Then think about this, Robbie," he said slowly, and I was sure I could hear his lips, his mouth, all of it forming a smile. "There's talk of another journal, Robbie. A lost Fadowsky journal."

And I slowly turned away from my screen. Turning around, toward the window, as if this man stood behind me.

"Fadowsky was a prolific note-taker, you know," he said. "It's always seemed so unlikely to me that he wouldn't have documented the formula behind his boxes. Don't you think?"

And again it was only that authenticity in his voice, the familiarity in his speaking, that kept me from hanging up. Although now I wouldn't have been hanging up out of annoyance. Now I would have done it out of fear.

This man was laying the groundwork to blackmail Core Communications.

It was not just the Fadowsky Boxes—and the Blue Boxes we plugged into them—that had made Core possible. And it wasn't just the shadow network. Just as important was the fact that Frederick Fadowsky had never documented his formula. Because without possessing this unknown formula, we appeared to have found a way to talk to the Fadowsky Boxes. This was what it meant to draw blood from a mainframe. And no one else had ever come close.

"Do you know what kind of effect a lost journal would have on the stock market?" the man asked, and I pictured his smile.

Now I was telling myself, *Don't show him you're afraid.*

"People like you," I said to him, staring toward the window, "call me all the time."

"Really?" he asked.

"Why would I believe your story?" I said, seeing myself in the window now. Seeing my eyes blinking, my hair strewn across my head, my mouth gnawing slowly on my lip.

"I think you already do believe it," he said. "I think you're just looking for a reason not to."

Don't show him you're afraid.

"Rumor," he said. "Possibility. That's all it takes."

Clearly he didn't even have a real journal. But that didn't matter. And he knew it. A substantiated rumor—a rumor that seemed plausible, possible, only maybe real—it could send our stock down by twenty, thirty, even forty points.

In a day.

Grace would be pushed back by months. Even a year.

And the shadow network, dependent as it was on the price of the stock, would be deeply wounded. It might even crash.

"People like you," I said again, "call me all the time."

"But how many of them," he said carefully, "how many do you talk to for more than a minute?"

And I couldn't answer.

"You believe me, Robbie," he said. "I know you do. I can hear it. In your voice."

And I couldn't speak.

And I'd realized who this was.

"You're right to believe me," he said. "You're right to be afraid. Because I want what's due to me," he said, and I realized I was leaning back in my chair, closing my eyes, hearing his voice turn dark, like the charismatic villain in a story of good and bad, a turn so comfortable, so predictable, and I could hear the simple joy in his words. "I want my share," he said. "You see, Uncle Frederick owes me. But I guess it's you who will have to pay his bills."

Again I was sitting in a child's chair pulled up to a low wooden table. This time I wasn't in Perry's office, though. I was in Whitley's office, where we'd immediately called a meeting of key SWAT members in order to respond to the call. And where Whitley had, for some reason, recently brought in a low table and set of children's chairs.

"Friday," Perry was saying quietly, "and I was sure we'd get through the week without being blackmailed."

I passed him a written note as others were speaking.

I thought you weren't allowed to leave your office?

He scribbled a response with only a glance at the paper, his face expressionless, eyes turned away.

Just don't tell Robbie.

Perry had been added to the SWAT team that day, Whitley insisting that he be made a member of the group given the severity of this threat. Perry had agreed without argument, a surprising decision on the part of my burned-out head of R&D.

I've asked you to join SWAT for two years, I'd written him in an e-mail.

Sure, he'd responded, *but Whitley never has.*

"I can confirm with ninety-seven percent certainty that you were in fact contacted by Eugene Fadowsky," said Ronald Mertz, our head of corporate security, now taking control of the discussion.

Ronald was a serious and intimidating man in a padded nylon jacket. He stood near the end of the table, towering above us all as we sat in our low chairs. He seemed not to have acknowledged that the rest of us sat in children's furniture.

"Certainly," Ronald was saying, "this is a move consistent with Eugene's profile."

Eugene Fadowsky was Frederick's nephew. That was why he'd seemed familiar to me. I'd read articles Eugene had written, had seen footage of him speaking, had even met him briefly at a Core shareholders meeting two years earlier. He'd been invited to the event by one of our PR people. No one had thought to check his background, instead assuming that as a descendant of the famed Frederick Fadowsky, Eugene would bring an air of history and consequence to our gathering. He didn't. A highly sophisticated and well-placed malcontent, Eugene had instead accused Core Communications of abusing his family's name, of making unauthorized and illegal connections to the Fadowsky boxes and of stealing profits that should have gone to the Fadowsky family.

To keep his phone call to me from being outright blackmail, what Eugene had done was simply offer to sell me the lost journal. "I'm thinking of this as a right of first refusal," Eugene had said to me. "Which is only fair to you, don't you think?"

The catch was that I had to buy the journal sight unseen. And I had to do it at a huge—and as yet unstated—price.

For now, we were all looking to Ronald for guidance.

Even at seventy-four years old, Ronald Mertz possessed a deep and obvious limberness, a strength that always hinted at the inevitability of rapid, sudden action. Moreover, Ronald was one of those people who stand. He stood through staff meetings, he stood eating lunch in a break room, he stood while talking on the phone in his office. Even now, as he spoke, he paced the carpet at the head of our low table.

Ronald was noting that Eugene was actually the nephew of Fadowsky's brother-in-law, the former electronics salesman who'd first sold Fadowsky Boxes to corporations worldwide. Eugene hadn't been born with the last name Fadowsky. But, upon turning twenty-one, he had changed his last name—the first in a series of steps he'd taken to try to make himself chief representative of the Fadowsky family.

The family had made hundreds of millions of dollars off Frederick's invention. Frederick's death and the ensuing realization that the formula could not be found had done nothing to slow the brother-in-law in his selling of the Fadowsky Boxes. Upon his retirement in 1989, the brother-in-law had placed the rights to the Fadowsky Boxes into a family trust, which in turn paid the entire Fadowsky family a substantial licensing fee.

"But," Ronald said now, "the share of this fee that young Eugene receives is, apparently, not enough."

Whitley closed her eyes, hand slowly crossing her lips, breathing quietly but sharply. Julie pressed both her hands flat against the table, pushing hard, and I thought the table might break. Leonard's dense legs looked so large, so very large near the floor, the weight of them barely held by the tiny chair on which he sat. And Cliff, he'd crossed his arms and hands over his chest, as if trying desperately to keep them from jerking away from his body.

Ronald had begun passing out copies of a document stamped CON-

FIDENTIAL in bright-red ink. One of SWAT's duties was to run response scenarios on a wide range of potential security threats. Developed in conjunction with former security experts from the NSA and CIA, the scenarios covered everything from terrorist attacks on local power supplies to routine break-ins of our field and home offices to black-mail by people inside and outside the company.

"Is all this *really* necessary?" I'd asked Whitley eighteen months earlier, when Ronald had first presented me with the request to de-velop these scenarios.

"Ronald makes a compelling cost/benefit analysis," she'd said flatly, then paused, pushing her black hair from her face for a moment, eyes held upward as she considered a thought. "And, just as appealing, maybe they'll form a kind of window on our future."

As I scanned the security document now, I saw that there were nu-merous blackmail scenarios. This possibility—a direct approach by a member of the Fadowsky family—had not only been explored, it had been identified as the most harmful to us.

"It's as if," Perry said quietly, eyes scanning the pages of the secu-rity scenario, "young Eugene has read this paper himself."

Ronald stopped in place, turning carefully toward Perry. "Are you suggesting there has been an internal security breach?"

"No," Perry said, turning a page, fingers moving slowly, the rest of his body so tremendously still. "It just struck me as the most dramatic comment I could make."

"I would ask you to take this more seriously," I said to Perry, "if we weren't all sitting in children's school chairs." I turned to Whitley. "What in the hell is going on around here?"

"Pure envy," Whitley said flatly, nodding toward Perry, whose low desk and chairs were, in fact, being emulated companywide, people hauling children's chairs onto the elevator or exchanging as much as six months' worth of favors to get a full set of chairs and a table deliv-ered to their offices.

I started to respond, but Ronald interrupted our digressing ex-change. "As you can see, Eugene's offer does almost exactly match that described in this scenario. And, as you can see, the scenario concludes with the following recommended response." He turned to the last page, pausing for a moment before reading aloud. *"Keep the contents, nature and all associated information regarding the threat completely secret. Do not contact outside authorities. Do not negotiate. Pay the family blackmailer any amount up to and including $75 million, which, weighed against the enclosed benefit analysis, is a less expensive option than the fallout that would unquestionably follow the disclosure of the story."*

A look of disgust passed over the faces of the people at the table. Julie seemed ready to put her hand through the floor, Cliff's head began to move in a circle, Leonard sat back in his small chair, his face frozen in an extended wince.

"Rumors of lost journals have floated into view for three years," Whitley said, voice fading even as she spoke, trying lamely to convince herself of what she was saying. "We've never paid off anyone else."

Perry shook his head, smiling only slightly. "Except."

She threw a pencil at him, clearly aiming it directly for his eyes. "Except none of the stories came from Eugene," she snapped.

The pencil careened off the wall. Whitley lowered her eyes, let her hair fall forward slightly, finding a half second of privacy in the fray.

Over the next twenty minutes, everyone in the room made attempts to convince themselves of some reason why we did not need to follow the advice of the scenario document. But each point was as weak as Whitley's, and each point had already been examined and then discarded within the scenario we all held.

The problem, in the end, was that even if we tried to fight or discredit Eugene, his name and relationship to Fadowsky would carry enough weight to give him credibility. Credibility would make people consider the possibility that Eugene's journal was real. And at that point they'd realize how dangerous a real journal—or a fake one—would be to Core's now dominant position. In turn, the market would not only demand that Eugene's claims about his journal be validated, it would also demand a response to the possibility that another threat might surface in the future. The more we fought Eugene, the more the issue would remain in the market's mind.

And so he had us. Just as the scenario document described.

And of course Eugene had me in a worse position than he could possibly have realized. Because of what the dramatic dips in the stock price could do to the shadow network.

As I listened to everyone's increasingly weaker attempts to dispel the reasoning behind the scenario document, I realized, as I had in Perry's office a week earlier, that the child's chair was actually quite comfortable. And, in their way, the low table and chairs were somehow refreshing, this new and unexpected view from the near surface of the floor. The chair was comfortable enough, in fact, that I could keep myself from dwelling on the possibility that Perry, Whitley and anyone else who might soon buy chairs like this, all of them were reaching their own limits. All of them were nearing some state of regression.

My phone clicked, and I checked the screen. It was a message from Eugene, who'd insisted I give him my direct e-mail address and cell phone number.

By the way, his message said, *I forgot to mention that if I don't sell the journal to you, the first company I will offer it to is based in Finland. A company called Regence. Ever heard of them?*

I closed my eyes. I shook my head. The group had turned to look at me.

"Eugene," Whitley said.

I nodded. I read his message aloud. And there was quiet then, the absence of movement. Finally, after a moment, Perry looked away, toward the window. Ronald Mertz sat down. Julie very carefully, very slowly, without noticing what she'd done, pulled her pen apart, blue ink now pouring into a pool near her hands. Cliff simply stood, then had to leave the room.

Eugene had thought all this through very, very carefully. Because by involving Regence—even by using their name with me—he'd reached a position stronger than even the security scenario had contemplated.

Founded by a onetime Finnish postal worker born Reginald Toralon, Regence was, on the surface, a multi-billion-dollar international supplier of telephone and networking equipment. In the business world, though, Regence was in fact a high-tech thug, a multinational phenomenon grown to prominence through an always ruthless mix of fast-paced innovation, technical superiority, blatant price gouging, largely illegal but entirely unproven product dumping, and the periodic hostile takeover. Known to the world as Chairman Tor, Reginald had leveraged the company's Cold War position as primary producer of computers, networking supplies and communications systems for the Finnish military to generate a huge reserve of money, influence and intellectual capital. Technical innovation, marketing creativity, top-quality service and support—these things had unquestionably aided the company. But few analysts or observers saw those as the essential reasons for Regence's dominance. Competitors were undercut into bankruptcy or acquired through hostile takeovers that, once completed, resulted in a complete liquidation of the business. Governments were lobbied, stroked, paid off or attacked in order for Regence to buy the best position for itself and its services. The few Regence employees who'd challenged Chairman Tor's vision or his methods had been immediately cast out of the company, stripped of their compensation, sued for breach of contract and held in limbo by their stifling noncompete agreements.

In all, Regence was an archetypal villain of the electronic age, with its blitzkrieg attacks on markets it sought to dominate anywhere in the world, with its deeply devout legions of multinational workers, with its mysterious but charismatic leader, Chairman Tor, pictured always as a windswept sixty-five-year-old in black Polarfleece and silver sunglasses.

A reporter working for a Swedish newspaper had once drawn connections between Chairman Tor and former top officials of the KGB. Though neither Regence nor Chairman Tor ever publicly responded to the article, the reporter was said to have moved out of Sweden just weeks after the article appeared. Such stories about Regence's personal intimidation of its detractors were not at all uncommon, although I often thought the articles were manufactured by Regence's own very powerful public relations machine. Either way, the effect on the outside world was the same. Regence did not accept attacks or criticism—and so it was not attacked or criticized very often.

In the United States, Regence maintained eight campus-style offices nationwide, each staffed by hundreds of American workers but run by top-level Finnish executives imported from the company's headquarters in the hills outside Helsinki. They were metallic, fenced-in campuses located in heavily wooded, entirely faceless communities. In essence the campuses were highly manicured compounds, with their multiple security checkpoints, their black four-by-four vehicles roaming parking lots and access roads, their cameras peering out from hedges and trees. Their lobbies were staffed by guards in long trench coats, by unnaturally beautiful men and women sitting calmly at austere reception desks.

As in all the countries where it operated, in America Regence paid its workers the highest salaries in the tech world, though in return it demanded not just the longest hours but also the most stifling confidentiality and noncompete agreements. It was that mix of demands that allowed Regence to breed a cloistered and arrogant culture of exceedingly devoted employees.

Parking lots filled with black sedans. An enticingly familiar yet ultimately meaningless company name. Deep-rooted paranoia that reached greater depths each day.

Very few workers had ever left Regence. Those who did leave were not only barred from discussing the work they'd done, they were also essentially barred from continuing to work in their field. So insular was Regence's culture that former workers never again spoke to their onetime colleagues. So powerful were Regence's campuses that former workers were soon forced to leave their homes—shunned by neighbors who worked for Regence themselves, stigmatized by community leaders who'd quickly grown dependent on the company for tax revenue and political support.

It was said that, back in Finland, Regence employed an entire division devoted to nothing but the monitoring of these former workers. Wherever they moved. And, especially, wherever they next went to work.

Leaving Regence was a bit like entering the witness protection program.

And yet, as big and powerful as it was, as many products and services as it offered, Regence had never drawn blood from a mainframe. Which had made Core Communications an obsession for Chairman Tor. He had been putting hundreds of millions of dollars into mainframe research. He had been acquiring mainframe networking companies worldwide. He had even unsuccessfully attempted to buy the rights to the Fadowsky Boxes from the Fadowsky family. Regence was desperate. Tor wanted our clients. He was jealous of our success. And so I knew—everyone within SWAT knew—that Regence would jump at the chance to buy a fake journal from a member of the Fadowsky family. Tor would play right along with Eugene, spreading rumors about the journal, giving credibility to its contents, calling it "promising" and "worthy of extended study." All of it would be done with a single goal—to undermine Core in any way possible.

"The decision's been made for us," I said now, for a moment watching Julie, with her shoulders pulled so high, so hard and tight, but her fingers, those smooth, dense fingers, pushing lightly against the edges of the pool of ink on the table, delicately feeding the ink back on itself.

Perry sat so still, impossibly still, like me staring at the ink on the table.

Leonard worked his thick lips against the outer edges of his teeth.

Cliff returned to the room, hand clutching his calculator like an old man gripping a cane. He bent slowly down to sit in his low chair. I realized he'd gone to throw up.

"There's no better solution," I said slowly, "no better solution than the one presented here."

I was watching that pool of ink again. Watching Julie tend to its edges, keeping the dark fluid in place.

But something had happened. People had turned to me. Others looked down at the butcher-block tabletop.

And I realized that, when I'd said there was no better solution, my voice had gone quiet. Hearing my voice again. It had been an almost shallow voice. Weak. Because I had, in that moment, shown I was scared. Scared of Eugene's threat. Scared, especially, of Regence.

Whitley's hands were stopped at her lips. Julie held her fingers still, a dam against the drifting ink. Cliff appeared ready to leave the room again. Only Perry smiled slightly, slowly tilting his head to the side, clearly taking a picture of an image he'd never seen before.

I leaned back in my child's chair. I smiled at them all. I tried to break the spell I'd cast over the room. "We go with the expert advice," I said finally, tapping the scenario document on the table in front of me, standing now, trying to speak quickly, confidently. "We dodge a fight with Regence. We pay Eugene his money."

I came inside her.

Eugene's lost journal. Regence with an opportunity to hurt the company. My moment of fear. Trevor roaming the world's airports, phone at his ear, pushing aside any traveler who stepped in his way. Rogue sections in the DMZ. Whitley's SWAT team scanning servers, tracking accounting codes, watching for any anomaly in the chaos. Shimmer turning, spinning.

Beautiful. Above me. Hair black and falling across my face. Ends just brushing my forehead, my eyes.

She leaned down. She whispered, "Again?"

Thirty-five million in purchases for the shadow network. Three new companies in the Caymans. One more in Budapest. Lawyers out of Bermuda. Contract technicians from India.

She whispered again, "Again?"

Breasts just touching my chest. Thighs so light against my sides.

Again.

What is it that makes this my release? What is it that led me to this solution? Can you stop, can you think, can you take a moment to consider? Can you find the reason?

Again.

"Again."

Another day. We had made it.

I came inside her again.

And she doesn't love me. Doesn't know me. Doesn't care. And I like that. Want that. Need that from her.

Again.

She has a sense she is almost there. A sense that there is a point in time. Some last level achieved. Some long-held goal finally met. It's more than stock. More than bonuses.

To Whitley, for months it has felt as if Core is finally about to reach some place of permanence. And success.

She drives at nearly a hundred miles an hour, one hand on the wheel, hardly aware of where she is, the West Side Highway to the Henry Hudson, a quiet dark car passing the lights of the cars around her.

Within the company she calls it winning. Finally, she says, we will win.

But here, alone, it is something else.

Safety.

And she can't say why she feels they've almost reached it. The work isn't done, there are new markets to launch, there are offices to open in all parts of the world. And there are threats, so many threats, from outside and inside the company.

But she feels it. It's as if finally she were reaching the end of a search.

The events of this company, this place she has managed and led and organized and shaped, are finally coming together. They are about to make sense to her, to her people, to everyone around her.

She needs to sleep.

She needs to go home.

But she can't sleep, she can't go home, she can't explain any of this to her husband.

If she stops, if she pauses, if she hesitates at all, she is sure the momentum will end.

Although he doesn't understand that. And really, she's stopped trying to explain. Just as he has. They don't talk. They don't touch. They don't even go through the motions anymore. They share an address, holiday dinners—sometimes they both find themselves in the same room, awkwardly happening upon one another, finding a few empty words to say. But it died two years ago. Two years in which she's made a thousand decisions at work, in which he's probably made a thousand decisions at his firm. And yet neither of them can make this decision.

End it. Say the words. End it.

The car changes lanes. The dim lights of the dashboard just beyond her hands. One hundred. One hundred and ten.

Markets to open, products to launch, people to hire, acquisitions to make. Threats to explore. Rumors to investigate.

SWAT, Eugene, rogue sections. All are about security threats to the company. But for Whitley, they've also become something more. A slowly shifting, carefully layered view of Core itself. Moving and distorted mirrors pointed inward on the people who work here. On the actions they take. On the life they've created.

And what they show her is something she could never repeat out loud. Something she can only describe in the margins of her notes, recording these things almost absently, then crossing them out as she rereads them. Because in those moments she sees a place that is strange and flawed and unknown in so many ways and so beautiful in others. It is only an office. Only a company. But it so much more. These people all living together, not just working but living together in a community they've created. Finding outlets for work, for ideas, for creativity and for themselves.

She needs to sleep.

It is only a company.

But it is so much more.

And it means so much to her.

And it is nearing this place she can see but not describe. An end to this time, she wants to think. An end that opens onto something more.

Cliff told her that grace has moved closer. A full month closer.

One hundred and ten is not fast enough. One hundred and twenty is not fast enough. She's not out of control. She's not careening up the highway. She's just driving, midnight, and soon she'll turn back, toward the city and the office.

An end that opens onto something more.

Onto an answer.

Why is something at Core not right?

So many times she's started to tell Robbie. So many times as they've sat together in his office, late at night at the end of another of these longest days, and she's thought about telling him. About trying to describe what is only a feeling. A blank spot in her understanding of the company.

There's only one way she can come close to describing it, describing it even to herself.

I'm not quite sure how the Blue Boxes work.

She can explain all parts of the Core system, has refined and rebuilt and remade so many parts of the process. She is, in the industry, an expert on all facets of mainframe computing.

How did Robbie make Core work?

How did Robbie understand Fadowsky?

And it's more than simply not having access to Shimmer. It's about some part, some step in the logic, that she doesn't understand.

Passing cars. Passing every car.

She needs to sleep. She needs to end her marriage. She needs to not be afraid anymore.

Whitley is afraid. Afraid at home. Afraid at work. Afraid of things she does not understand.

People are afraid of her. She knows that. Used to like it. But she thinks that maybe now the fear will end too.

She'd rather not be feared.

And when she thinks this way, she thinks about Robbie. About the thing in him that she cannot understand. Something about Robbie that does not quite make sense.

She's worked with him for these three years. Spent so many hours in meetings and on the phone and exchanging messages and reports. And still it's as if she barely knows him. And still there's this thing that she can't quite make sense of.

One more car to pass.

Afraid.

It's a thing she'd rather not think about now. Or ever.

A thing unproductive. Unhelpful. Unhealthy. Maybe sad.

A thing that, late at night, in the dark, makes her smile.

I need to sleep.

CHAPTER 5

"Mr. Case," the voice said, "there's been a problem with a Blue Box."

I'd been woken up on the couch in my office, and already it seemed like I had not been asleep. My driver was standing in the doorway, speaking with his back turned to me.

It seemed like, all my life, I'd been waking up fully dressed.

"What time is it?" I asked.

"Four A.M., Mr. Case."

I stared at the dim ceiling, blinking. Trying to remember what day it had been when I'd gone to sleep. In a moment, I thought to ask, "Is she gone?"

He spoke again. "She is gone," he said.

I was wearing jeans. I could see dim white light cast across the ceiling. The highest ceiling.

I heard him saying, "Leonard said you should forget about Eugene."

And now I was slowly pushing myself up from the couch.

"He said to tell you this is worse than Eugene."

There was a sound like a hailstorm as I entered the DMZ. Twenty men and women were typing rapidly at keyboards, their bodies and features lost to the shadows in the room. Their faces were turned blue with the reflection of the screens. Their eyes flickered white and silver from the series of tall, wide displays mounted on the front wall.

The noise of it all, the unusually dense feeling of so much motion among the people and computers and screens in front of us, all of it left me just slightly short of breath.

I still didn't know what day it was.

"A Blue Box in Tulsa," Leonard was telling me, not looking up from his seat in front of three large computer screens, his body and presence as large as it had ever been, filling the chair, the desk, enveloping the screens. I had to remind myself he was only six feet tall. "A processor failed," he said.

I'd never seen someone type so fast, a blurry and disconnected motion made more disengaged by Leonard's tangible sense of calm.

I scanned the main status board, a twelve-foot-high by twenty-foot-wide screen that filled the center of the front wall and that was bordered by ten more large screens. The separate monitors and main status board showed a range of rapidly shifting graphs, recalculating numbers, rotating maps, and scrolling text codes, all of which painted an ever-changing, multilingual story of the company's network and computer systems. In just the few seconds I'd spent scanning the screens, I registered the current level of data flowing to and from our clients, read updates on all our international networking outposts, checked the positions of most key satellites in the system. And I could see the problem immediately, shown now as a string of rapidly growing numbers and a series of small, flashing red lights near the center of the main status board, which now displayed a very large map of North America. Most of the continent glowed a healthy blue. It was Oklahoma, Arkansas and Missouri that flickered red.

"Processors have failed before," Leonard said. "But this time," he said, "both backup processors failed. That has never happened."

"Actually, they don't seem to have failed outright," one tech said, her voice coming from a dark and unidentifiable area to my right. "The processors appear to have simply rejected the incoming data."

"Although, for some reason, the Blue Box doubled the data before rejecting it," said another tech, this one a male voice, rising from my left.

"And then this doubled data from Tulsa bounced off to the nearest Blue Box," yet another tech said, so that now they'd become some multiheaded person, speaking with different voices, words coming to me from all corners of the room. "It found a federal payroll processing center in Oklahoma City."

"Which not only rejected the data," a tech said, "but suddenly rejected its own batch."

"After doubling its data," another said.

"Now combined, the two batches bounced off a satellite and found a Blue Box in Broken Arrow, a suburb of Tulsa. Which doubled its batch, then rejected it all."

"Think of it as a tidal wave," Leonard said, not looking at me as he continued to type so rapidly on his keyboard, eyes staring at the code, reports, numbers and maps all scrolling across multiple windows on the three screens in front of him. "It surges forward," he said, "wiping out each ship, each swimmer, each sea wall in its path, getting larger, gathering mass, made stronger by the very destruction it has caused."

I couldn't help but be impressed by his seemingly off-the-cuff, highly rhythmic analogy.

Iowa went red, a firestorm spreading across the heart of the status board. For the first time I noticed that Perry was in the room, leaning against a wall, staring up at the board, the left half of his face glowing crimson with the reflection of the failed machines. I knew he had to have been here, in the building, when the problem started. He wouldn't have had time to get here yet if the tech team had called him at home.

And Leonard, I now realized, must have been here too.

"Where is the wave going?" I asked.

"We think it's coming here," Leonard said.

And then one of the techs spoke quietly. The words almost inaudible. "The wave just split in two," the tech said.

Leonard leaned back, the motion at the keyboard stopping abruptly. It was like an unfinished question hanging in the center of the room. Leonard turned to the tech who'd spoken. "Say that again," he said carefully.

"The wave of data split in two," the tech repeated. "Into two separate waves. Near the Indiana-Ohio border."

Leonard turned back to his screens. He typed just two commands. I saw him close his eyes, and for the first time I felt fear. Real fear, sudden and unexpected and total.

Leonard nodded, then licked his lips. "The two waves just split again."

Pennsylvania went red.

"Before the wave split," Leonard asked, "had anyone figured out how much time we had till it reached the DMZ?"

"Fourteen minutes," answered a voice gone pale and anxious. "Fourteen minutes till it reaches the DMZ."

"Although now it will arrive much sooner," said a different voice.

"The four waves split again," said another voice. "We have eight separate waves."

"Sooner," said a voice. "Even sooner."

"And the Blue Boxes that have been hit," I said, "what's happened to them after the wave bounced off them?"

There was the silence of typing for a moment, another.

"Each one," Leonard said, "appears to have been erased." He turned to me. "Essentially destroyed."

My phone clicked. A message from Shimmer. A wave had reached the shadow network.

Whitley and Cliff entered the room behind me, both looking tired and confused, clearly with no idea how bad the situation was.

"I want to do a full reset," I said now, loudly, and again the room was quiet.

"No, no," a tech said quickly. "We have not tested that. We have no idea what a reset would do to the system."

Leonard turned to me again. Silent now. Staring.

"We have sixteen waves," a voice said.

"What is a full reset?" Whitley asked, trying hard not to show any worry. Any fear.

"It's a complete restart of the entire system," Leonard said to her, but he was staring at me. "Which should take it back to the last moment of normal operations. Back to square one, in other words. Which, in this case, is the moment before the first Blue Box failed in Tulsa."

"Do you just push a button?" Whitley asked.

"I just push a button," Leonard said. "Which launches a series of drones out into the system. The drones will reset, reboot or restart every piece of equipment on our network—every computer, router, switch, Blue Box and satellite uplink. Everything."

California went red.

"At least," Leonard added, "that's what is supposed to happen."

"We have thirty-two waves," a voice said.

"Isn't there some way to protect the remaining Blue Boxes?" Cliff asked.

"We cannot protect the Blue Boxes," I said. "Essentially, given the situation, we can only turn them on and off."

"Why the hell is that?" Cliff asked, and although the typing continued, the room did seem to go quiet. It was a bad question in a confused moment. Cliff knew why. Everyone knew why. Only I had access to Shimmer. And only from Shimmer could such major changes be made to the Blue Boxes. But, in the next few minutes, there was no way for me to access Shimmer and, from there, protect each Blue Box.

And there was no way I could let Leonard onto Shimmer anyway. Because of what he might see.

Leonard was still turned to me. Staring, but not speaking.

"We have sixty-four waves," a voice said, "one of which has reached the DMZ."

I nodded.

"Essentially," Leonard said, "what we're left with is pulling the plug."

I nodded again.

The whole board was red.

"We have one hundred and twenty-eight waves," a voice said, "eight of which have reached the DMZ."

"What is happening to Shimmer?" Cliff asked, looking toward the door to the room holding the machine. Our corporate secret. Gateway to all the data in the system. Secret gateway to the entire shadow network.

Leonard shook his head. "I don't know."

"What will happen to the data now in the system?" Whitley asked.

Leonard shook his head. "I can't guarantee it will be okay."

"Will the reset do even more damage?" Whitley asked.

"It's possible."

"Will the Blue Boxes restart?" Cliff asked.

Leonard shook his head. "Honestly, I have no idea."

This twenty-six-year-old man was not only about to shut down our $20 billion company, he was about to put our entire future at risk.

"We have two hundred and fifty-six waves," a voice said, "thirty-two of which have reached the DMZ."

I leaned forward, staring at Leonard's screen, but suddenly all I really wanted was to be closer to him, to touch him, even hold him, put my arm around his wide shoulders, press my face against his heavy neck. I said quietly, "I blinded you to everything, didn't I, Leonard?"

He was tapping a finger on the desk. He smiled some. "Of course you did."

I nodded. I looked toward Perry. He started to speak but stopped. I thought for a moment he might move, might step forward from his place against the wall. He was in some way hiding a smile, I thought, not smiling at this failure or danger but smiling at something below it all. But he only stared at me now and, in a moment, nodded.

I turned to Leonard. "Reset the system," I said.

Cliff looked away. I saw Whitley close her eyes. I saw Julie, reaching the DMZ at just that moment, staring at the board, not knowing what was happening. But feeling it. Feeling it from every person in the room.

Leonard typed three passwords. Then another. Leaned aside and had me enter two passwords. He typed three lines of code, then one password. Then one command.

The hailstorm of typing stopped as the techs turned to the board, the silence seeming to pull the last of the air from the room. The red lights still flickered bright. But then, a second later, the board went black. Every screen in the room went dark. The computers shut down. The phones all began to ring in unison, then went silent. Even the ventilation system went quiet, the whisper of moving air now removed from the silent room.

"This is expected," Leonard said quietly, his voice like some announcer to the darkness. "This was expected."

The green lights of two battery-powered exit signs shone somewhere behind us.

Twenty seconds. Thirty. Sixty seconds. Silence.

I found myself expecting the floor to drop out from beneath our feet.

"This is expected," Leonard said again, still a kind of unseen guide to us all.

Two minutes. Three. No one moved. No one spoke.

"All of this is happening as planned," Leonard said quietly.

And in my memory I pictured these people I worked with, Perry and Cliff, Julie and Whitley and Leonard. Realized that Julie was like some older sister to me, the sister who was a better person, who would fight for me, who told me the secrets of adulthood, who I liked so much I wanted only to sit with her, quietly, in the comfort of the mailroom. Realized Cliff looked so tired, so gray and so tired, and realized he had a silly pink bracelet on one arm, the remnants of a temporary tattoo on his cheek, all the weekend markings of a tired, loving dad. Realized for the first time how beautiful Whitley was, how she hid this, tempered it, kept it from her days as COO. Realized how much Perry worried about me, about this company, about everyone in his group, this building, how that worry and care were what kept him in the darkness of his office till nights as late as mine. And in that moment I wished that Trevor were here. Wished he could have found a way to fit into this picture. And I thought of Trevor's question: *Do you want this to end?* And I didn't. Not at all.

It was a moment later that I realized Leonard had stood up in front of me. I barely recognized him in the darkness, his size irrelevant, and now he was already out of my view.

One terminal in the room—not the phones, not the floor lights, not the status boards—just one screen of one terminal had begun to glow. White light spread across the small, thin face of the tech sitting in front of it. It was almost a minute before the rest of us all began to move toward the light. Slowly, though. Carefully. Testing the ground at our feet, the space at our sides.

The tech said quietly, "Tulsa is up."

Leonard was standing behind the tech. He leaned forward toward the keyboard, one hand on the tech's shoulder, with the other typing a few commands. He said in a moment, "But it's not responding."

"It's live, though," the tech said, pausing, silent. Then he added, "Isn't it?"

Leonard typed a command, then another. "It's all live," Leonard said, now turning to me. His face looked unexpectedly small in the bare, white light from the screen. "And the waves have ended. But it is not responding."

"Tulsa?" I asked quietly.

"Any of it," Leonard said, eyes flashing white with the light from that one computer. "The whole network. I'm afraid we've completely lost contact."

And so the rescue began. We had twenty-four hours. Twenty-four hours, and the Core network had to be operational again.

It had been four o'clock Saturday morning when I'd told Leonard to launch the reset. Most of our clients passed relatively little information over the weekend. Those who tried now were receiving a message that the Core network was in the midst of a routine service and upgrade that would delay their transfers until Sunday. By Sunday morning, though, massive amounts of client data would start to hit our system as our clients—first in Asia, then Europe, then in the United States—began to prepare and process information for the week ahead.

If we didn't restore the network before the clients started passing information Sunday morning, then the world's confidence in the heretofore unstoppable Core network would not simply be shaken, it would be wounded forever. We would be contractually obligated to cover a huge percentage of our clients' costs. Word would get out to the sales prospects Trevor and his staff were pitching. The press would fall into the easiest and harshest possible attacks, pushing us from the pedestal they themselves had helped build. With the press assailing us, with sales to new customers falling off even slightly, with confidence fading among observers and analysts of all kinds, the stock price would drop dramatically.

Grace would be pushed back indefinitely.

Which wouldn't matter anyway. The crashing stock and falling sales would cause an almost immediate collapse of the shadow network.

Leonard's expectations for restoring the real network were cautious at best. "We do not understand how the waves began," he told an assembled group of the senior staff, Perry and the top tech people. Five A.M., and already six hundred tech staff worldwide were being put onto the task of restoring the Core network. "We don't know what kind of damage the waves have done," Leonard said. "We don't know what kind of damage the reset itself may have caused. And, of course, we've never restored the network before."

"Give me a percentage chance of success," Julie said.

Leonard leaned back against a wall, staring at the ceiling. "Less than thirty percent," he said after a moment, and his top tech people shook their heads just slightly. Leonard spoke again. "Probably less than twenty."

Julie leaned back, turning her face to the ceiling, eyes open wide and staring. Cliff left the room, would return a few minutes later, lips wet, face pale. Whitley breathed deeply, hands at her lips as if smoking five cigarettes at once.

As the meeting ended, Leonard stayed in the room for a moment. Staring at me.

"Are you okay, Leonard?" I asked.

He nodded, then again, his huge chin swaying down, then up.

"I'm not sure—" he started, then paused.

"Not sure how to do this?" I asked.

He closed his eyes, leaned back against the window. "Yes," he said.

I stepped toward him, his size growing as if I were approaching some statue or monument.

He opened his eyes, and I smiled. "I'll show you," I said.

In a way, there was little I could do to help Leonard. He and his people knew the systems far better than I did. But what they didn't know was how to make the decisions—the hundreds of decisions— that would have to be made. Decisions made quickly.

And recklessly.

But that was something I did know how to do.

We left the room and saw immediately that around the DMZ, and throughout all the groups on the five floors that made up the tech group, people were moving into position, as if Leonard's proverbial tidal wave had in fact washed through every floor of our office. Employees entered the building like rescue workers pouring into a disaster zone. But rather than filling sandbags or scrambling to evacuate refugees, these workers were handling hard drives and backup tapes, transferring data from nearly destroyed computers to new servers set up in conference rooms, break rooms, even wide areas of the halls. They were stringing cable off spools like detonation wire. They were sketching out maps and instructions with pencils and pens, many tearing open sealed plastic envelops holding disaster-recovery plans that, although they did not contemplate a system crash this severe, laid out a series of steps to be followed, directions to be taken, roles to be filled.

In all, it looked like a complete assault on the office.

I soon determined that rather than fix those systems frozen or damaged by the waves and the reset, Leonard and his top people should simply replace the computers completely. There were roughly fifty now-defunct servers and mainframes that needed to be replaced in order to manage the essential components of the Core network. In some cases, there were near exact copies of those machines working in test environments untouched by the waves. Those machines were now being moved—physically or virtually—onto the network. But in other cases, Leonard was going to have to rebuild the machines almost from scratch—software, hardware add-ons, networking components, everything. And so I sent his people in search of high-end machines throughout the building, commandeering servers, stripping them of their components or rapidly backing them up, then erasing them, then connecting them to Leonard's new network or, in some cases, rolling them into a conference room or hallway or office near the DMZ, then plugging them into the network from there.

Along with the fifty high-end servers and mainframes, many of the less sophisticated but still essential PCs used by techs and programmers companywide had also been damaged by the waves and reset. Already groups of employees had been sent out to discount computer superstores and low-price electronics warehouses in the city, out on Long Island, out in Jersey and even Connecticut, waiting in the cold morning parking lots, ready to buy a stockpile of new computers on corporate gold cards, then bring them back to the office in rented moving vans.

The crazed morning shopping sprees of desperate computer professionals.

All these machines were being brought to the area around the

DMZ, then placed on designated desks, on conference tables, on two-by-fours laid out on the floor. Techs were rapidly sketching out the details of the new network, giving directions to anyone who could help. There were people running wire between machines, between rooms, in some cases stretching cable down hallways, across lobbies, down stairwells and off into a room three floors above or below the DMZ, each room seized without apology, each seizure driven by some unwritten version of eminent domain.

Just outside the DMZ, on six huge whiteboards that had been rapidly attached to the wall, Leonard and I had created a master list of the fifty key machines that had to be replaced and the networking needed to link them to the Core network. Already the heat from those machines that had been restarted was raising the temperature around the DMZ—a serious and growing danger to the new and old equipment. Those of the building's air conditioners that were working were immediately turned up to high, fans were brought in from all areas of the building, mobile air-conditioning units were being purchased from the same discount electronics stores where we were buying so many new computers.

And still, by eleven A.M., disaster plans were being cracked open.

Still, maps and layouts were being drawn, then redrawn, then refined again.

Still, wire was being run down hallways and stairwells.

Still, new Blue Boxes were being shipped out to clients to replace those destroyed by the waves.

Still, servers were being rolled toward the DMZ on hand trucks, carts, skateboards and scooters.

Still, I stood near Leonard, telling him, *Yes, make that decision, move that forward, take that chance, it doesn't matter, somehow, Leonard, somehow we'll make it work.*

And still, the building was filling with people. Some had only now answered their home phones or turned on their cell phones. Some had flown back from vacations or weekend getaways. Most were techs, network administrators and software programmers called in to rebuild the network. But people from Marketing, Customer Service, Legal, Finance—all had been called to the office as well. The marketing teams were forming contingency plans to repair our image in case of the worst. The customer service groups were being prepared for what could be a surge of angry, threatening calls. The legal and finance teams were developing plans for a response to clients, partners and, of course, the market.

All of them, everyone now entering the building, were motivated by some varying mix of pride, fear, responsibility and greed. Because even though no one knew what this would do to the shadow network, everyone understood what could happen to them, and to the company, and to grace, if we missed the Sunday deadline.

Back in my office for a moment, checking on the shadow network for the fifth time that morning.

So far, Shimmer was fine. So far, those parts of the shadow network I could see were fine.

Shimmer, shining gold, the numbers still, the motion quieted. A picture of the shadow network waiting simply to restart.

The secrecy of the shadow network would, now, be its salvation. The shadow network was made up of thousands of independent parts. Server farms. Test centers. Satellite uplink stations. All had to operate on their own. Not because they were built to withstand something as severe as the waves or reset that had brought down the real network but because I'd known from the beginning that the only chance I had of keeping the lie alive was to have each part of the hidden system operate independently. And so now all those parts were unaffected by the waves and reset.

The shadow network was undamaged. But I had no idea if it would reconnect to the new network.

———

Toward one o'clock that afternoon, with the smell of Chinese food and coffee mixing together in slightly dank, sweet-and-sour winds, three techs and two security officers arrived on the eleventh floor with a small wooden crate. Two of the techs carried the crate, the security officers walking in front of it, the third tech following behind. A hush spread through the people, the crate being moved very carefully across the floor, the escorts slowly leading it toward a specially prepared room near the DMZ.

It was the Blue Box from Tulsa. Ready now for immediate analysis.

An hour later, Leonard had gathered enough information from the box—and had laid out a clear enough plan on how to restore the network—that he could give the senior staff, Perry and other top managers a summary damage assessment.

"The costs are in the eighty-million-dollar range so far," Leonard was saying.

Cliff held his calculator above his lap, working the buttons with both his thumbs, almost on the verge of cracking the small machine in half.

"However," Leonard said, "that's before full reporting from all the field offices."

Cliff's attack on the calculator paused, then resumed with even greater force.

"But word is that damage was light in Asia, correct?" Julie asked.

Leonard nodded. "And Europe. The damage was minimal."

"Did the wave even hit Europe?" Perry asked.

"No," Leonard said. "Not Asia either. The damage overseas came from the reset. And none of it was debilitating. That fact certainly helps with costs and the speed at which we can restore operations." He looked down at the notes in his hands, ready to start up with his damage assessment again, but Perry interrupted him.

"Did the wave hit Canada?" Perry asked.

Leonard looked over his notes. "No," he said. Then he looked at

Perry. Staring now. Realizing something. Speaking more slowly. Almost quietly. "Not Mexico either."

"But Hawaii?" Perry said, part question, part comment. "Alaska?"

Leonard's eyes were opening wide. He sat down. He nodded very slowly, carefully. "Yes."

Perry turned to stare out the window, face made gray by the very distant fall day.

I had lowered my head as Perry spoke. Realizing. Realizing what Perry saw, realizing something very obvious but something no one had had a moment to consider.

"What?" Cliff asked, looking up from his calculations. "Tell the money guy what this means."

Leonard started to answer, then paused, biting his lip, as if he couldn't bear to say it.

"The system," Perry said when it was clear Leonard was not able to answer, "our system, has little sense of countries or borders. It just knows data. It passes data from a mainframe in Berlin to a mainframe in LA, from a satellite over Mexico to a transfer station in Canada. If the waves were simply a failure in the system, why would they stay within the United States?"

Cliff squinted for a moment. Then he blinked. The last one in the room to see it. "The Blue Box didn't fail," Cliff said. "We were hacked."

Leonard shook his head, a motion so large, so involved that I had to stare at the structure of his neck for a moment, concerned that maybe it could not support Leonard's skull. "No," he said quietly, his voice falling toward a whisper with each word he spoke, "we were assaulted. We'd thought about hackers. But this, this was something else. It was a calculated, comprehensive assault by a very sophisticated group."

There was silence then, for a long moment, a room without breathing or motion or sound of any kind, and it was Julie who said the word. "Regence."

"Scramble the bombers," Perry said quietly.

This wasn't some kid in a university computer lab cracking a password on a Blue Box. An attack by Regence was something else completely. Regence had near infinite means to attack our system. It could have invested in a company that was a client of ours, in so doing gaining access to a series of our Blue Boxes, creating a beachhead for itself inside our network. It could have loaded the attack software on one of the millions of cell phones it manufactured, then arranged for that phone to be sold to a Core employee, specifically someone who would plug the phone into our network in New York.

It was corporate espionage, really. Illegal, unethical, extremely risky. But possible. Very, very possible.

Whitley was standing now. Very tall, pulling her coat from her chair, sliding white-shirted arms into the black sleeves. "We've got to notify the board of directors," she said. "About the attack. And about the risks."

"I'm not sure of that yet," I said. "I'm not sure how I want it presented to them."

She paused at her chair, hands at her cuffs, dark eyes turned to me. "Robbie," she said, "I'm not—" She stopped, then started again. "I'm not asking. I'm speaking as head of SWAT. We have to notify them. Now."

And it was a moment before I could respond. The room was quiet. Whitley glanced around. For that second, our world had shifted. A tangible passing of control, of power. To Whitley. And away from me.

I nodded. Smiled. I nodded again.

Even Whitley didn't seem to like it. Because what had shaken the room was not that Whitley was reporting the disaster to the board now. It wasn't just that she'd asserted her authority so directly, so quickly, and in a way no one had seen before. What had shaken the room most was that this kind of demand was what SWAT, the board, auditors, lawyers and so many other people would pursue on a daily basis if we didn't get the network restored in time. Because then our world would shift completely and forever. The isolated life we'd created for ourselves, our deeply removed world of work and money and jokes and friendships, it would be invaded, broken and quickly brought to an end.

———————

"Security?"

"Certainly."

"And containment?"

"Absolutely."

"Restoration?"

"Soon."

"When?"

"Soon enough."

The board, speaking to Whitley and me via a speakerphone on Whitley's desk. Whitley answering their questions. Questions for the past thirty minutes. Questions from board members spread out across the country, talking from cars, from weekend getaways, from their homes, from their apartments, from hotel rooms and airplanes.

But, as was always the case when we held these phone-based meetings with the board, the board members soon became one for me. One opinion. One entity. One voice.

"I can't believe we will be able to keep this quiet, Robbie," a voice from the board now said.

"It's in everyone's interest to keep this quiet," I said. "Every programmer, every customer service rep, they all know what this could do to grace."

"That's the power of grace," a voice said in agreement.

"Grace," I said, blinking, telling them what they wanted to hear.

"That's the power of the company," a voice said in agreement.

"Power," I said, blinking, telling them what they wanted to hear. "And we're already preparing the spin for the press and the market. There will be some ugly rumors in the papers, some fear among investors. But as long as the network comes back up, we will weather this."

"And if it doesn't?" the board asked.

"Then," I said, pausing, waiting, feeding the subtext of drama with no particular purpose in mind, but knowing drama was called for, needed, necessary. "Then I will go in front of every TV camera, every reporter, every client, everyone who will listen. And I will explain.

Apologize. And most importantly, if our suspicions about Regence are, in fact, true, we will blame them. We will attack them. We will make them the villain."

"*It'll be ugly,*" the board said.

"It will be war," I said.

"*It'll be war,*" the board said.

"A war," I said quietly, pausing, waiting just an extra moment again. "And a war we will win."

"*Yes,*" the board said.

"*Win,*" the board said.

Whitley shook her head, smiling slightly. She wrote a note on a piece of paper. *Fucking brown-noser.*

I nodded. "Whitley has just passed me a note," I told the speakerphone, "reminding me that we are due back in the DMZ. But I want to make sure all your questions have been answered."

"*Absolutely,*" the board said.

"*Certainly,*" the board said.

"*War,*" the board said.

The board hung up. Whitley shook her head.

I shrugged.

I was ready to stand, leave, move back into the motion and work in the DMZ. But Whitley was staring.

"Do you believe any of that?" she asked.

I sat forward for a moment, gnawing my lip, readying an answer. But I looked at her before I spoke, Whitley with her head tilted forward, her hair across her eyes, not pushing it away, not blinking or sitting up. And I sat back. "I don't know," I said quietly. "Actually, I'm far too scared to know what I believe."

"That's not helping," she said, lowering her eyes to the table, hiding for another moment. She looked up again, eyes that were green, something I certainly had never known.

I smiled slightly. I shrugged. "I get a moment of honesty."

"A moment to be real."

I nodded.

"We're dead if we don't get the network up tonight," she said. "There's no saving us. No fighting what will happen. We'll be, at best, some two-bit networking company with a handful of clients."

I wanted to nod. I thought about agreeing, about simply saying, *Yes.* But in a moment, I found myself asking, "Don't you believe what I said?"

Whitley nodded slowly, smiling barely, a vision so kid-like in its uncertainty. "I have to, Robbie. It's what gets me through each moment."

I nodded.

"A favor," she said then, "a favor for me." And I saw her smiling past me, like a kid again, holding back. Holding something back. "Tell me you believe what you said."

I stood. I nodded. "Of course I do," I said. "I believe it completely."

It was three o'clock when I remembered Eugene and the blackmail. I found Whitley near the DMZ, saying, "Eugene. We need to pay off Eugene. And we need to do it today."

After we'd managed to gather most of the key SWAT-team members into a free conference room, I told the group that we needed to pay off Eugene immediately.

"Even when we restore the network," I said, "we'll have a nightmare of rumors to address. Word will get out that something happened here. Something bad. We don't need Eugene causing trouble in the middle of that."

"How much?" Cliff asked.

I waited. Thinking through the numbers. I said finally, "Ten million more than the maximum in the scenario."

Julie was motionless. Perry smiled sickly. Whitley nodded slowly. Cliff had pushed himself away from the table, head now bowed over his knees. I thought he might begin to cry. Although I saw that, on the floor between his feet, he was managing to push keys on his small calculator.

Trauma aside, no one disagreed.

I called Eugene from my phone, standing at the end of the conference room, looking out toward New Jersey, toward the Hudson River, toward streets not far from this building. On the windowsill in front of me was a set of final documents spelling out the terms of our purchase of Eugene's journal. Two hundred pages pulled together by our legal team in the twenty-four hours since Eugene had first called. It was codified blackmail, really. Clear-cut, well-defined and made legal by these pages.

"Eighty-five million," I said to Eugene. "But only if you agree by midnight tonight."

"You are not the one who's here to negotiate," Eugene said.

"I don't have time for this," I said. "And so I am making you a very lucrative offer."

"With a catch," he said. "There has to be a catch."

"You have to agree not to offer to sell us, or anyone, a journal again," I said. "Essentially, that's it."

"I don't believe you," he said.

"It's formalized blackmail, Eugene. Legal, contractual, very straightforward."

"Are you taping this call?"

"Sign the documents I'm going to send you, Eugene. Take the money. And walk away."

"And if I wait till tomorrow?" he asked. "Or the next day?"

"Then don't bother calling me back."

And I hung up the phone.

The group around me was quiet. Cliff seemed frozen over his knees. Whitley had stood, pacing near the window. Julie held a pen so tightly in her fingers, the body of it bent, and it seemed that the slightest motion would break it in half. In a moment, she said what the rest were clearly thinking. "I'm not sure that's a threat you can carry out."

It was Perry who turned to her, just his neck moving, his body so still. "I don't think Robbie's got any choice."

Five o'clock, and my cell phone rang. And finally I saw it, the name *Trevor,* displayed on the screen. I told myself not to answer. All day I'd been waiting for him to call. I knew I shouldn't talk to him. Knew the kinds of things he would say. And yet I'd answered already. Pushing a button, saying, "Yes, Trevor," into the phone. Because I needed to answer. I had to answer Trevor.

"Tell me you've at least hidden your money under your mattress," he said, "because it looks like judgment day is here."

And I could see the smile. The wide and thin grin on his sharp face. I could see him drinking in some tall, easy bar in a distant hotel. Or wandering through his suite in a huge and bright metropolis, near the headquarters of another conglomerate, this just another client he'd sold. And I was angry.

"How did you find out?" I asked. I walked down a hall, stepping into a dark break room, and as I spoke I could feel my tongue in my mouth for what seemed like the first time in my entire life. My teeth, each ridge on my tongue, and I started to wonder when I had last slept.

"People tell me things, Robbie. I do know other people in the company."

"Are you out celebrating yet?" I asked, stepping farther into the break room, toward a narrow window looking out on three bright buildings nearby. "You'll be able to move on to something else if this fails. Cash your checks. A very rich man."

And for a moment I remembered my feeling of wanting to see Trevor here. That feeling I'd had in the seconds before Leonard had reset the entire network. That wish, a somehow generous but undefined wish that Trevor could be a part of this, that he could be my friend. Now that feeling was gone. Erased in the moment when I heard his voice. When he stepped in on me again. When, simply, he became real, the problem cousin I had always known him to be.

"I want Core to continue, Robbie," he said, and his voice was slightly quieter.

"Then why did you call? To offer your help?"

"I'm not sure why I called."

"I am, Trevor. You called to enjoy this moment. You called because I am powerless. Weak. You could smell it from wherever the fuck you are."

"No," he said. "Not really."

"I would believe you," I said. "I really would. If it weren't for the fact that you're lying to me."

"I'm not lying," he said, pausing, waiting it seemed. Pausing another moment. Awkwardly. For Trevor, it was awkward. "I just called," he finally said. "I think I just wish I were there."

"Stop it," I said, leaning forward, one hand touching the windowsill, my forehead pressed lightly against the glass, saying it again, saying, "Stop it," nearly whispering. "Stop it. You wish you were here? Why? So you could watch and laugh and sit off to the side counting the money you'll have made when all this collapses? Stop it, Trevor, because I don't need this from you."

And for a moment, in my anger and in the exhaustion I could feel in my eyes and through my body, in all that, I noticed a restaurant down on the street. On the first floor of one of the buildings in front of me. Hundreds of feet away. And I thought about how I used to have lunch there. How many weeks had it been, months, since I'd had lunch there?

"When it does fail, Trevor," I said quietly, turning my head, pressing it forward, now wanting to see the front door of that restaurant, to see the menu in the window, the three best tables, all facing out on the street, "when this company does fail, Trevor, today or in the future, when it does I'm going to come and shoot you in the head, Trevor. I'm going to shoot you dead."

He didn't respond for a moment. "You don't mean that," he said lightly.

"I don't, no, you're right, you're completely right, but that is how I feel, Trevor, that is all I want right now. I want you dead."

I pressed closer to the window, forehead against the glass, but couldn't see the restaurant any better. The menu. The tables.

Trevor's voice was suddenly very small in my ear. "All I said was that I wish I were there."

"Unless you can fly to New York in the next twenty minutes," I said into the phone, "and rebuild the entire Core network, including reconnecting it to the shadow network I've spent three years building and maintaining, then no, you don't need to be here."

"I'd just like to see," he said.

"See the whole thing fail? Oh, it'll be beautiful, Trevor. A celebration."

"No," he said. "That's not what I want. I guess I can't say it." He paused for a moment. The phone went quiet. "Is everyone really there?" he asked now. "Someone told me there are hundreds of people there. I'm sorry I called, Robbie. Really. Just tell me. Is everyone really there?"

And now I found myself closing my eyes, leaning back against the counter, wishing I hadn't answered Trevor's call. Wishing I had just stayed in the fray of rebuilding the network, of talking to the board, of meeting with the senior staff. Wishing I'd stayed in those places that had become so safe for me. Known and controlled. Not just today. But every day. Safety in the well-defined chaos and blurring, indistinct sounds and constant forward movement of every day at this place. Safety, which was so unlike these circling conversations with Trevor. Conversations where I went from anger to something else. Hearing his voice, like his kid's voice, Trevor my cousin talking to me from the top bunk, leaving me now feeling something like sadness.

"Stop, Trevor, all right?" I said, wanting my voice to be louder. "Just stop," I said, feeling something like regret.

"I'm in Renton," he said. "Or maybe Burien. Near Seattle. I'm near the airport, I do know that."

"Trevor," I said.

"Meeting with an airline tomorrow," he said. "Then to Tokyo. Then Singapore. I'll call you from there."

I was staring out the window. "And you haven't slept," I said.

"Actually, I just woke up. I couldn't even remember where I was. Not till I just said the words to you."

"Trevor, what do you want? Really. From me. From any of this."

"I think I'd been asleep for a few hours," he said.

I was speaking very quietly now. Slowly. Eyes open. Staring up, past the buildings, past the rooftops. Seeing some break in the sky. Blue, and passing clouds. "And how long had you been awake before that, Trevor?"

"Days."

"How many?"

"A few."

"More than two?"

"Probably."

"Why?" I asked.

"I was selling," he said, and I knew now that Trevor was in a dark room outside a city, sitting in modular furniture in another hotel near another airport, near some shopping center with its familiar stretch of brightly lit stores, the best room he could get but as faceless and gray as the rest he'd stayed in that week and month, Trevor leaning forward now, on the phone, eyes closed, calling to see what was happening. What would happen.

"Some woman came up to me in an airport yesterday and told me she was my mother," Trevor said, voice near the phone but seeming not to listen again.

"How did it feel to be me?" I asked, knowing the woman had confused Trevor with me, having seen us both in an article or on the news.

"Fine," he said.

"Why don't you sleep?" I asked.

He didn't answer for a moment. "I don't know, Robbie."

"We think Regence might have done this," I said.

"Probably they did," he said.

"I just updated the board," I said quietly.

"I'm glad I don't do that," he said.

"I'm sure they're glad too," I said, smiling some.

"When you tell me about talking to the board," he said, speaking away from the phone, "I almost feel bad for you."

I touched the window. I pressed so hard with my fingers. "All this is getting to be more than I can take," I said.

"I know," he said quietly.

"Do you? Can I believe you?"

"I guess you can't," he said.

"I guess not."

"I hope the network comes back up," he said.

"I know," I said. "I know."

"I'll call you from Singapore," he said.

"Call me from Tokyo."

"I will," he said.

"Good-bye."

Eleven at night, and Leonard was standing in the doorway of a conference room. "I think we're ready," he said to Whitley and me.

His tone was so pleasant I would have followed him anywhere. His motions so calm that, for a moment, I forgot what we were about to do.

But as Whitley and I followed him toward the DMZ, the weight and risk of the situation did come back to me. We were about to restart the system using a network strung together on the fly, laid out in the hallways and conference rooms, pieced together by techs still checking their pencil-drawn diagrams. As Whitley and I walked behind the dense, wide figure of Leonard, it seemed that all of the twelve hundred employees who'd come in that day had made their way to the eleventh floor, all crowded into the hallways and workspaces near the DMZ. And now they parted slowly, letting Leonard pass. Whitley and I were just followers at this point. Privileged bystanders tagging along in Leonard's biggest shadow.

"Given the obvious time constraints," Leonard was saying, speaking over his shoulder as he led Whitley and me through the still-forming path, "I haven't had a chance to tell you about all the specific hazards associated with what we're about to do. I suppose it's a bit of an understatement to say we've never done this before. And again, given the time frame, it's been hard to take all the precautions we'd like."

Whitley glanced at me, smiling slightly. Struck not only by the concerns Leonard was now raising but by the matter-of-fact way in which he could discuss these issues.

"In summary," Leonard said to us, thick hand brushing against his ear, "we could damage the network even more by trying to restart it."

I saw Whitley's mouth open, not sure what to say, her eyes wide as we continued to wend our way through the people all looking at us. "That's important for me to know, Leonard," she said. "Can you maybe fill in some details?"

"Rather than take up a lot of our time with the particulars of the various negative scenarios," he said flatly, hands raised as if holding a large ball, or maybe the world, "it's probably best if you picture all those bad movies you've seen where the mad professor is desperate to give power to the broken machine." He turned his head full around, walking backward, and it was amazing to see so much girth turn a circle. "He flips a switch. The lights dim. Sparks fly. There is smoke. Tears. Failure."

"Except that instead of smoke," Whitley offered warily, "we'll just see the system go dead?"

"Actually," Leonard said, still walking backward, in some ways seeming to tumble easily toward the DMZ behind him, "there could be smoke. And however this turns out, sparks are pretty much a given."

"This is a terrible time for you to develop a sense of irony," Whitley said to him.

Leonard squinted. "I hadn't noticed."

"Maybe we should wait a little longer before doing this," Whitley finally said. "Run some more tests. Explore some more of those precautions you would normally take."

Leonard shook his head. "I don't think so," he said, his wide face pinched and serious. "If it doesn't work now, we'll still have a few hours to try some more drastic measures. Assuming, of course, that we don't destroy every working computer in the building."

Whitley could only pull hard on my sleeve, the scared child clutching for safety and protection.

"And besides," Leonard added, turning to us again, another slow and fluid motion as his face opened into a smile, "we're all pretty eager to see what's going to happen."

Leonard opened the door to the DMZ.

The seats in the DMZ were filled with techs, some terminals doubled up with wide-eyed administrators waiting now for the restart. Along the back wall stood just a few people, Perry and Cliff and Julie, now joined by Whitley as I followed Leonard to the middle of the room. He took his seat very slowly, gently fitting himself behind the narrow desk, now carefully checking the height of his chair, the position of his keyboard, the brightness and contrast of the three screens in front of him.

At many companies, Leonard would have been blamed completely for this. But everyone knew it was only because of Leonard's abilities that we had even a chance of restarting the system. Leonard couldn't access Shimmer, the most critical element of our system. And so this was not Leonard's fault.

Yet suddenly, for the first time that day, I wondered if Leonard understood this. Because now, standing behind him, seeing the faintest reflection of his face in each of the three bright screens, now I did see Leonard blink his heavy lids an extra second, saw him tap extra hard on the keyboard, and I knew that of course Leonard was not calm, knew he saw no humor in any of this. Leonard was simply scared. Hiding it better than anyone else. But scared. Because this job, this system, the people all taking direction from him, the thousands more dependent on his next move, together it all formed the very center of the life of this twenty-six-year-old boy. This was his existence, summed up, in total.

For Leonard, there was nothing more.

I leaned toward him. I said quietly, "Let's give it a go."

Leonard looked at me and said, "Yes," as he turned from me to the computer, reaching to the keyboard to send off the drone that would attempt to restore the system. But before he touched the keyboard, he turned back to me briefly, and I said a few words to him, and in a moment I was already quietly laughing, laughing before Leonard touched his keyboard again, before the drone was released, laughing and smiling, both of us smiling, and the lore that would surround that moment became a story repeated companywide, a Core fable no two people remembered quite the same way but that every person knew, all of them saying I'd laughed simply because I knew the network would be restored. Knew it as if I knew everything, knew it because I was the founding CEO, the top visionary who whispered some blessing in the ear of one of his most important prophets before our miracle was sent out into our world.

I never told anyone this wasn't true. Never told anyone that I hadn't laughed because I'd known Leonard would make this work. Never told anyone that I'd laughed simply because of the way Leonard had turned to me, blank-faced, wanting something, wanting simply some warmth and support, and I'd said only, "I know, I know," and he'd smiled then, quickly, child-like in his satisfaction, almost giggling as he nodded toward me, taking a moment to raise his hand to me, delaying the salvation of the company by just a second or two as he touched me, firmly, on the arm.

I do not like to be touched.

But now even Leonard had decided to get in on the joke.

And so I had laughed. Laughing that spread to the crowd of fifty around us, then the crowd outside the DMZ, then the people on other floors, all laughing as the board lit up white, then green, the terminals flickering, shining, glowing back at us all, the network responding, all processes, all steps, unfolding as planned.

It had worked.

There was drinking then, even music, even dancing and most of all a steady, sometimes frenzied, only barely exaggerated repetition of the story of the crash and the effort to restore the network, people who'd worked side by side for twenty-four hours now retelling each step they'd taken, nodding rapidly at one another, reliving each moment, retelling it again, nodding and smiling and lost to the pleasure of the work they had done.

And I was laughing. Telling stories too. Celebrating with each person I could.

Cliff almost bouncing, bouncing in place, from room to room, a few times lightly bouncing off a wall or desk.

Whitley and Julie seeming to teach Leonard his first dance, pulling him into the center of the happiest of groups, all of them now reaching to touch Leonard's mass, patting his shoulders, pulling at his arms, and he danced and spun and smiled.

Perry staying with the group, this rolling late-night party, staying with it till the end, off to the side, sitting alone, but staying even when all eyes had turned away.

And everyone laughing.

And me, I was laughing too.

Laughing even when I'd gone back to my office, checking the shadow network, seeing each part of it working, seeing each part of it unscathed, untouched by the crash.

Laughing as I watched Shimmer shine so bright, numbers spinning, lines spread evenly, multiplying once, twice and again.

Laughing, although silently, as Eugene called me on my phone, telling me he had accepted the offer. Saying he had signed and returned the documents to us.

Laughing because of course we'd won that battle too.

Laughing because, although Regence was still a threat of unknown scope, it seemed right now that there was no way we wouldn't conquer it too.

Laughing and thinking about Trevor, my sometime cousin and would-be brother, still lying awake in one more hotel out there, and once more I wanted him to have been here, to have seen this, to have been a part of something he had never experienced in his life.

Laughing with the group again, the programmers and the vice presidents and the admins and everyone, all gathered around the DMZ, in the offices and hallways and conference rooms they'd commandeered, drinking beer with the cables still running under their feet, strung over the desks, taped to the ceilings and chairs.

Laughing and talking and drinking with the hundreds of people still there, all night, till one o'clock, then two. Laughing till I went up to my apartment. Alone and staring out toward the skyline of Manhattan around me. Laughing till I was quiet. Till it had passed. Till all that was left was the picture of Leonard's child-like grin as he'd touched me. And the smile of every person celebrating our success. And the laugh of every person who knew we could never be stopped.

And only now did I cry.

It had worked. It had worked.

My God, it worked.

And soon I would destroy them all.

It's his stomach, really. He was born with a weak stomach. As a child he got carsick, seasick, airsick, all of it.

It's Cliff's stomach more than anything.

He sits on his back porch, kids all playing. Ten kids, more, his kids and their friends and some parents from the neighborhood. It is sunny and warm and the kids roam in laughing, screaming packs across his yard, in and out of his house.

He is trying to eat, but he can't.

And he is trying to forget work, but he can't.

Network collapse, Eugene and his journal, Regence a threat they can't fully see or understand.

There is someone talking to him on the porch. Cliff responds, says words, but he is not really there.

And he doesn't want to think about work. Doesn't want to talk about work.

But he can't put it away.

Usually it's a game to him. Accounting and finance, some funny game he came upon. He liked history, and English. But math was easy. A funny, easy distraction from the things he liked to read.

And then he needed a job. And it all got even funnier. These people grinding numbers on spreadsheets on their screens. Talking gibberish, their accounting lingo. Rollover, cash flow, receivables, net. He liked it. And she was pregnant. And so he took a job, and fifteen years later, he was CFO of Core Communications.

Even through the first few years at Core, it all made him smile. He could see everything, this company and the ones they acquired. The turning of the money, the flow of cash among so many divisions, the lines of credit and stock transfers. He saw it all. Consolidations of the income statements, and depreciation of the assets, and amortization of the interest.

For those first years, Cliff could see each part, each function, each activity in the finances.

But now he can't see it all. He can't pull each piece together anymore. It all balances. It is all checked and audited, and it conforms to the highest standards he can impose. But there is something underneath it, some untouchable movement that even he can't see.

An auditor in the UK asked him a question he could not answer. About money paid to a vendor. About the timing and source. He knew the answer, the source of funds, the bank account and purpose. But. He couldn't answer. Because the payment was slightly off. The timing was wrong. The money hit the account, then moved. Moved sooner than it should have.

He could have answered that auditor, put the question away. But he didn't. Because he didn't understand.

He takes a bite of food, chewing slowly, carefully. It is just bread.

He's already quietly started an internal audit in the UK. So that he can understand.

He calculated grace this morning. Less than three months away.

He knows he is talking now, responding to what this person is saying.

He smiles as he talks, still chewing, still looking around at these children, all of them, roaming so happily in the light around him, movements for a second slowed in his eyes, and he has to blink, needs to finish this food, needs to sleep. At grace he will sleep.

Why would the money move that way?

CHAPTER 6

Now there was the spin. Spin for the press, the clients, the market and investors. Because, by Monday morning after the network had been restored, the rumors were spreading. There were questions from our clients. There were rumors among reporters. There were half stories being passed between brokers and analysts. Although everyone in the company knew the network failure had to be kept a secret, still it was impossible to keep something like this completely quiet. Some VP speaking to his family, some security guard talking to a friend, some rogue section playing a joke. There were thousands of ways whispers about the network crash could spread.

By ten that morning, there was a growing number of e-mails to our PR department. Stories in the chat rooms devoted to rumors about stocks. Questions from our contacts at supplier companies. Phone calls from stock analysts hearing and spreading these same rumors themselves.

And by eleven, our stock had dipped $6. The first decline in eight months. The first substantial decline ever.

By noon, the stock had fallen another $4. The calls and messages mounted. Hits to our Web site were doubling every five minutes—the press, the brokers, day traders all looking to our site for information.

Our response companywide was that, at this time, we had no response.

Because this was what I had said to do. I said to wait.

"The uninhibited nature of the favors offered to me today in exchange for information about the stock," said Julie, staring into her computer, clearly skimming through e-mails, deleting them as she moved on, "borders on the scandalous. The profane. Even for me."

The stock fell another $2.

By one o'clock, the senior staff had all brought their laptops to my office, ostensibly to discuss the ramifications of the stock drop but really seeming only to want to be together, in my presence maybe, at the very moment I gave the nod. The moment I told them it was time to respond.

By one-thirty, the stock had fallen another $4.

All five of us—Cliff, Leonard, Julie, Whitley and I—tried to go about our work as usual. But none of us strayed from my office for long. All of us clinging to the security of our combined presence.

The stock fell another $2.

I handed each of them a piece of paper with a very short description of what we should say.

The stock fell $4.

I handed each of them a piece of paper with eight names on it. Each of us would call eight different people.

I watched as Cliff left the room very quickly.

Two o'clock. Two hours before the market would close. Board members calling me. Analysts e-mailing. Our nonresponse still being distributed to anyone and everyone who asked. Critics saying a nonanswer was worse than any answer we might give.

Wait, I said. *Trust me. Wait.*

Outside my office, people were gathering along the aisles and hallways of the twentieth floor, all of them quietly seeking the security of the senior staff.

Cliff left the room again. He returned a few minutes later, mouth damp. Julie passed him a mint.

Two-thirty. I picked up a phone in my office, moving toward a window, making a call. And starting to spin.

"We can't say what happened," I said into the phone, speaking to a lead Wall Street analyst, staring out the window as the rest of the senior staff listened. "I'm not even supposed to be talking to you. All I can say is that the bettors on Wall Street have it completely wrong."

I was nodding slowly, listening to this person ask questions I wouldn't answer, pulling at my lip with my fingers.

"All I can say is that sure, it's a better story if Core had a problem," I said. "It's a great story. We've been untouchable. And that gets boring. But the bettors have it all wrong."

I absently pulled at my lip.

"All I can say is that we're a company whose actions are frequently bound by secrecy," I said. "We handle a tremendous amount of financial information. Personal information. And so we can't announce every good thing that happens, every positive development that takes place."

I absently pulled at my lip.

"All I can say is that we're a technology company," I said. "These people on Wall Street know finance. They don't know computers, and they particularly don't know mainframes or satellite communications or high-speed networking. So how can they tell a good development from a bad one?"

I absently pulled at my lip.

"All I can say is that whatever happened, it was a testament to the strength of this company. Its staff, its market position, its technological edge. And if we could announce the full story—and I may just find a way, given the shit I'm hearing out there—if we could announce it, then I'd be the first person to let it be known."

I nodded, I listened, I turned back to the four of them and raised my hand, then one finger. This was it, I was telling them—of all the points on our sheets, this was the one we had to get right. This was the line we had to sell.

"All I can say is that sometimes we're bound by issues more important than rumors and stock prices. I mean, for God's sake," I said, finger still raised, "why the hell else would I do something so stupid as to wait all day, till the market is on the verge of closing at a record loss for us—why else would I wait till now to respond?"

In another moment, I hung up, still staring out the window, staring now in the direction of Wall Street. Staring as if I could watch the reaction. In a moment I turned to them and said quietly, "Make your calls."

Everyone started to call the people on the lists. Analysts, reporters, suppliers, customers. We delivered my story. We sold it as hard as we could.

By three-thirty, the stock had regained $10. At closing, it ended up another $5. By closing on Tuesday afternoon, the next day, it had jumped another $15, ending at an all-time high.

And so we'd won another battle.

By Tuesday night, when the market had closed, the analysts had all certified the stock's recovery as nothing short of amazing. I was walking with Whitley, the two of us crossing through the remnants of our disaster. There were cables still strung along corridors, running into and out of offices near the DMZ. There were whiteboards leaning against walls and doors and desks, all filled with checklists and next steps related to the continuing restoration of the network. There were people, some in shorts, some in overalls, each monitoring the activities and status of the patchwork system Leonard had built.

And all of them, the people here now, the people who I'd seen in hallways and in meetings and in elevators for the past two days, everyone in the company who I'd talked to or gotten e-mail from, all of them were the same. Happy. Not just pleased. Not only relieved. But happy in a way that was total, complete. These hundreds of people who'd worked straight through the last four days, consumed and encircled by the work they did, all were deeply, purely happy.

"This all has meant a lot to me," I said to Whitley now, stepping over the cables, reaching out to touch a whiteboard. Seeing my hand for a moment, a hand that for a second seemed very removed from my body. "Maybe too much, I suppose."

"Too much?" she asked.

"It's a job."

She shrugged. She seemed so comfortable, so at ease. "Not really," she said. "It's more."

And as I walked, talking with her, I had half thoughts and a list of notes already scrolling across my eyes. Things to do, transactions to make, people to hire, markets to explore, a shadow network that had to be maintained.

"These people have always had a sense of ownership," Whitley said. "But it's even more so now. A sense of place. A sense of belonging."

I needed to go back to my apartment. I needed to sleep. Tonight, sleep. Get ready for tomorrow. Keep the company afloat. Keep the shadow network alive.

I noticed that Whitley's hair was less straight today, somehow messy in a way that suggested she'd slept in late, and only now did I realize that Whitley was wearing jeans and a sweater.

My mind worked through the next steps for the shadow network, a growing list, twenty items to finish, twenty transactions to make. Buy twelve mainframes through the third Cayman company, the one with the extra cash from the sale in Dublin. Buy satellite time from the company in France. Begin the transition of the Asian accounting systems, creating the float accounts and expense pools.

Each item was a point to complete by the morning, to finish off so I could move on to the next. Although, as I walked, I knew that maybe more than anything, what I really needed was to sleep. If I could sleep, I would make it. I would see some solution.

"The rebound in the stock," I said to Whitley. "The spin. Thanks for your help."

Route more Scottish data through the French satellites. Lease two more satellites through the company in Denmark. What's the name of the company in Denmark?

Go back to your apartment. Don't even stop in the office. Go back and sleep.

"What I did," Whitley said, walking slowly, Whitley setting a pace so oddly slow, "what we all did, is made easy by what this place has become."

Moving through the office. Crossing wide corridors, passing through areas in darkness, then bright. Passing people working late, people playing games, people drawing madly on whiteboards and notepads and computers.

Send the new Indian code to Santa Fe. Send it through the consultants. The new ones. The new ones from D.C.

Go back to your apartment. Sleep, all night, in bed.

Release the lawyer in Salt Lake. Forward all documents to the attorney in St. Paul, subtract the fee from the account, forward the money, close the account, terminate the contracts with the agency in Twin Falls. Tomorrow. Put that in motion first thing tomorrow.

And find a way to sleep.

Find a way to sleep.

Shift more cash into the Caymans. Swap bank accounts in Tampa. What's the name of the company in Denmark?

Go back to your apartment.

"In a way," Whitley was saying, "I could have said or done anything."

Go back and make the call.

"I don't believe that," I was saying, saying it because this was what I was supposed to say. Because my mind was racing fast. And because I already knew what Whitley would say next.

Maybe a college girl.

And I would like it when I heard what Whitley would say. And I'd fear it just as much.

Maybe dark hair.

What's the name?

A beautiful woman. Dark and near silent, and slow.

What's the name of the company in Denmark?

Go back and make the call. Go back, and call, and sleep. Then find a way to save this company.

"What saved us," Whitley said, touching her lip, then her ear, then touching me on the arm to reinforce her point, and smiling just a second as she did it, and I smiled back at her, lifted for a moment by the silly joy of an ongoing joke, but, still, wanting to crumble under the truth of what Whitley would say, "what saved us is that, ultimately, no one wants to believe that Core Communications can fail."

Inside her.

Against her.

Above her.

Against.

"Like that?" she asked quietly.

Like that.

"There?" she asked quietly.

Slow. Slower.

Slow. Slower.

The white light of buildings, shining on the pillow, then the sheet. The muffled roar of a helicopter somewhere beyond me. White light lying easily across her perfect face.

Across her black and empty eyes.

"Like that," she said quietly.

"There," she said quietly.

Inside her. So slow.

There.

It was everything. All of it. Everything gone. Only here, above her, against her. Nothing else. Nothing.

"There," she said quietly. "Once more, there."

Ronald Mertz wore slacks so tight you could see the outlines of the quarters in his front pockets. He was so detailed in his work, so thorough in his analysis, that today, as always, the rest of the SWAT team sat spellbound in his presence.

Ronald, our head of corporate security and day-to-day manager of Whitley's SWAT team, was reporting on Regence. Network restored. Eugene paid off. But Regence still out there.

"We have confirmed," Ronald was saying now, thumbs hooked on the pockets of his maroon nylon jacket, staring toward the ceiling as he spoke to key members of SWAT, "that the attack on us was launched from a series of computers owned by the Dutch subsidiary of an American-based logistics firm. That firm is, as we suspected, one of Core's clients. Additionally—and more importantly—the Dutch subsidiary is a strategic partner of HXT, LLC, out of Bermuda, a shell operation which, according to a report just filed with SWAT, maintains very close ties to certain individuals living in Macao. Said individuals, according to another confidential report submitted to SWAT, maintain very close connections to a series of Regence executives."

"Do we have black-and-white photographs shot from long distances?" Julie asked seriously, sitting forward on the edge of her chair, barely able to hold in her joke. "Do we have grainy photographs of said individuals getting into unmarked sedans?"

Ronald turned his gaze from the ceiling toward Julie. "In fact," he said warily, "we do."

Julie beamed widely. Perry smiled just slightly. Ronald seemed to make a mental note to check in on Julie later.

"Although the attack was intended to shut down our network," Ronald continued, "it's clear that their primary goal was to understand how a Blue Box works. In that respect," he said, hooking a bony thumb in his belt, "we believe they failed."

Cliff seemed to take his first breath of the morning. Whitley tapped three times on the table, smiling behind her falling black hair. Julie's square shoulders did, just slightly, go soft and low, and as small as the motion was, I thought for a moment that she might melt through her chair, reassembling herself in a warm, sleeping ball on the floor.

"Do we know yet if Regence did any other damage?" Whitley asked.

"I think Regence saw that our network was experiencing a massive failure," Leonard was saying, now standing next to Ronald. "And so they did launch another assault."

"On another Blue Box?" Cliff asked, leaning forward, relief gone already, and in the middle of the file folders he'd brought to the meeting I thought I saw an airsickness bag.

Leonard shook his head. "On the headquarters. Here."

There was a shifting, movement in our seats, all of us waiting for Leonard to continue.

"Well," Whitley finally asked, "did they get in?"

Leonard squinted, confused. "Absolutely."

Julie was standing now, and almost yelling. "For how long?"

"Actually," Leonard said, "I'm quite certain they continue to monitor us right now."

Whitley and Cliff both stood. Perry stared at Leonard with a look part frightened, part entertained. Ronald Mertz stepped toward me, one hand pushing open his jacket as if he were going to draw the gun he kept in a shoulder holster, the other hand raised in an apparent effort to protect me. It was if we'd been told Regence was not only watching and listening to the seven of us in this room but that Regence's own security force was ready to break through the door in black jumpsuits and boots, guns firing rapidly as they methodically eliminated everyone in their sights.

Leonard was completely confused by our reaction. "Wait," he said in a moment, after our concern had fully registered with him. "Let me clarify. Regence has seen nothing of substance. We just found them this morning. They've done no damage. They simply made an inroad into a database used by internal operations."

"Internal operations?" Ronald asked.

"Janitorial supplies," Leonard said. "Lightbulbs, paper towels, soap refills."

"Toilet paper?" Julie asked.

Leonard nodded. "That too."

"This," Perry said quietly, "cannot go unchecked."

"When it happened, our security systems immediately isolated the intrusion," Leonard was saying. "In other words, although we only just realized where they are, Regence hasn't been able to escape that particular area of that particular database. And so we're watching them. Studying their tactics. Recording their movements and attempts to break into other areas."

"Do they know you're watching?" Cliff asked.

"No," Leonard said.

"Can you put them on a false trail?" I asked. "Let them jump from internal operations to some kind of fake system?"

Leonard nodded. "My team has already sketched out a number of scenarios to that effect. Initial ideas include false specifications for a Blue Box or inaccurate diagrams of Shimmer."

"A fake set of financials," Cliff suggested.

"The secret formula for Coca-Cola," Whitley said.

"Naked pictures of Perry and Cliff," Julie said.

Perry shook his head. "Not without a credit card."

"And so," Whitley asked, quietly now, pausing, and Leonard turned to her, "and so as a result of the attack, Regence learned nothing important?"

"Correct," Leonard said.

"We won," Whitley said.

"So far," he said, nodding, a motion I wanted to support with my own hands, cradling his wide brow as it dipped forward, then back, "so far, we have won."

Maybe it was the relief of knowing that Regence's attack had failed. Maybe it was the success of having restored the network in time. But one week after the attack, I had what I can only call a vision.

It only lasted a moment. But in that moment, I had a revelation. A revelation that came from Frederick Fadowsky.

In the week since the attack, I'd taken to rereading Fadowsky's published journals late at night, poring over the pages as I waited for the sun to light my living room. Three years earlier, when Trevor had first brought me the idea for the Blue Boxes, I'd read the entire published set of annotated journals. Now, as I came back to them, Fadowsky struck me as more visionary than ever, an arrogant but brilliant man haunted by wildly prescient, deeply inspired insights into the future. Fadowsky had foreseen a networked world and had seen it in a light so separate from any of the purely technical issues.

What he'd seen was an entirely new relationship between people and time.

"The future network," Fadowsky had written back in 1977, "a truly robust and high-speed network made up of a near infinite number of interdependent machines alters completely and forever people's relationships to one another. Fundamentally, a network such as this alters time. It renders distance meaningless. It renders physical space unimportant. It renders such artificial constructs as time zones and borders irrelevant as it recasts the very notion of human interaction."

Wordy, self-important, filled with an inflated sense of his place in the world, Fadowsky was nothing if not arrogant. But he was also right.

And so it was that as I entered a Friday meeting with Whitley, my head was filled with Fadowsky's thoughts.

Although, thinking back, I know it was more than Fadowsky's writings that inspired my vision. It was also the game of putt-putt.

I was playing with Whitley, the two of us discussing an expansion plan for Eastern Europe. Like all the putt-putt courses spread throughout the building, this one was as much an obstacle course as it was a golf course. Furniture, printers, potted plants and the nearly endless movement of people through the building.

Through the first few holes, I was too occupied with the plan Whitley and I were discussing to notice how well Whitley was playing. By the fifth hole, though, I'd realized what was happening. Playing with care, speed and purpose, Whitley had built an eight-stroke lead over me. By the seventh hole, she was ten strokes ahead of me.

"I'm a one handicap," she said to me as we walked down the hall.

"Which means?" I asked her.

She tapped her white teeth. She pulled at her black sleeve. In a moment, she said quietly, "I'm the highest-rated player in the building."

"I had no idea," I said.

Whitley shrugged, smiling lightly now. "It's true," she said, pushing that sharp black hair from her eyes as she gripped her club. "I'm a badass."

For most of the first nine holes, I had been barely hanging in the game, totally unfamiliar with the course and obstacles. But that began to change, inspired as I was by Whitley's methodical commitment to the game. By the twelfth hole, I'd cut her lead to six. By the fifteenth hole, I'd cut Whitley's lead to four.

"So much promise," Whitley said, watching as I sank a twenty-foot shot. "So much hope."

To the seventeenth hole, then the eighteenth, Whitley and I tied as we neared the final hole.

"What's riding on this game?" Whitley asked, looking at me.

"Pride," I said, "honor, the unspoken glory of individual accomplishment."

"Bullshit," she said. "We forgot to bet."

"Money?"

She shook her head. "I've got none to give, and you've got no incentive to win it."

"I guess there's no bet," I said quickly, wanting to take my shot before anything serious was at risk. I lined up and swung my club, my ball missing the hole by a foot.

Whitley had her fingers at her lips. Inhaling. Release. "The bet is still on," she said.

"Lunch?" I suggested.

"Not quite," she said.

She took a practice swing. If she made the shot, she would win.

"There's a currency more valuable than any of that," she said, leaning over the ball, but I could see that she was smiling behind the hair hanging across her face. "It's the most common currency in use in this building."

I nodded. I smiled just slightly. I remembered what Perry had told me a few weeks earlier.

"Favors," Whitley said.

I nodded again. "What favors?" I asked.

"Unnamed favors," she said, lining up to take her shot. In a moment, though, she stepped back, looking at me again. "Three of them," she said.

"Three wishes," I said.

She took a last practice swing. She turned for a second and smiled at me brightly, kid-like in her excitement. "Three wishes," she said, then turned back to the ball and swung.

And in what to me would seem like one long second, one motion, one thought, one vision of all the space around me, I saw Whitley swing, saw elevator doors opening behind her, saw people slowing as they turned to watch her, and I saw myself there, putt-putt golf club in my hand, thinking for that moment about this section of this floor of this building in New York, two people here for this short second as work went on around them, Core Communications passing data to its clients worldwide, its employees talking to coworkers, suppliers, partners around the globe, its shadow network bouncing data between satellites and hidden outposts, all of it in motion in that frozen second as I watched Whitley.

And I saw it.

Fadowsky was right.

The kind of high-speed network made possible by the Fadowsky

Boxes changed completely how we had to view time. The shadow network working simultaneously in every hemisphere, above the north and south poles, in just seconds passing information from a western day to an eastern night. Time meant something else completely.

I saw the network. Saw myself. And I saw an answer. A way to take so much pressure off the shadow network. A way to extend its life by months or more.

The details of what I needed to do were immensely complex, so complex that the idea could easily fail. Already I knew that executing the change would be a huge effort, made worse by the fact that I could involve very few people, and none would know the scope of what was being done.

Still, the idea itself was simple. The shadow network would collapse when it finally choked on the ever larger amount of data that was being sent—at ever faster rates—through the satellites, cable, switches and mainframes. Ultimately, no amount of money or hardware or people could change this. But what I'd realized was that Shimmer, by default, hadn't ever allowed for transferring data not faster but slower. If I had Shimmer upload data to the satellites at a slower rate—just fractions of a second slower—and download it at the same speed I downloaded it now, I could, essentially, create more room in the network. The difference in speed between upload and download, that fraction of a fraction of a second, created a lag time. And that lag time would grow every day, increasing slowly and in turn creating more capacity in the storage units, in the land-based cable, in the mainframes and servers, everywhere except the satellites themselves.

I couldn't do this forever. The system would choke when the lag time got too big. Even ten seconds would crash the network. But for now, the lag could buy me time.

Judged against the standards of a normal business, it was a crazy idea. But the Fadowsky journals had reminded me of the tremendous scope and speed of a network like this. In so many ways, it existed in a time created by and for itself. I would simply alter that time very, very slightly.

And I know now that there was something besides the Fadowsky journals, something I'd been reminded of not by Fadowsky but by the game of putt-putt. This was not a normal company.

Core was best helped by an inherently failed idea.

"Three wishes," Whitley said again. And I realized I was looking at her. Realized she had finished the game.

Realized that, of course, she'd already sunk her shot.

Into meetings. Crossing corridors. On the phone and answering e-mail. Walking alone or with a team of six, sitting at my desk or sitting at a table with twenty. Talking with investors, brokers, analysts, the press. Agreeing to buy three companies in south Florida. Sitting through two interviews with British TV. Seeing the light, everywhere, broken or filtered—shafts of light or angled shadows, all falling across doorways and conference tables and the faces of accountants and programmers and senior product managers.

And, all the while, communicating with the thirty groups worldwide working on the changes to the shadow network. Assessing their results. Adjusting their plans. Talking to them via a hidden trail of half-informed contractors, shifting intermediaries and redirected e-mail addresses.

For a week I'd been working on the changes. It would be another two weeks before I could roll them into the shadow network. Only then would I know if this would work, in part because none of the people working on this were aware of what I really wanted them to do. *Slow data to the satellites,* I wanted to say. But I couldn't, was instead only able to relay the responses of one group to the next, translating and recasting their comments to suit my secret purpose. It would be another two weeks of this, monitoring the groups' progress, waiting for the conclusion, doing it all in and between the mix of critical, important and sometimes trivial moments that made up my life.

Tuesday, in my office reading a letter from my mother, a onetime waitress now living in the suburbs of Toledo. She'd been forced to give me up for adoption by my father, the domineering night manager of a densely packed Toledo trailer park. I sat back in my chair now. For a second, closed my eyes. Pictured my father, a rotund dictator roaming the asphalt streets of the Thirty Pines trailer park, his estranged wife staring wistfully toward the nearby on-ramp to Interstate 80.

The letter was heavy with emotion. Details, however, were—as always—a little sketchy.

It was just one of forty letters from would-be parents, all stacked neatly on a table in my office. My assistant tended to bundle up all these parental claims, hanging on to them in a file locked away in his desk, letting me have them only reluctantly, and only after I asked for them repeatedly. Often I would have to go to his desk and open the drawer myself.

"I want to see what's come in," I would say.

"Actually," my assistant always said, "you really don't."

It was only his sense of loyalty that kept him from throwing away every one of the letters.

So now I looked them over. A letter from my father, a karate instructor in Michigan. A letter from my mother, a customer service supervisor in North Dakota. A letter, with photo, from my father and mother, co-owners of a diner in Arizona. A very distinguished-looking Asian man and lovely Indian woman, they did not even bother to explain the racial discrepancy between us. "We have found you," the letter began. "What's done is done."

I looked at the letters and thought maybe they were standard packages sent to all the world's wealthy adopted children. *Playing the odds,* I thought. *At some point, maybe someone will bite.*

Most all the letters did ultimately end up in the trash. But some I kept, putting them in a file locked away inside my desk. Because maybe. Maybe that woman in Toledo really was my mother. Maybe that man in Michigan really was my father. It wasn't that I didn't believe what my father had told me before he died. That my birth parents were both dead. But maybe, somehow, he'd been wrong.

And maybe someday I'd decide I wanted to know for sure.

Eating lunch in Ronald Mertz's office, and getting an update on Regence's inroad into our facilities database. In the past week, we'd let Regence's spies learn that we planned an expansion in Cologne, Germany, told them that Core used high-quality paint in all its renovations, revealed that the company's Asian soap dispensers averaged a 96-milligram output per user.

"It can't hurt," Julie said, and Ronald and Leonard nodded sincerely.

"However," Leonard added, "I must report that, twice, a number of documents have appeared in the facilities database containing the words *Regence Sucks*."

All eyes turned to Julie. She swallowed quickly, then shrugged awkwardly. Ronald frowned deeply. Leonard turned a page.

Stopping by Cliff's office and using a quick conversation about the French stock market to confirm a rumor I'd heard from numerous sources—a small stack of airsickness bags lying on Cliff's windowsill.

As our conversation about the markets came to an end, there was a silence. I pointed vaguely in the direction of the bags. In a moment, I asked quietly, "Trouble?"

Cliff shrugged. "Age."

"Take a break," I said. "A few days. A week."

His thumbs began to twitch. He crossed his arms against his chest. He held his elbows in his palms. "It would only make it worse," he said. "Just get me to grace."

And so I smiled. And nodded. And left.

Passing by a conference room on the twelfth floor, the meeting attended solely by women dressed in green.

Construction on Perry's expanded office had begun, his only semiserious request for a raised floor and antechamber having been approved. Walls for the chamber had been drawn out on the carpet near his door. Chalk lines had been marked along the inside walls of his office, the dim blue marks delineating the height of the new floor.

"How does this happen?" I asked when I saw the preconstruction.

"I submit a request," Perry said, shrugging. "I trade favors, and the work begins."

It was Thursday, and Leonard and I had come to sit in Perry's darkness, here to discuss the status of nearly forty new products and services we'd released in the last six months.

"The ideas have proven themselves," Perry was saying now. "Everything we've released is selling at or above projections."

But even as he spoke, there was an awkward silence forming among the three of us. Because we knew. Knew I was dedicating as much money as possible to R&D, to products wholly unrelated to our Blue Boxes. Knew I was spending this money at the risk of worrying the board of directors, our banks and investment firms, even the brokers and Wall Street analysts, all of whom had invested in Core because it was a high-margin, one-of-a-kind service, not because of our new products.

And we knew that, so far, the sum total of the new products and great ideas had barely paid for the research itself.

"And a new Blue Box?" I asked, referring now to Leonard's team of programmers who, for two and a half years, had been working solely on replicating what our Blue Boxes did.

"They've given up sleep," Leonard said. "I've made sure of that."

But again there was that silence.

"They're still trying, though," Leonard said.

"Of course," I said.

And for that moment, we were quiet. A silence that lasted just a second too long, creating a pause no one knew how to break. An awkwardness so unnatural for our office.

The silence of failure.

Outside the door, we heard two golf balls slamming into a potted plant, a putt-putt game making its way down the hall, one player letting out a high-pitched scream. The three of us smiled some. Then adjourned. Then found our way back into the world beyond our disappointment.

In my office, on the phone, asking for changes to a new technical security plan. In a conference room rejecting three proposals to invest in software start-ups in Silicon Valley. In the hallway approving marketing plans aimed at our expansion in Asia.

In my office, watching the stock climb.

In my office, reading a report on two rumors about lost Fadowsky journals—rumors since dismissed by SWAT.

In my office, reading, at the end of an e-mail from Whitley, *And I'm still thinking about my favors.*

In my office, working on the changes to the shadow network.

Late at night, reading the conclusion of a weekly confidential report from SWAT—*Analysis of Eastern European facilities continues as part of the investigation of the DMZ rogue section.*

Late at night, working on the changes to the shadow network. The communication flowing through me as I sat at my computer from midnight till four, sorting through e-mails and documents, relaying the information to another group and yet one more consultant.

"You can't say *beaver* in a meeting," Julie said.

"You can't say *erected* in a meeting," Whitley said.

"You can't say *swab* in a meeting," Cliff said.

Monday, a senior staff meeting, just days from rolling out the changes to the shadow network. Once more we were coming to the end of our management meeting, the gold light of the sunrise shining cold and bright on the New Jersey shore. Once more we were joking with each other. Once more we looked ahead and were sure we could not be stopped. We'd restored the network. We'd bought off Eugene. We'd let Regence know that our use of cellophane tape was experiencing a massive and unprecedented upswing.

As we talked, I thought back over the weekend—forty-eight hours preparing the most difficult of the upcoming changes to the shadow network. I'd slept a few hours Saturday, an hour on Sunday. But otherwise I'd been on the phone or at my computer, still managing the rework and testing. So far I'd found no problems with the idea of a lag time.

And I'd realized I was excited. Excited by the thrill of building something big, of doing something I hadn't thought possible, of engineering an insane and creative solution to an impossible problem.

Inside, I felt good. And, inside, for a moment, as I sat there in the sunrise with my senior staff, I had a thought. A glimpse, really. Coming to me, then gone, like the hundreds of dreams I'd had in my few hours' sleep that weekend. What I'd seen in that glimpse was something much more than us not being stopped. More than the obvious happiness felt by everyone in the company. More than the invented daydream in which the staff around me were now immersed. What I saw was a glimpse of this, all this, continuing forever.

And I sat back. And in that moment, it was better than floating. Better than sleep.

Better than the thing I called sex.

"You can't say *foam* in a meeting," Cliff said.

Leonard hesitated, ready to speak, all of us waiting. "You can't say *sordid* in a meeting," he said.

Julie blinked, turned away, then turned back to Leonard. She started to speak, paused as Leonard squinted, then said kindly, "Why would anyone need to say *sordid?*"

After a few moments' hesitation, Leonard responded to Julie. "But we were listing inappropriate words," he said, his voice part response, part question.

"Actually," Julie said in a deeply helpful, even encouraging tone, "we were listing words that you *can* say but *shouldn't* say, because, for juvenile professionals like us, such words have sexual, uncomfortable or otherwise inappropriate *connotations.*"

Despite the glimpses of irony he had exhibited during the restoration of the network, Leonard was, as he'd always been, a bit out of sync with the joking around him, his highly organized mind somehow unable to identify the shape and texture, the underlying rhythm and tone, of the bantering conversation he witnessed.

He stared at Julie now, squinting, puzzled. He bit his wide lip. He rubbed a massive ear. He reminded me—probably everyone in the room—of a kind and overgrown child.

Julie stood, rapidly moving to the whiteboard at the end of the conference table, beginning to write out two separate lists of acceptable and unacceptable words.

Leonard scanned the board, eyes jumping from one column to another. He nodded, slowly at first, then faster. "You can't say *tasteless* in a meeting," he announced.

I sat back in my chair. I turned toward New Jersey and smiled.

Forever.

"By the way," Whitley whispered to me, leaning toward my ear, "you look like shit."

Word would come any minute now. Weeks of work complete. Thursday, and within the hour I would get an answer. Whether the changes to the shadow network would work.

Cliff, Whitley and I were ninety minutes into a conference call that should have taken just five. And yet the three people on the other end of the call—all managers of a venture capital firm in Newark that had invested heavily in Core during our IPO—were screaming so loudly, so forcefully, that there was some question whether the call would ever stop. They were screaming at Whitley and Cliff, at each other, at me. Screaming in unison, then seeming to take turns. Screams filled with anger, then happiness, with gloom, and even hope. In the muzzled, amplified projection of their voices from the speakerphone on my desk, the managers alternately sounded like gleeful revelers at a New Year's party, then dying passengers on a crashing plane.

There was no point to their anger. No reason behind it. They simply called us once a quarter, wanting, it seemed, to hear themselves yell.

"Is it not possible," Whitley was now saying into the speakerphone, the first of us to speak to them in more than five minutes. "Is it not possible," she repeated, neck straining as she leaned down toward the microphone, trying to be heard over the din coming back in her face, "that you are overreacting?"

The speaker went white with noise, a crackling blur of renewed accusations and an unbridled, albeit digitized, passion.

Whitley frowned. Cliff shook his head. I shrugged and turned to my computer. Waiting for an e-mail about the shadow network. Trying not to stare too frequently at my screen. Trying not to let Whitley and Cliff see how distracted I really was.

Cliff looked at Whitley, then me. "I've forgotten what we're arguing about," he said, his voice unheard by the screaming men at the other end of the line.

"They'll lose their steam soon," I said.

Cliff threw a binder clip at me. I shrugged again.

"Haven't they made millions off us?" Whitley asked.

"Tens of millions," Cliff said. "Maybe more."

"I picture them standing in a concrete room," Whitley said, staring into the phone as if she could peer down inside it. "Or locked up in a pen. Cyclone fencing. Chains on the gates."

The sound from the speakerphone increased, then tapered off, then spiked to a near impossible high. A kind of ebbing then rising tide from a four-inch-by-four-inch box.

I clicked on my mouse. I checked for new messages. I was waiting for just a few numbers. Transfer speeds, network capacity, repositioning of eight satellites. I would drop the numbers into the model. Work the changes into Shimmer.

No messages.

I squinted my eyes. I stared at Whitley. Thinking back on something Whitley had said. "You say *cyclone* fence," I said, part comment, part question. "Not *chain-link*."

She thought about it for a second. "Yes," she said.

"Interesting," I said.

"Really?" she asked.

"Given the context," Cliff said slowly, and as I glanced at him I saw that he'd attached a black binder clip to his lower lip.

He seemed unaware of this fact.

"Tell me again where you grew up?" I asked Whitley.

"Houston," she said.

"Do they say *soda* or *pop?*" I asked.

"Neither. We just say *Coke.*"

Cliff shot binder clips toward the window. Whitley stared up at the ceiling. I clicked absently on my mouse.

"What's wrong with you?" one of the managers was yelling, apparently having pushed aside the other partners in order to dominate the phone. He was like a nine-month-old who'd found his voice, a baby forming words, finding joy in the wavering tones he could emit by screaming at full volume. *"Tell me!"*

Whitley leaned forward toward the phone. "Nothing at all," she said flatly.

The noise from the speaker seemed to erupt in front of her, a sound almost visible, bright and solid and so loud that I half expected her black hair to blow back from her face.

I clicked on my mouse. I quit my e-mail program, then opened it again.

I said to Cliff, "Barf bags."

He nodded. He detached the binder clip from his lip, for a moment staring at it, clearly having no idea where it had come from. In another moment, he'd attached it to his thumb. He turned to me. "Barf bags," he repeated, nodding. "Unused for three days," he said.

I nodded.

He nodded.

"I'm glad," I said.

Whitley had leaned to her left, as if the sound from the speakerphone was a fountain she had to look around. "Do you want to know whether I say *crayon* or *crayon?*" she asked, pronouncing the word as *kray-on,* then as *cran.*

Cliff shot a binder clip at her, missing her head by a few inches.

I nodded, now also leaning to the side, looking at Whitley around the invisible tower of noise.

Whitley thought for a second. "Cran," she said.

I mouthed the word. I clicked on my mouse.

"Do you want to know whether I say *sneakers* or *tennis shoes?*" she asked.

I nodded again.

Cliff had begun using the plastic body of a pen to shoot spitballs toward the open door.

"Tennis shoes," she said.

"Is it tennis shoes," I asked, "or, really, *tenny* shoes?"

She moved her head side to side, squinting, thinking, clearly repeating the words in her mind. "Somewhere in between," she finally said.

I nodded. She nodded. Cliff shot giant paper clips toward the door.

And then I saw it. An e-mail from Scotland. Sent to me via three blind e-mail relays. I tried to click on the message without showing Whitley and Cliff how anxious I was. I saw two rows of numbers. Flipped open the model. Saw Shimmer launch itself behind the spreadsheet. I entered the numbers into the model. Let Shimmer absorb them. And then I simply stared.

It was a minute before I realized that Whitley was talking to me. "What?" she was asking.

It was another moment before I could even shake my head.

"What?" she asked, smiling now. "You don't smile like that. Robbie Case doesn't smile like that."

I shook my head.

Shining, bright then brighter, the screen blinking white, Shimmer blinking white, Shimmer gone pure and perfect and clean.

"*Tell me!*" a single voice screamed out at us, once more distinguishing itself from the otherwise blurring, constant noise. "*Tell me now!*"

Shimmer one color, one number on the screen.

Twelve months.

"You should smile like that more often," Whitley said. "They say it's good for you."

The changes had worked. But Shimmer had done more. Shimmer had used the changes to calculate the exact date of the collapse. And the collapse was twelve months away.

I turned away from Whitley, turned back, wanted to stand, to hug her, hug Cliff, wanted to tell them both what I'd just found out, what had happened, what this meant.

"Why won't you tell me?" the voice was screaming.

I turned away again. Looking out the window. Knowing I had to stop smiling. Knowing I couldn't tell Whitley and Cliff what I'd learned. Knowing I had to get back to the conference call, to the next meeting, to my life at Core Communications. But that world I would return to, already I knew it would be so very, very different. And all I wanted was to share this with them. To come out from under my lie.

"Good news," I said slowly, turning back to Whitley. "I just got good news."

"Tell us," she said, smiling, leaning sideways in her chair, hair falling across her eyes.

"Why?" the voice was screaming.

Shimmer, on my screen, filling in lines, and colors, and numbers.

Twelve months to find a solution. Twelve months to find a way to keep the company alive.

Twelve months was forever.

Whitley was still staring at me, saying, "Tell me. Tell me, Robbie. What happened?"

"Twelve months," I said, although I hadn't meant to say the words aloud.

"Till what?" she asked.

I shook my head. But this time I decided I wanted to hear the words. I wanted to say them. "Twelve months."

I came inside her.

It had surprised me when I called. I'd thought I only called when things weren't good.

She was twenty-one. Twenty-two? Maybe she was twenty-two.

Maybe she could be young, the woman had suggested when I called.

Young, I said, not sure what to say.

Small, she said. *And daisies, maybe.*

Daisies?

Her panties, her bra. Daisies.

I see.

The girl next door.

Next door.

Maybe twenty-one.

I see.

A yellow sundress, sandals. Hair pulled off her shoulders. No makeup.
Maybe lipstick. Maybe not.

I see.

For a change?

For a change.

Exactly.

For a change.

The girl next door. Damp with sweat. Smiling up at me. Whispering something, quietly, sweetly, close to my ear. Still with her daisy-
speckled bra across her small, perfect breasts.

I wouldn't have thought I was a person who would call now. Now,
when I'd found a date for the collapse. Now that the collapse was a
year away.

But I had called. Like always. And, like always, it seemed as if this
had been put in motion before I'd even picked up the phone.

"You're twenty-one," I said quietly, speaking out loud without realizing it, speaking toward this girl a few inches from my face.

"What?" she whispered. Only whispering. I'd made that clear. Like
always. No talking. Whispers, at most.

I shook my head.

"What?" she whispered again. The girl next door does not talk. She
whispers.

I shook my head. I moved her hand to her chest. I had her slowly open her small bra.

Had I ever really slept with the girl next door? I tried to picture girls from high school. Women from college. But all I could see was this image beneath me, this young woman under me. What had it felt like the first time I'd had sex? What had it felt like, in high school, in college too, when I had been in love?

"I've never done this," she whispered, and it was a good thing to say. It was a good part of the scene. And maybe it was true.

Maybe, I told myself, *maybe it's true.*

It had surprised me when I'd called. I hadn't called in two weeks. So many nights spent working on the changes.

Maybe it wasn't a release this time. Maybe I wasn't trying to sleep or escape.

Maybe this was a celebration.

"Am I pretty?" she whispered, and I moved my hand slowly across her, feeling her, this girl here so damp on her knees and thighs.

I see now that to lie, to lie about everything in your life, to do that you have to deaden yourself. And I had been deadened, separated from the things that happened around me and to me.

Sex on a schedule, sex that was prepared, then completed, that was fully contained.

"Am I beautiful?" she whispered.

Twelve months.

Before this, before this company, before Blue Boxes and Trevor's lies and my lies and money, before this, what had I wanted? Where had I wanted my life to go?

There'd been a time in my life when I'd have never touched a prostitute. Never called one to my home.

"Please, tell me," she whispered. "Tell me you like it."

What had I wanted? Who had I been?

Twelve months.

"Please."

Finding myself back inside her.

"Tell me," she whispered. "Tell me you like it."

Holding her, under me. Holding all of her, at once, completely. Whispering, "Okay."

"I'm eighteen," she said. "I've never done this."

"Okay."

"Never."

"Okay."

"Never, Robbie. Never."

He wishes Eugene's journal had been real. Not because of what it would have done to the company. Leonard does not want that at all. But because of what a real journal would say. What it would explain. What it would reveal.

How this works.

How the Fadowsky Formula works. How these Blue Boxes work. How Robbie's system works.

Leonard wants to know.

He sits in a dark conference room. Pretending to sleep. Staring up at the ceiling. Sitting in a chair pressed into a corner. Staring at the dark ceiling, then at the floor, then at the dark shapes of the table and the chairs and the door and the shades pulled down across windows along the wall.

It is so quiet in here.

His life is never so quiet.

He's been putting the network back together, each day since the attack. Rebuilding every part of it, re-creating each piece destroyed in the reset. And he wishes more than ever that he understood. Fadowsky and Blue Boxes, Shimmer and the systems only Robbie can see. It works. All of it works. But the edges, the angles, the shapes don't make sense.

He shifts slowly to the left, his chair creaking as he moves.

Twenty years of creaking chairs.

He thinks about changes he's wanted to make to Shimmer. Improvements, upgrades, an expansion of what Shimmer can do. He wants to connect Shimmer to the entire company, wants Shimmer to reflect the company back to him and all of the senior staff, wants to use Shimmer to understand how to improve productivity, improve security, improve every aspect of the operation. And he wants to make Shimmer a self-teaching entity, a program that learns from what it sees, that operates independently of the tasks it is given.

He is sure it can be done. He is sure he can make Shimmer do all of this.

Leonard stretches out his long, heavy legs. He stares down at his thick, wide hands.

He wonders what time it is. He wonders what day it is. He tries to remember when he last went home.

He'll be happier when he gets to grace. He hates to admit it, but he will.

He's wanted to make these changes to Shimmer since he and Perry finished it two and a half years ago. But Robbie has never let them near Shimmer again. Robbie has said there are more important things to do.

His hands are so big. His legs. His body, his head, all of it.

He closes his eyes.

Leonard wants to do this because it would be so helpful to the company.

And Leonard wants to do this because he can, because he is that smart, and because he needs a success right now. Needs to do something well. Something right.

I wish I weren't so big.

CHAPTER 7

The parties had become one of those New York events. They'd started as office parties, held quarterly or every other month—company-funded drinking gone unreported to our insurance provider. In the last year, though, the parties had become one of those unidentified events known to people across the city. They drew programmers from software firms city wide, founders of breakaway ad agencies holed up in Chelsea and Tribeca, brokers and investment bankers working late on Wall Street, even an unlikely sampling of junior moviemakers, directors and actors and actresses all talking up their new script, their new project, their next even better idea.

I was handed a drink. I thanked the stranger who'd already turned away, disappearing into the mix of people and music and easy warm light, all of it spread across the lobby of our building, four stories high, now filled with a few hundred people.

Friday.

"In the last six months," I said to Perry, who was sitting next to me in a low, heavy chair on the first of two mezzanines above the lobby, "two hundred people have claimed to be my parents."

"Sure," he said, slowly crossing his bare feet on the table, "but at least a hundred of those claims came from me."

His bare feet, his legs, all were motionless. His whole body was. Perry's tremendous capacity for stillness. Especially now, stillness so obvious as the room moved steadily with people and light and sound.

In front of us were the groups laughing, the pairs drinking, the people shooting cocktail straws from one mezzanine to the next, and each person, each shooting straw, each image reminded me that my changes to the shadow network had worked. Now we had time. Now I had so much more time to find a solution.

And not one thing reminded me of the girl next door. I can see now how I sat there and did not think about her at all. Not a memory or a vision of the eighteen-year-old prostitute I'd been inside twenty-four hours ago.

"A new kid from my group," Perry said, nodding in the general direction of the mezzanine across from us, "is able to shoot toothpicks with astounding accuracy."

I saw two toothpicks shoot forty feet into the back of the head of a programmer from R&D, the kid who'd shot them very discreetly lowering the straw to his side. I heard myself saying, "Nice."

Ronald Mertz viewed these parties as management-sanctioned breaches of corporate security. Outsiders roamed the halls of the floors just above us. They joined baseball games played across unprotected workstations. They lined up for putt-putt golf tournaments that led in and out of conference rooms and offices—notes, plans and reports covering the tables and whiteboards that surrounded the games. And, worst of all for Ronald, the outsiders joined in on any number of multiuser, networked computer games—killing, hunting, joking, plotting, driving and swinging their way through an immense electronic universe hosted on Core's computers.

Despite the Regence attack, despite restoring the network and Eugene's blackmail with a fake Fadowsky journal, I'd said the party would happen. Security had been tripled, access to the network essentially eliminated, the layout of the putt-putt courses curtailed.

But Core would have its party.

As we sat in our chairs on the upper mezzanine, Perry and I had tiny earphones in our left ears, both of us listening in on the security team as they talked to one another. The sounds of urgency coming through the earphones were so disconnected from the easy, happy scene in front of us. It was an urgency that flowed directly from Ronald, who had a large force of uniformed and plainclothes security officers stalking the perimeter of the lobby, roaming from mezzanine one to the fourth floor and back to mezzanine two, issuing commands over the tiny microphones pinned to their collars, listening for instructions via the earphones hidden in their ears.

"Hansel, this is Gretel, please identify," Perry and I heard an officer saying over the radio. *"Repeat. Hansel, this is Gretel. Please identify."*

"This is Rapunzel," said another voice. *"Sector two is clear."*

As he had throughout the night, Perry spoke without turning to me, his voice instead drifting out into the space in front of us. "We have a sector two?" he asked.

I nodded. "Of course."

I was handed a drink. I thanked the stranger who'd already turned away.

"I heard you got some good news," Perry said.

"You've been talking to Whitley," I said.

"And Cliff. Both said you lit up yesterday."

I nodded. I shrugged. I hoped the topic would pass.

"Does it affect me?" Perry asked.

"Some bad conference call with an investor," I said, smiling some, trying to answer him without giving an answer. "It would probably have gone better if I'd just gone to visit them."

"You hardly travel anymore," Perry said.

I took a drink. I shifted in my seat. "There never seems to be the time."

"And you didn't answer my question," Perry said. "Why is it you were smiling?"

"Someone forwarded me an e-mail," I offered lightly, "with a couple of really funny jokes."

And there was a moment where he smiled.

"Up until a few days ago, Cliff was using barf bags," I said.

"Julie was sleeping in her chair at night," Perry said, and I hadn't known that.

"Whitley seemed on the verge of finally taking up smoking," I said.

He paused. I thought he might turn to me. "Even Whitley," he said.

A toothpick stabbed into the armrest of my chair.

"I'm still worried about Regence," Perry said.

"We seem to win every battle, though," I said. "We seem like we can't lose."

I waited a moment, but he did not respond. In another moment he raised his hand, two toothpicks bouncing off it.

"Bold young man," Perry said of the new member of his group who, apparently, was fearless in his chosen targets for cocktail-toothpick war.

"Trevor did sixty-five million in sales last week," I said.

"I know."

"How do you know?" I asked.

"I can still access the sales reports."

"We need to get that fixed."

"I'm sure SWAT will find me someday."

"Only if I sell you out."

"It's a good thing, right?" Perry asked.

"That you're able to get into those systems? No."

"The sales. We want sales, don't we, Robbie? Or did I miss that meeting?"

I nodded. I glanced at him. I saw him sitting motionless in his chair. "Yes," I said. "Yes, we do."

And for the next five minutes, then ten, we only watched the party, saw it unfolding, growing, turning louder and brighter, and for me it felt good to sit next to Perry, saying nothing, a few times both of us pointing at scenes for which each of us knew the joke, smiling silently, all the while ignoring the half lie I'd just put between us. Because, in not answering Perry, not telling him what message I'd gotten during the call, I was certainly lying.

We watched the toothpick sniper move about the room. We watched the people still arriving, through the entrance, from the elevator, from offices and floors upstairs. We watched the senior staff, watched managers and assistants and coordinators and VPs all loosely circling the room, Julie near the bar and Whitley up above us on the second mezzanine and even Cliff's white-shirted accountants and analysts and legal counselors, all of them were sharing their jokes with their boss, all of them sharing their take on the moment, the day, the week, the network attack and restart.

"We restored the network," I said to Perry.

"Yes," he said. "I was there."

I nodded. I took a drink. I watched Perry's eyes slowly follow the motion in front of us, drifting side to side with the flow of the party. "I wasn't sure it would work," I said.

"You're not allowed to have those thoughts," he said.

"I only share them with you."

He nodded. "Personally, I'd bet a year's worth of favors on the system winning this one."

"Never bet against Leonard."

"Never again."

"Sometimes," I said to Perry, pausing for a moment as I shot a toothpick from a straw at the unsuspecting kid from R&D, "I really like my job."

The toothpick bounced hard off his neck. He buckled over, wincing in pain.

Perry nodded slowly, now shooting a toothpick of his own, the kid dropping for a moment onto one knee before scurrying into the crowd. Perry asked absently, "But do people still try to touch you?"

"I'm able to dodge most of the attempts."

"The people here are beautiful," Perry said. "Everyone here is so beautiful."

I looked out, and it was obvious. All the people, each of them, seemed attractive and fit and beautiful.

"I'm not sure I like it," I said. "Something inhuman, unreal."

"No," Perry said carefully. "I thought that too. But it's okay. Because, if you look closely, it's not so much that the people are beautiful. It's the place. The lobby. The quiet music and steady light. The stone floors and bright metal in the walls. Look at that woman near the entrance, the man by the door. That whole group on the stairs to mezzanine one. None of them are pretty or not pretty. It's just that here, in this place, they are beautiful."

"So maybe it's a good thing."

"Maybe it is," Perry said.

The kid from R&D had positioned himself behind a column, just twenty feet away. Perry spoke quietly into the security radio. In a moment, the kid was surrounded by two very humorless security guards.

"The power," I said, and Perry only nodded.

"I'm watching Whitley on the mezzanine," he said.

I looked, then found her, in black suit, white shirt, a group of cocktail straws placed carefully in her front pocket.

"I can't see her clearly," Perry said. "Too close, too familiar. Like Cliff, like Leonard or Julie. Like you. I can't see any of you separate from my mind's own vision of what you look like, who you are."

And I couldn't answer for a moment. Only because he was right.

"Can you see her, Robbie?"

I shook my head. "I suppose I can't really see any of them."

"I should probably help you see her," he said. In a moment, he stood up. "But now I have to go."

"Home?" I asked.

"Work," he said.

"Big project?"

"Among other things, Whitley's people are on the verge of shutting me out of a number of the European accounting systems."

"Can't let that happen," I said.

"I'd have nothing to do," he said.

"Never bet against Leonard," I said again.

"Usually," Perry said, "I like my job too."

"I'm glad."

"What I hate is the lying."

"When do you have to lie?" I asked him, leaning backward, wanting to sink into my chair, disappear into the cushions.

Perry blinked, a slow and drawn-out blink that was almost a wince. "I don't lie, Robbie. I never have. At most I remain silent. Which, for me, can feel like a lie."

He slid his feet into his sneakers without looking down. "Are there bigger lies, Robbie?"

"Join the senior staff."

He turned away, then turned back to me. "Really, Robbie. I'm not joking. What I hate is the lies."

And as he spoke I only pictured Shimmer, glowing, spinning, showing the shadow network, now extended, but still a lie, my lie, supporting us all.

And I didn't know what to say.

"The people are beautiful," Perry said, "because this is a place without cynicism, Robbie. These people, all of them, at some level, they can be their best selves here."

I could only blink. And nod.

"I realized that," he said, "sitting here with you."

"It's a powerful thing," I said. "If it's true."

"It is true," he said, staring at me now, somehow studying me. "These people have commitment. Community. The possibility of achieving at the very extreme of their potential. They restored the network, Robbie."

"Yes," I said. "Yes, they did."

"They did the unknown. They did it for themselves, for each other and for you."

I searched for some response, some typically restrained and sarcastic response, but couldn't find it.

"Growth is good, right, Robbie?" he said. "Trevor's sales are up. The stock price is rising. The company expands. Grace comes closer."

"Join the senior staff," I said.

"Is there an end to this?"

"To what?" I asked.

He shrugged. He looked around the room. Women said he was good-looking. To me he looked mild, still, a presence that floated between the cracks and empty spaces in the glowing, turning light. "This," he said.

"I don't know."

"It seems like there should be an end," he said. "A predetermined end. Expected and planned for."

"In essence, foretold," I said, trying to smile, trying to joke with him.

"Yes," Perry said, smiling some, but waiting. Wanting that answer.

"I don't have an end."

He nodded.

"I haven't left the building in four months," I said, and it was something I hadn't spoken out loud. Something I had barely said to myself. Knowing it but not admitting it. And so now the words hung distantly in my mind, as if I'd overheard someone else talking about a person I didn't know, but a person who seemed very familiar to me.

And it sounded strange.

"Four months," I said, but quieter now.

Perry stared at me. His face held an expression I didn't know and had never seen. A face I still see now, thinking back. Kindness.

In a moment, I said, "Maybe I'm here searching for an end."

"Should I be worried?" he asked.

"I don't know."

"Go outside," he said. "There might be an answer there too."

"I know," I said.

"Leave the building."

"I will."

"Tonight," Perry said.

"We'll see."

"Tell me if I should be worried," he said.

"I will."

"Tell me," he said. "Tell me anything."

And the party was building, Perry disappearing into the crowd, nodding at the people who tried to approach him, head ducked slightly, shoulders pulled high, like a man caught unexpectedly in a violent rainstorm. My sometime alter ego running from the dance floor to his dark office on nine.

And the party was building.

Julie stood smiling, laughing at the center of a swirling group near the reception desk, and I saw that she was absently pressing the *Start* button on a small desktop copier, bright light from the edges of the machine periodically flashing across her soft face.

Cliff's arms waved rapidly as he clearly talked finance with a group on the upper mezzanine, the people around him standing just a step or two away, listening intently, but wary of being knocked across the face.

Whitley found me standing, watching the others. "Get me a drink," she said.

"Is this one of your favors?" I asked.

"Not quite," she said, face half hidden behind her hair.

"Am I underestimating the weight of your upcoming requests?"

She was staring at me. "That and worse."

I nodded. I smiled. I didn't know what she meant.

"I have questions," she said. "I don't understand."

"Understand what?"

"How they work," she said, staring at me, talking slowly, oddly. "I don't understand how you made this all work."

I tried to stare. Tried to nod.

"Someday you should tell me," she said, slow, and I saw how many cocktail straws were in her front pocket, and I realized Whitley was half drunk.

She was smiling now. "Or maybe," she said, her words slowed, not slurred but slow and very deliberate, "maybe I could just tell SWAT to find out."

She turned away.

I was so scared of Whitley.

And the party was building, louder and darker and people moving, smiling bright and moving close, and I could see Cliff moving so smoothly now, fluidly, not dancing, just moving, and could see Julie leaning close to Leonard as she spoke to him, Leonard almost wide-eyed as Julie entered his massive presence, the people, all these people, all moving and talking and turning and laughing, all here and so happy and all of it, all of it happening in the cavernous lobby of a supplier of networking services and equipment to mainframe computers worldwide.

I did not go outside that night.

It's not that I was afraid of what I might see, or find.

It's not that I was afraid of crowds or open spaces.

It's not that I was afraid the shadow network would collapse if I simply left the building for a few minutes or hours.

It's just that I didn't have a reason to leave.

There'd been a time when I went out with friends almost every night. When I went to apartments on the upper West Side for dinner and parties, out to Montauk for the weekend, went to bars and clubs with a group of people I'd known from college and California. But, over the past two years, that had stopped. Invitations slowing as my declines increased. Until finally, although I received printed invitations to holiday parties hosted by those people, to weddings between people I'd lived with in school, art openings by women I'd dated off and on, really now I was so separate from that life.

An executive who'd rarely slept more than two hours at a time in the past three years.

A liar searching for an end he could control.

A thirty-five-year-old with an addiction to prostitutes. Closeness, for a fee. The only closeness other than what he found at work.

I did not leave the building that night. Because I'd already made a call.

She wanders through a forgotten storage area on the fourth floor. Pretending to look for files on a series of acquisitions the company had completed in Spain. Here in these dimly lit rooms, filled with boxes, ten high, hundreds of them, each labeled so clearly and carefully by someone on her staff.

But really, Julie just needs some time alone.

One more fight with her husband. One more time telling him he does not understand. One more time being told she is doing the wrong thing, putting the wrong things first, putting her family last.

One more time knowing he is right.

Get me to grace. It will all be better at grace.

And she finds herself sitting. On a white cardboard box. Staring forward blankly. And she wants to cry. Wants to sleep. Wants so badly to go home. Wants so badly to stop fighting. Wants so badly just to crawl into bed with him, and sleep a while, and have sex, and sleep some more.

He is right. She'll tell him tonight. As she always does, about this at least, a day or two later telling him she is working too much. It's all too much.

And she leans forward a moment, lets her eyes close, lets her face hide deep in her hands.

Somehow she should have been able to protect the company from everything. Regence, blackmail, everything.

And she knows that each threat means there will be one more problem.

It means all this will never end.

She's known this for years. But this morning it is so clear.

Regence means this will never end.

Eugene means this will never stop.

Network failures, Fadowsky journals, new markets and unexplained changes in production facilities in Asia, and this will never end.

Grace won't change that.

And so she tells herself to face this.

Tells herself to remember this will not end.

Tells herself to realize this is the life she wanted.

Tells herself she will have to choose.

You can choose to leave.

CHAPTER 8

As always they'd set the meeting up through a series of vague and circular phone conversations. As always they'd had to see me in person. As always I'd never met them or seen them before.

Anonymous representatives of some large company or investment firm, here to try to buy Core Communications.

A few times a month I listened to the circling, probing questions of people interested in a purchase of the company. No one at Core knew how many offers there had been. I'd revealed only a few to the senior staff and the board. The others I'd kept secret. Because a sale was impossible, no matter the price, no matter the buyer. The shadow network made a sale impossible.

As always I was giving these emissaries no encouragement, no hope. As always I met with them only to spread the word that Core was not for sale.

And for me, especially after we'd restored our network, especially after the life of the shadow network had been extended, today, especially, we were not for sale.

The woman was quite beautiful, probably forty, the carefully prepared image of financial savvy and street smarts. The man was nearly seventy and somehow perfect as well, this image of late-life fitness, stamina and experience.

"So where are you from?" I asked them.

The man sat back, turning his palms to the ceiling. Smiling wide. In a moment, he said, "I'm here at the request of a friend of a friend."

"Who," I suggested, "is really more a friend of someone else's friend."

He tapped his hand on the table, moving it side to side as he weighed his response. Finally he said, "True."

"You're a consultant," I said, part comment, part question.

He shrugged. "Confidante."

"Sounding board."

"Go-to guy."

"One thing I didn't mention," I said, "is that you have just two more minutes before we're done."

He held his lips awkwardly tight, beginning to sit back, then carefully leaning forward.

"A buyer," he said. "I'm here at the request of a buyer of companies. Companies like yours."

"Ninety seconds," I said, smiling only slightly.

"Throw out a multiple, Robbie," the woman said to me, then slowly, so slowly, she began to lean back in her chair. She appeared to not be breathing, still moving, back not yet touching the chair. "Give us an absolutely absurd, top-of-the-top, beyond-hypothetical multiple you might use to put a value on this company."

"I'd have no idea where to start," I said.

"Then paint a picture for us," the man said, also leaning slowly backward, suspended in his own space, seeming to use the last of his breath to form these words. "Draw out the future. Sketch out a path."

"Describe a scenario, maybe?" I asked.

They both smiled wide, letting their backs touch their chairs, taking what seemed like their first breaths in minutes. "A scenario," she repeated, exhaling easily.

"Give us the highest price you could ever imagine," he said. "Then add another billion."

I said nothing. Stared down at my hands.

"We would pay cash to your senior staff," I heard him say.

"We would buy you a home," I heard her say.

"We would accelerate grace," I heard him say.

I closed my eyes. I leaned forward toward them both. I tapped very slowly on the table near his notepad. "Tell your friend that Robbie said, 'No.'"

"No?" the man repeated tentatively.

"An unequivocal no."

"An unequivocal no with an invitation to talk later?" she asked carefully.

"No."

I reached out slowly, grasping the table, ready to stand. "Thanks for coming," I said.

"Can I tell you something?" the woman asked, and I waited. It took her a moment, twice starting but stopping. A softness passing over her as, finally, she gave up.

When she did speak, her voice was much quieter than it had been, natural, the gloss of her sales pitch now gone. "You've performed a miracle," she said quietly. "You know that, don't you?"

My first reaction was to make a joke, some response about her only stroking my ego with bits of praise and wonder.

But she leaned forward, staring now, talking now as if we were sharing some secret. "You know that, right?" she asked. "You did something no one else could do. These are the things that fables are made of. Fables of the new millennium, I guess. And whatever happened to this company a few weeks ago, whatever Core went through that weekend, it only increased the aura even more."

The man sat forward, breathing easily. The spell these buyers always cast upon themselves, it was long since broken for both of them. "I guess," the man said, "I guess you're thinking you'll get that much richer without us."

And what I said next was incomprehensible to two people like this. What I said next should not have been spoken to two anonymous emissaries, two people who could take my words back to buyers, brokers, analysts and investors. But I said it.

Today I told the truth.

"Actually," I said, "it's not about the money. This has nothing to do with money."

And I was already in motion again, walking back to my office, passing through the swirling hum of the building. Reading messages on my phone. Seeing people, seeing paper, seeing games in the hall.

What I'd said was, for people like that, impossible to believe. They were words I could not say. Could not think. Could not even hear.

But it was the truth.

This has nothing to do with money.

As I reached my office five minutes later, Whitley walked in quickly behind me, the black suit flowing out from her sides. She stared at me. Waiting. Finally saying quietly, "Who did you just meet with?"

It was a moment before I responded. "I can't tell you."

She logged on to one of the extra computers near my conference table, opening a browser onto our intranet, entering a password, then clicking through a series of security-camera views of our building.

"Here," she said, opening the image to full screen. "Look at this."

It was a video recording of the lobby, people walking in and out of the building, some in pairs, some alone. I saw that the images had been recorded just a few minutes earlier.

"Security was running the standard background checks on your visitors," Whitley said, "and something came up."

In a moment, I saw the two people from my meeting. They were leaving an elevator, talking quietly as they made their way to the front door.

Whitley had turned to me, staring, smiling a little. In a moment, she said, "He's with Regence."

"Not her?" I asked, slightly scared, unsure, thinking something was about to happen. "Just him?"

"SWAT says only him. They're already retracing every step he made in this building. Looking for anything he might have done, anything he might have left behind."

I turned back to the two people on the screen, both these images of Wall Street finance, suitcases and overcoats carried easily out the front door. Whitley switched the browser to another camera, this one pointed at the street. The two of them shook hands, the woman walking quickly down the sidewalk, the man getting into the backseat of a waiting silver car.

Whitley was pulling at her sleeve. She stared directly at me. "What was the meeting about?" Whitley asked.

"An investment," I said quickly, knowing already that I did not want to tell her about their offer, just as I hadn't told her or anyone about so many other offers for Core. "Nothing came of it," I said. "Probably this was just a way for him to get into the building."

"What investment?" she asked.

"In some company," I said, lying, lying so easily.

"At some point," she said, "you'll have to tell me more."

We were quiet a moment. I didn't nod or disagree. She only stared.

The video was set to loop, so that once more I could see the two of them walking out the front door, shaking hands, the man turning toward the car.

"Look," I said quietly, reaching for the mouse, already half smiling, shaking my head, entirely confused by what this meant. I rewound the video. "There," I said as the man turned toward the car, and Whitley saw it too, and she was smiling just barely, shaking her head very slowly.

"What the hell is going on?" she asked quietly, and she rewound it herself, to the moment he turned away from the woman, and we watched as the man looked directly into the camera, a hidden camera mounted behind a glass fixture on the outside of the building. He couldn't have seen it. He should have had no way of knowing a camera was there. But he looked right at it. And worse, his hand was at his side, his thumb flipped up.

"What the hell is going on?" Whitley asked again.

I realized what it was, now calling Leonard on a speakerphone. "Check the security cameras," I said to him. "Check for some kind of intrusion."

"Hang on," he said above the noise of his office, people talking to him, typing at computers, each now joining Leonard's search.

In a few minutes, I heard one of Leonard's people say, "There. That. Damn it, that."

"Oh, no," Leonard said quietly, and I don't think he meant to say it out loud. In a moment he said into the phone, "It's a shadow."

"A what?" Whitley asked.

"They got into the cameras," he said slowly, voice fading, then rising, as if he were looking around, or shaking his head. "Regence can see through our security cameras."

"And so what is he doing?" Whitley asked, turning to me. "Why is the man giving a thumbs-up into a security camera? Did the meeting go exceptionally well?"

"The meeting went nowhere," I said quietly. "I think what he's doing is giving the go-ahead. To something."

"Why wouldn't he just wait till he got into the car and then call his people back in Helsinki?"

I thought about it for a moment. Shrugged. "Regence is a company that understands the value of drama," I said.

She nodded. She smiled just barely.

The video looped again.

"Did he give the go-ahead to another attack?" Whitley asked.

I shook my head. "I don't know. But be ready," I said, then turned to the speakerphone. "Leonard, don't shut them out of the cameras yet. And everyone needs to keep this absolutely quiet."

Leonard started to speak. "I'm really—" he said slowly, then stopped. "Right. We're checking. We're checking where else they might be." He hung up.

"At some point," Whitley said to me again, "you'll have to tell me more about the meeting."

"Would that qualify as a favor?"

She tilted her head back, hair falling away from her face. Smiling slightly. "It's about to qualify as a formal request." In a moment, she left.

I stood alone, wondering what reaction the senior staff would have if I told her the truth about the meeting. If I were forced to admit that this was one of many offers I'd had this year. I wondered how they and the board would react.

And I wondered what any of them would say if they knew what I'd told Regence.

This has nothing to do with money.

I stared at the screen, SWAT team members all around me, and there was the shadow network in front of us.

Monday morning, and Leonard had called SWAT to a conference room near the DMZ. There had been nothing on any screen as he'd called us into the room. No sense there was anything I should fear.

But I could see immediately that there was something wrong with Leonard. His large hands flat against the tabletop. His eyes turned away, not looking at anyone as they entered the room.

"I want to talk about Shimmer," he'd said quietly as he'd started the meeting. "It's time. Given the threats, the attack, it's time to discuss Shimmer."

And slowly, everyone in the room had turned to me.

Leonard was not asking for access to those parts of Shimmer that controlled the Blue Boxes. What Leonard wanted to do was point

Shimmer at the rest of the company, using it to view the very insides of the operation. Leonard and Perry had long said that Shimmer could dramatically improve the productivity of every area of the company. Shimmer's representations, its ability to assimilate so much information, all would allow managers companywide to streamline their areas, Shimmer pointing out holes and gaps and breakdowns and strengths. Most important of all, Leonard wanted to make Shimmer self-teaching, adding code that would make Shimmer an almost independent entity, a thinking, learning machine scanning all areas of the company, suggesting changes, highlighting problems, representing the company in all its complexity and detail.

And, of course, this self-teaching component—something Leonard had never been able to complete—would be able to find and decipher all types of security problems in the company.

"You know my concerns about this," I now said carefully.

"I know them," Leonard said. "But I believe they've been rendered meaningless in comparison to the current and recent threats. Only Shimmer can definitively show us if we have been compromised by Regence. Or by anyone or anything else."

"Actually," Whitley said, pausing awkwardly but saying it nonetheless, "I think the severity of the attack and the new risks posed to us by Regence do justify an expanded implementation of Shimmer."

SWAT wanted Shimmer. And SWAT was going to have it.

I was looking up, toward the ceiling. "So you're telling me to give Leonard the go-ahead?"

"I can't tell you to do it, Robbie. You know that. I can only recommend it."

"To me. And to the board."

"And to the board," she said.

Perry spoke quietly. "It's time, Robbie. You knew it would come. And now it's time."

I was thinking quickly, trying to anticipate problems, to think through the threats to the shadow network, but trying to do it without anyone seeing my defensiveness, or my plans. "Okay," I said slowly.

"Once you've completed the self-teaching component of Shimmer, we can move forward with pointing it at the whole company. How much longer before you solve the remaining programming issues?"

"Actually," Leonard said, "I solved the problems last night."

Perry turned to him, slightly wide-eyed. "How?"

"I've decided to give up sleep," Leonard said slowly, pausing, his heavy lips working against each other, preparing the words he would then say. "Once I eliminated the softness in my mind that, in hindsight, came only from being rested, I saw the answer to the remaining problems quite clearly."

"And so this new Shimmer works?" I asked, trying to speak evenly, carefully, without fear.

"And so this new Shimmer *should* work," Leonard said. "I haven't hooked it up to the live systems. I'd like your permission to do that right now."

It had been Leonard's request that the group meet in a conference room near the DMZ. Now I knew why.

Leonard led the group into the DMZ, asking all but the most essential admins to leave. They filed out quickly, locking down their machines with a few commands, leaving just eight techs to administer the entire system. Leonard moved through the dim light of the room, the glow of the main screens casting green and red and a barren white across his body as he sat down in his usual place in the center of the room. He immediately began to type rapidly on the machine. "Probably," Leonard said absently, the rest of the SWAT team gathering around him, his voice almost lost to the flurry of noise from the keyboard, "probably there will still be a few bugs."

He hit three keys. He stared at the screen. He leaned to the side and had me enter a series of passwords that gave him very limited access to Shimmer.

I realized I was taking short breaths, blinking rapidly.

I was opening the door to my own unwitting executioner.

Leonard hit a key, then another. "And there it is," he said slowly, looking up at the main status board. The same board that had, a month ago, shown the Core network going red in the face of the attack. "Hello, Shimmer," Leonard said quietly, and it was almost a whisper.

Already everyone in the room was silent, staring at the board in front of us, lost to the quiet images on the screen. On the board was the company we'd created, displayed to us now in shifting, blurring colors, rapidly moving numbers, the simple turn of squares and circles and lines.

If the standard information on the status board—the usual mix of numbers, codes, maps and graphs—was a multilingual story of Core Communications, this, this wide mix of graphs, colored bands, interconnected circles, curling numbers, this all was almost telepathic. For the people in the room, people who already knew Core so intimately, Shimmer's representations were immediately clear. It made sense.

Later, that was what everyone in the room would say.

It just made sense.

Even for me, a person who'd spent so much time using Shimmer, the images on the board—representing now the entire company, not my shadow network—were breathtaking.

Two circles near the upper left corner of the board, pale blue, barely moving, seemed simply to be the heartbeats of the people in this room.

The rogue sections were easy to see, pulsating vortexes that spun in on themselves, sending out only intermittent tentacles. I could see Ronald looking at each of them, his lips moving slightly, probably considering which sections were already under investigation, which had been rumored. It made sense that the rogue sections were so easy to identify. Even a rogue section that generated high volumes of e-mails, memos, reports and plans was not in real, two-way communication with anyone else. And so, inevitably, the rogue sections generated no results, and thus no connection to anything else within Shimmer.

"Black holes," Leonard said absently, standing now, stepping up onto a long platform that ran the length of the status board, his body silhouetted against the screen, "each separated from the other stars in the galaxy."

"You need some sleep, Leonard," Whitley said.

"Actually," Perry said as he continued to stare up at the board, "I think he needs even less."

"So what is all that?" Julie asked, pointing at four dense circles in the upper right corner of the screen, their colors steady, the darkest blue, unchanged.

"I'm not at all sure," Leonard said slowly.

I knew, though. I knew exactly what they were.

"There's Regence," Perry said quietly, nodding toward a pinpoint of light on the other side of the board, people's attention all shifting from the dense circles. Regence's presence in the facilities database was a bright pinpoint of light, lines then shooting outward from the screen, some radio beacon hidden in our territory on a war map.

"And there they are again, in the cameras," Leonard said, pointing to another pinpoint and lines, all of us following Leonard's voice, this our massive tour guide through a new but very familiar world.

And everyone stared, and nodded, and some people smiled.

"I'll need further access to Shimmer," Leonard said quietly. "And the Blue Boxes. Need to get closer to the Blue Boxes."

"I'm not sure that's possible, Leonard," I said.

"I understand," he said, fading almost, his attention, even his mind it seemed, all being absorbed into the images in front of him. "I understand. But we'll have to talk."

Again Julie pointed to the four dense circles. Perry turned his head slowly, carefully, staring at them as well. Shaking his head. But staring.

I knew, though. It was the shadow network.

Even with this limited access, what this new version of Shimmer had done was pick up on the massive overcapacity in various parts of Core's system. It was represented in the dense circles Julie had seen. Circles so dense with information that Shimmer couldn't yet make sense of them. So for now, even Leonard couldn't recognize what they were. And really, Shimmer was only showing a tiny fragment of the company, and a tiny fragment of the shadow network beneath it. But that could be enough. That could be all it took.

And of course Shimmer itself was getting smarter, learning, adjusting itself as it studied each part of Core.

"There will have to be more testing," Leonard was saying, staring, talking absently, probably to himself. "Quite a bit more refinement before we can give access to the senior staff and other managers. But this is promising. Very promising."

I stared at the glimpse of the shadow network.

"That's your company," Perry said quietly, standing next to me but maybe not even speaking to me.

"That's it," I said.

My God, I thought. There it is. The spinning, drifting image of shapes and lines and colors.

And the image was beautiful.

Regence. Shimmer. SWAT.

Shimmer spreading out through the company. Seeing more. Learning more. Getting smarter every second.

With Shimmer, SWAT could find me.

With Shimmer, the shadow network itself could even be empowered to speak back to every person it secretly supported.

I could see myself in the window. Could see my hair that needed cutting, my jaw working slowly on my lip. I turned in my chair, away from the image. Leaning forward, elbows on knees, staring down at the floor. At my feet. And the base of my chair. Wanting simply to lie down. Wanting simply to sleep. Finally, sleep.

Shimmer was my real enemy.

Shimmer.

Inside her.

A beautiful woman. Always a beautiful woman.

Shifting pressure there. Then there.

Regence. Our spies watching them. Where could their spies be? In Marketing, maybe. In Programming. In Sales. Production. Security.

"Come now," she whispered, between the slowest movements, talking, then not, all of it one motion, one thought.

This, my release. This, my answer to Shimmer. To SWAT.

"Come in my mouth," she whispered, between, then talking, then not.

And why was this what I wanted? Why was I here in my home, naked on my bed, a woman paid to fuck me now moving so carefully, so perfectly, across me?

This, the answer to my life.

I'd spent part of that night panning through the live security-camera views of various parts of the building. Wanting to see the views Regence itself was looking through. And I'd stopped on the camera pointed at the sidewalk outside our lobby, the one on which I'd watched the man from Regence get into that silver car. And through that camera I watched the people plodding through a cold New York night, racing toward a train, searching frantically for a cab. Or just wandering down the street. Wandering through their evening. Some of them alone, more of them in pairs. Wandering. And at some point I caught a clock in a store window, a store across the street from our building. And I realized I'd been watching that camera for nearly an hour.

I couldn't remember the last time I'd been outside. I remembered that I used to go outside. Remembered whole days in the New York streets. But I couldn't remember the last time I'd been out there. The time I must have walked back into the building, thinking—knowing—that I would go out again. Never imagining that I wouldn't go outside again for months.

"Come now," she said.

I had to have known why this was my answer. This, my release. If I stopped for a moment, thought about it for a second. Thought about the day two years ago when I'd made the first call. Called to have a woman come here. Have her here, see her, see what it would feel like. Be like. Look like.

But if I did know then, I'd forgotten it by now.

Motion so slow.

A woman paid to fuck me.

Our fantasies, everyone's, somehow attached to a fixed place or moment. Something gone wrong. Something very good. Something scarring. Something wonderful.

Something.

Why can't I remember?

And of course it was about sleep. Wanting some way to sleep.

What happened to sleep?

And of course it was about work. About Shimmer, the shadow network, the collapse.

What happened to work?

I'd seen an ad in the paper. Called that place. Then another. Then found this one.

Why had I been looking in the paper?

And so now I think that maybe, even then, I didn't tell myself why I'd chosen this. Maybe, even then, I wouldn't tell myself.

The warm, damp surface of her mouth.

Why this?

The wet, narrow corners of her lips.

Tell yourself.

The very end of her tongue.

There was a reason. There is always a reason.

The very edge, lightly dragging, her teeth, then tongue.

But I honestly didn't see it.

Maybe it was time. Like so many things. I just didn't have the time. Time to answer the question. Time to figure out why.

Didn't have the time. Didn't have the focus. Didn't have the will.

And that was it, there, her there. Her.

Regence. Shimmer.

Shimmer.

And that was it, there, her there. Her.

And for a second I could see that the answer was lost in that same place that didn't really know why or how I'd started this fraud. The same place that let me sustain the lie now called Core Communications.

Mouth, then tongue. Then coming.

What is this woman's name?

There was something wrong with me.

Coming.

There is something wrong with you.

Coming.

You know that. There is.

Trevor walked into my office at three A.M. the same night. I was sitting in the gray and white light from the buildings nearby, watching the faded glow of three tugboats move slowly up the Hudson.

Trevor leaned against a table near the window. Half standing, half sitting. Leaning his thin back against the glass, his whole presence so much thinner, narrower than I remembered.

"You have bad news," I said, barely hearing my voice.

He smiled some, looking away. "Do I only ever come to see you with bad news?"

"Yes."

He nodded, still smiling. "Sometimes I bring good news," he said. "And always I bring sales."

I could hear the empty sounds of the city drifting up toward the two of us in this building, the sounds of a downshifting truck, a speeding subway, two barking dogs, each barely penetrating the windows of my office.

"Even the best news you ever brought me," I said, feeling small and light and like some kid in a chair, smiling and blinking slowly, and wondering if I would sleep that night, "even that has been the worst thing in my life."

He nodded, turning to look out the window. Hair hanging across his face for a second, over his eyes, and he didn't bother to move it. "I have no news, Robbie. Good or bad. I'm just here."

The shadows in my office left walls gray, glass black, the table a dim silhouette, the chairs a puzzle of vague angles and turns.

I turned back to Trevor. Always, with Trevor, there was that sense of wanting to yell at him. To blame him. To attack him for everything that had gone wrong. But tonight I couldn't.

"I don't think I can take any bad news, Trevor," I said.

"You don't look like you can take any news, Robbie," he said.

Above us, the ventilation system quietly started, the near silent hum just touching the sound between our voices.

He nodded, crossing his arms over his chest, one hand on an elbow, the other on a shoulder, and it was as if he were holding himself.

"Cliff is vomiting four or five times a day," I said. "Leonard has given up the act of sleep. Julie often works from the mailroom for two or three hours a day. Whitley is smoking three packs of imaginary cigarettes. This is not a healthy time."

He nodded. Turning toward the window.

"Sometimes I think the only thing holding them together is grace," I said.

He nodded. Leaning forward and, for a second, pressing his forehead against the glass. I heard him say quietly, "I am really sorry."

That ventilation system, so quiet, below sound, the non-sound.

Still his head was pressed lightly against the glass.

"Leonard pointed Shimmer at the whole company," I said. "A new version of Shimmer. It's self-teaching. Learning. Right now, learning."

He stepped back from the window. Still looking out at the night. He nodded.

"Do you understand what that means?" I asked.

"I understand enough."

"We need a solution."

"Can you cut Leonard off?" Trevor asked. "Just flip a switch on him?"

I shook my head. I tapped my teeth. "No," I said. And all I wanted was to sleep.

"Every few days I hear rumors of lost journals," Trevor said.

I nodded slowly. "I hear them too."

"I always want to believe it's true," Trevor said. "Want to believe I can simply find a journal, pay for it, and solve every problem we have."

"I do too."

"But it's Shimmer," Trevor said, turning his head, "Shimmer that could destroy this faster than anything."

In a moment, I nodded.

"Shimmer is our enemy," he said.

He was pushing his thin hair from his eyes. His hand moving along the sharp angle of his jaw.

"It's not just grace holding this place together," he said.

He stood up, leaning close to the window, again slowly scanning the New Jersey horizon. "Go to sleep," he said.

"When do you leave town?" I asked him.

He nodded absently. "Now," he said. "I leave now." And he turned and touched me on the arm, and left.

It was twenty minutes later, as I began to think I should stand and move to my couch, that I realized I was sitting in my chair wrapped in a blanket from my bed upstairs.

It was another ten minutes when I remembered the firing in Omaha.

And it was yet another ten when I remembered that I don't like to be touched.

Leonard did not look well. His body seemed even bigger, heavier, the mouth and arms and shoulders pulled downward. His eyes not just wide, not just heavy, but red and wet and turned now toward the surface of his desk.

"One of the waves," Leonard said slowly. "From the Regence attack. One of them made its way out of the country."

"We were wrong about the attack?" I asked. "It was bigger than we thought?"

"I think this is something else."

I nodded, glancing around the room, waiting for him to speak again. All I wanted was to run my hands along every angle in the room, every desk and book and stack of papers and files, all of it placed so carefully around us.

"I think this was a mistake," he said. He was pushing his lips together between words. Eyes still so red and wet, but now staring at me. Wanting something, I realized. Some word maybe. An answer. "The wave triggered a mistake."

"Where did the wave go?" I heard myself ask.

He pushed a thick hand across one ear. "To Budapest," he said.

I stared.

"Why did it go to Budapest?" he asked, light from the windows now casting sharp angles across his face.

"I was going to ask you," I heard myself say.

"I'm out of ideas, Robbie," he said, and it was like he'd touched me, this biggest of employees squeezing me on the knee. Because Leonard never used my name. Leonard never called me Robbie.

"There's a test center in Budapest, right?" I was asking.

"There is an anomaly," he said, glancing down, slowly, his head seeming to fall forward, as if soon it would slide off his neck. "In Budapest. Across all of Eastern Europe."

I could only nod.

"It comes and goes," he said.

"The wave?" I asked quietly.

He shook his head, staring down. Still with that look of wanting on his face. "The anomaly," he said.

"Maybe," I started, then stopped. "I don't know," I said emptily.

He shook his head. "It looks like something else." And carefully he was raising his head again. "I thought maybe it was something you might have left in the system. From the beginning. When I saw it, I thought, maybe Robbie knows what this is."

I heard myself saying, "And what is it, Leonard?"

"I think you know," he said, looking at me again.

I couldn't speak. Leonard still staring, still wanting something. Something from me.

"I'll call it a tunnel. A hidden tunnel. A second data highway," he said. Had Leonard's hair always been black? "A shadow thread," he said.

"A shadow thread."

"Do you know what happens in Budapest, Robbie?"

I shook my head.

"Robbie, tell me why there's a hidden link between Shimmer and Budapest."

I shook my head.

He looked away. Nodding toward the wall, then toward his lap.

"Shimmer," I said.

He nodded. "I saw it with Shimmer."

"I don't know," I heard myself say. "It is not a thing I know."

"Then I hate to say this, Robbie. But I think I know what this is, if you don't. We need to call in SWAT."

I shook my head.

"It's the worst yet," Leonard said. "This is another one from my group. Has to be. Because this is the worst rogue section I've ever seen."

In all the times I'd imagined the beginning of the end—the end of my lie, the end of the shadow network, the end of the company itself— never once had I pictured it being launched by seven adults sitting quite comfortably in a set of children's chairs.

But that was exactly how the end was now seeming to begin.

"And where did you buy these?" Julie quietly asked Whitley, clearly planning a purchase of her own.

We were in Whitley's office on the sixteenth floor, the SWAT team sitting around her low child's conference table, our legs stretched out straight or knees pulled up high, all of us discussing the ramifications of the rogue section Leonard had just discovered.

Leonard's assumption—that this was the work of a rogue section— bought me some time. But how much I didn't know. Because what Leonard had found—what he'd called a shadow thread—was really just one tiny thread of the hidden system around us. The thread had been active only intermittently when Shimmer had found it. I'd even had time to begin to shut it down, phasing out that thread's use over the next twenty-four hours—fast enough that Leonard would not have much of a trail to follow, but not so fast that the thread itself seemed to shut down immediately following his meeting with me. Still, it was enough for Leonard and key members of his team to follow.

And with Shimmer, all this could be enough for Leonard to catch me.

"I could get a set of these chairs for you too," Julie said, looking at me.

"Just two of them," I said, leaning toward her, "for the mailroom."

She smiled. I felt like I couldn't breathe.

"The shadowing this rogue section is doing," Leonard said now, "is extraordinarily sophisticated. It hints at a very deep understanding of the company's network."

"Meaning?" Cliff asked.

"Meaning," Perry answered, speaking for the first time, "that this rogue section could possibly be doing much more than generating this one thread of activity."

"I'll be leading the investigation myself," Leonard said, in confirmation of Perry's assessment.

"And continuing to rebuild the network?" I asked quietly. "Watching Regence? Aren't you putting yourself in the lead there too?"

"Yes," he said, looking down at the table, then out the window, then at the table again. "And that's how it should be."

I realized Leonard hadn't looked at me since we'd entered the room, that pained expression from our earlier meeting still so clear on his face, in his motions, his body. It was more tempered now, less severe. But still there. And only now did I understand it. Understood why Leonard had barely looked at me back in his office. Understood why I'd felt like he seemed to want something from me.

"I should be responsible for all of it," Leonard said.

Leonard wanted me to forgive him. Forgive him for yet another rogue section, another security breach, another mistake, another failure. All these things that he'd put himself in charge of in the last few weeks, all of them were related to his group. They weren't his fault. He couldn't have controlled any of it. But he thought he was responsible. Felt it completely.

Over the next thirty minutes, I watched as SWAT agreed to a full investigation of Budapest, agreed to a deep historical analysis of the Budapest systems and, of course, agreed to have Shimmer not only analyze the shadow thread created by this rogue section but also search our entire network for any sign of similar activity.

Shimmer, gaining access, building strength, readying itself to speak back to us all.

I sat in my child's chair. I agreed to the SWAT response. I suggested an investigation of the Warsaw office that fed data to Budapest and all of Eastern Europe. I smiled as Julie offered to parade naked in front of the Regence cameras.

And I noticed as Leonard leaned back from the group. Staring forward. Separating himself. Immersed in the problems he had to make right.

I was watching the shadow network when she came into the room. Alone in my near dark office at ten-thirty at night, Shimmer painting circles on a wall at the end of the room. This was the same Shimmer that Leonard and SWAT could now see. Projected ten by ten feet on my wall, the dense circles now larger, deeper, made up of even denser cylinders, Shimmer already deciphering the meaning of the shapes it found, seeing where the company spun in on itself, seeing the motion of the shadow network beneath Core Communications.

She came into my office now, in a dark suit, a white blouse, the mouth barely holding her unknowable smile. The reflection of the shadow network flickering across her eyes.

"You should be asleep," Whitley said.

"Yes," I said.

She sat down on the windowsill near me, watching Shimmer on the wall, the lights of New York and New Jersey behind her.

Whitley was a late person. One of those people who could accomplish more in the hours after six than she'd otherwise finish in a full week's work. She'd been this way since joining Core.

It was Monday night.

"Do you think there will be a time," I said, "when there's no more of this? No more living in the building? No more late nights wandering the halls of this office?"

She was nodding slowly as I spoke, hair across her eyes, still staring toward the end of the room.

"Can you imagine?" I asked quietly.

She didn't answer, and we sat in silence for a minute, my mind working through a hundred problems for tonight and tomorrow, racing as it always did, listing as it always did. I didn't even realize that Whitley had stood, turning to stare out the window.

"If you say it," she said carefully, her voice so slow and distant and I didn't know why, "maybe then you might still be right."

I stood up, standing next to her now, thinking she would say more. But she didn't. Only stared out the window. The light from outside, from the computer and Shimmer in my office, all of it touching then disappearing from her half-hidden face.

"What are you working on tonight?" I asked.

She shook her head, turning to me now, hand on my arm.

"You don't like to be touched," she said, smiling some.

"It's a painful thing," I said, half smiling as I looked down at her hand, seeing it like some threat beside me, a weapon touching another person's arm.

"Like heat?" she asked, and I think she was holding it just a bit harder.

I shook my head. "Invisible waves."

"Radiation?" she asked, smiling slightly.

"It's all I can do not to pull away."

"Right now?" she asked, hand moving again, holding my arm, seeing her fingers, feeling that pressure.

"Inside," I said, seeing my hands, both of them for a moment, and both looked like someone else's hands. "Inside it destroys me."

"You're not very good at this," she said, half smiling, half turned away.

I started to shake my head, not sure what she meant, glancing away, toward Shimmer, and realizing then. Turning back. Realizing.

"You're not very good at this," she said again.

Of course.

"This," she said, "is the first favor."

I was closer to her now, not sure if I'd moved or she had, her hand on my arm still, and I felt myself touching her then, hand on her side, touching just barely the smoothest white of her blouse, touching her, touching Whitley, touching someone I'd known three years and only now crossing into some other place, this place where she was, there, here, against me.

"So you know," she said, "I'm not so good at this either." She was reaching to me then, her face close, closer, kissing Whitley, my eyes open, then closing, fading, kissing Whitley.

I heard her say, "I'm married."

A crisp white shirt, close around her sides.

"Can you keep a secret?" Whitley asked, kissing me, then not.

I tried to say yes, but could only nod.

"This," she said, touching me slowly, "this has to be a secret."

I tried to answer, but could only nod.

"I was twenty-three when I fell in love," she said. "I believed I knew everything I would ever want," she said.

Her jacket pushed slowly off her arms. The faintest edge of a bra just visible through the shirt. Thinking, *Whitley in a bra.* Thinking, *Whitley beneath a hundred suits I've seen, a hundred pairs of jeans and sweaters.*

"This is only about touching," she said.

I nodded. Thinking, *Whitley naked.* Realizing it was possible. Realizing it was here.

"Nothing more," she said.

I nodded. Thinking, *Whitley against me.*

"Tell me," she said, breathing slowly now, mouth against mine, pulling away for each word, each phrase. "Tell me it's nothing more."

"It's nothing more."

She had pulled herself very close to me. She had her hands on the buttons of my shirt.

I heard myself say, "I'm afraid of you."

I saw her nodding, heard her say, "I know."

"Should I be?"

"I know."

"SWAT," I was saying, touching, feeling her arm beneath her shirt, her hand on me.

"I know," she said, pulling me closer, pressing herself against me.

"Should I be?"

And she was at my mouth, she was kissing me, and my eyes were open, and hers too, and I could see her cry.

And she kept saying something I could not hear.

And I kept kissing her.

And finally I heard her say, "No." Finally I heard her say, "Everyone, everyone is afraid of me."

And I was kissing her more.

"Be one person," she was saying, quiet, "please be one person who is not afraid."

And now, now I was light and warm and against her, all the motion so bright, so warm and full and bright, and now I couldn't think about why she was doing this, couldn't think about anything except her, there, Whitley's white bra, the edges of her breasts, my hands just inside the edge of her pants. Light and warm and for now this felt like everything.

"This is more," I heard her say.

"I know," I said.

"This is more than touching," I heard her say.

"I know," I said.

"I am not happy," I heard her say.

"I know," I said.

"I am not in love," I heard her say.

And I could only nod. Nodding. So close to her and nodding.

"There's word from Finland," she said, the shirt sliding, then down. "Regence drew blood from a mainframe," she said, the black pants open, then off.

We had moved to my couch. Her panties pressed against me. Her bra pressed against me. Whitley, against me. Whitley, taking down my pants. Whitley, hair hanging across my face. Whitley, three years, a thousand meetings, a million moments, Whitley, now with bra open, breasts against me, her panties sliding off.

Saying quietly, I said quietly, "How much time do we have?"

Above me, mouth close, breasts moving gently across my chest, moving now and it was like she was inside me and my breathing was gone and hers was gone and I only heard myself echoing, "How much time?" saying it only because it'd been said, echoing those words but really lost to the motion of her above me, across me, against me, inside me.

"A few hours," I heard her say.

And I heard it again, *a few hours,* not sure if she'd said it or I'd heard it, and I was breathless, moving, turning, breathless.

She was pushing harder against me now. "They'll announce it tomorrow."

Trying to breathe now. Everything seemed to be about breathing.

She was more beautiful than I'd ever known.

"I am not happy," she said.

And I was nodding.

"They'll begin sales tomorrow," she said.

Breathing. All of it had to be about breathing.

She was the most beautiful woman I'd ever known.

"I can't control this," I heard her saying, words all broken and light, drifting emptily through our breath and motion. "This time," I heard her saying, "this time no one can stop what will happen."

Their message comes by fax. And the messages, they never come by fax. Too insecure, they had said. Too susceptible to intercept.

Whitley had liked that, about the spies. When she had set up the system of corporate spying. She'd liked their lingo, their formality and importance. They'd called the system an apparatus. They'd called the information she wanted targets. They'd called themselves her assets.

Now there is the fax, coming through on the private machine in her office.

She has to enter a code before the message will print.

The message is short. Just a few paragraphs. Regence is about to unveil its Green Box. Regence is about to launch a system cheaper and faster than Core's.

She reads the message just once. She turns. Stares out her window. Holding her breath. Closing her eyes. Wanting simply to lie down now. To sleep now. To cry now. To give up now.

And she wants something more.

She wants to not be alone.

She is so tired of being alone.
She isn't sure she can take a breath.
She knows grace is moving. She can almost see it disappear.
And she knows that she wants something more.
She cannot manage to take a breath.
And she knows that she wants something more.
She wants to be with Robbie.
She wants to be close to him.
She wants to be so close to him.
She can't remember how to take a breath.
She isn't sure what will happen next.
She is so afraid of where this will go.
She is so afraid this is about to end.

CHAPTER 9

It was really only a coincidence that Trevor had a bad connection when he called me. His voice was breaking up, a constant popping and static on the line, the noise of an airport all around him. But somehow that noise, the bad connection, all of it seemed to have been caused by the introduction of the Regence Green Boxes.

"Where are you?" I asked, voice raised so he could hear me.

"I'm in fucking hell!" Trevor screamed back. "The world is collapsing out here! Regence had four or five hundred sales reps. Trained and ready. Pouring out of Finland. Suddenly they were fucking everywhere."

Friday, four days since the Green Boxes had been introduced. And four weeks lost off the life of the shadow network. It was a horror really, to see the date. The date Shimmer had found for the collapse. Because now Shimmer was continually recalculating that date. Seeing the fall in our stock price, forecasting a downturn in sales and recalculating a date for collapse that moved closer each time.

"They're undercutting us on price, on service contracts, on warranties, on delivery time," Trevor was yelling through the noise. "They're buying out our agreements, cash on the spot. It's an assault, Robbie. In every market, on every client we have or wanted."

Usually I had an idea of what country Trevor was in when he called me. But now Trevor was in the midst of traveling to every territory in the Core sales universe. Fifteen countries. Twenty-five states.

"They did it in one fucking day, Robbie," he was saying. "I mean, on Friday they didn't exist. Then I look around and they are everywhere."

Four days, and when I had slept I'd woken up in the midst of dreams about Fadowsky or my father, dreams where they simply walked through the building, or my office, or sat down in a chair near me, and I would wake up because they would not talk in the dreams, would not say a word, no matter how much I asked or begged or screamed.

Four days, and I'd had sex with Whitley four times. In my office. On my couch. Quiet, barely speaking, sex of the last survivors, clinging together as Regence threatened to reach us.

"We see them in airports, Robbie," Trevor said, voice shrill now, the phone pinching down on his words. "The Regence reps. All my people have seen them. In airports, getting into cabs. Checking into hotels. Entering and leaving offices."

Outside my window, it was late afternoon, the sky just turning from blue to black.

"You see them from a hundred feet away," Trevor said, a wind and roar all around him, natural or electronic I couldn't tell. "They're perfect. All of them are goddamned perfect. They're human clones, biologically engineered, handsome and beautiful and more confident than a person could ever really be."

A jet engine began to roar over the phone, wiping out Trevor's voice. Apparently he was outside, and I pictured him walking quickly, head bent forward and bags across his shoulders, fighting his way across some darkened airport tarmac.

"And these spineless companies I've been meeting with!" he was yelling, engine roar fading, Trevor's voice still broken by the interference from the phone.

"The price, though," I said quietly. "Regence's price is half of ours. Companies aren't going to sign up with us if Regence is so much cheaper. These are businesses. It's about money for them. Just money."

Outside my window, I could not tell how cold it was.

"Is this hurting us?" he asked now.

"Of course it is," I answered.

"No," he said. "The collapse. I mean the collapse. Could this cause everything to collapse?"

I didn't say anything for a moment. Not sure what I should let him know. But then nodded, nodded again and I found myself saying it. "Yes."

"I'm asking how much, Robbie. How much sooner?"

"Much sooner."

"Christ, Robbie, tell me. You know what it means. Tell me exactly what this means."

I nodded. Stared. Heard silence suddenly in his phone.

"We have eleven months. But some days, we lose almost a week."

And the noise from the phone was steady, loud, complete.

"Probably," I said slowly, not sure he would hear, "if we can't stop the fall in the stock, probably we'll collapse in just a few months. Or weeks."

His voice came a moment later, once more rising from the steady, perfect noise. "I know, Robbie," I heard him say, his voice now fading in and out of the noise, Trevor speaking quietly, unable to compete with the warring sounds around him, but finally he'd reached his airplane, his cab, his end point in the battlefield he'd been crossing through these last ten minutes. "I know that this is your release, Robbie," I heard him say. "This is your escape."

Outside my window, it seemed like everything had slowed to stillness, no movement. "I think," I heard myself start to say, saying something, filling the space, thinking Trevor could see this, thinking Trevor could see everything I thought and saw and heard.

"Don't take this escape," he was saying. "Don't go."

And I was nodding, touching the window, pressing against it and it was cold.

"I have nothing without this," he said. "My whole life, my whole purpose, my connection to you, to myself even, all of it goes through this."

I pressed harder against the window, harder and I thought I could feel the wind pushing back, a silent motion I could not see, now pushing back against that window. "There's more than this company, Trevor," I heard myself saying.

"Don't take it, Robbie," he said. "Please don't let this go."

And we watched the stock fall.

And we watched our sales fall.

And we watched the press, the analysts, all of them turn on us.

The board wanted a response for the markets and shareholders.

And I listened as the analysts wanted action, a response quick and severe.

And the shadow network needed room. Every bit of life I could give it.

In the morning I laid off a hundred people in Asia. I made the call to each of the six offices myself. Six conversations with vice presidents and managers. Hearing out their concerns, their sadness, their anger and regret.

I said, *Yes.* I said, *I understand.* I said, *This is what I had to do.*

Cliff, when he'd given me the list of names, said only, "I'm trying to give you the smallest numbers I can."

I could only nod. And when I'd done it, let them go, I was sure I would never sleep again. Each voice on the phone, each name on the paper, each person now placed so clearly in my mind, all of it was gone from the company. Yet all of it, all of them, the memory of each person had fallen to me.

I will never sleep again.

In the afternoon I laid off two hundred people in South America.

I looked at the pictures of each of them. Pictures in their files. Names on the pages. Names of daughters and sons and husbands and wives. And I fired them all.

You deny someone their hope when you fire them. You deny them the future they woke up expecting. The self that they, minutes before, had thought they were.

But I had no other choice. Except giving up. Killing the shadow network and walking away.

And I couldn't do that.

Please don't let this go.

I walked across floors. Heard voices loud and rapid as people dealt with the problem of Regence, the falling stock. Saw the desks and conference rooms filled even higher with documents, with plans, with work to be done. Watched the people so tired as they made their way through the hallways and toward the desks.

And as I walked I came to the unoccupied territories, those freshly painted, freshly set-up oases of pristine office landscape, now looking less like the promised and inevitably grand future of Core Communications. Instead they now showed a very different future. An empty one.

The future unfulfilled.

The people who would have sat in these chairs, these people who would have worked for this company, they could have done so much here.

In the morning, I laid off two hundred people in Europe.

And really it seemed like I did not know myself anymore. This boss of five thousand employees. This head of a company with a nameless, ceaseless aura. This liar partnered with an obsessive cousin. This sleepless thirty-five-year-old hooked on silent, scheduled sex.

And even those things were changing. People laid off, the aura wounded, the cousin seeming to want survival more than anyone, the sex now complicated by a face and a name and a person I called a friend.

I saw all this and I didn't know how my life had come to this place. Somehow here, on the twentieth floor. Somehow here, expanding the company to its impossible size. Somehow here, alone, looking at the end.

Because I didn't know what I would do if it collapsed.

Whitley, here in my office. The two of us so quiet, barely breathing, in the dimmest white light from the buildings around us.

It was nice to touch her.

In the morning, I laid off three hundred people in U.S. field offices.

And we watched the stock fall.

The new Regence Green Box was the lead story in all the business papers, on the financial news networks, on Web sites worldwide. It was the story the press hadn't ever predicted. It was the moment our customers hadn't ever thought possible.

It was the threat Wall Street had never considered.

For the brokers and analysts and shareholders who tracked and invested in Core Communications, this was a disaster. In just these few hours, Regence's Green Box had cast Core in an unknown light. All the benchmarks by which Core had been valued, all the metrics long used to forecast our growth and success, all of it had been destroyed.

"Clearly," one analyst said, "an adjustment is due."

We watched the stock fall.

And I felt slightly breathless and erratic and completely exhausted.

Morning, and I was in a meeting of the company's top staff, the New York managers all sitting in front of me, the managers from the regional and international offices hooked in via speakerphone. I was talking. Talking quickly. Confidently. Telling them we would weather this. Telling them we would fight off Regence's new threat.

"Our customer base," I said to the group. "Our lead over Regence," I said. "Our existing sales," I said. "Our expertise," I said. "Our people," I said.

Our people.

I talked clearly, the managers nodded fast, the voices from the field offices were marked by purely positive tones. Cliff even stayed seated in a chair near me, an almost healthy color across his face and hands. But, like the press, like the shareholders and the analysts, these managers also saw that Core was in an unknown place. Weakness revealed. Damage done. The company had been wounded. A wound now measured by the falling stock. A wound no spin and no talk could completely heal.

A wound that, they feared, would only grow.

Phones had been ringing and beeping and vibrating throughout the meeting. All were ignored—these the calls and notices to the top managers in the company, *Core is falling, the employees are scared, your own finances are already in descent.*

I talked. Still, talking.

Competition. Stock. Technical edge. Traditional strength.

Continued fall.

And in my mind I was calculating numbers, running through lists, thinking back on the results Shimmer had given me that morning. The shadow network continuing to reel. Shimmer dimming at the edges, the shapes all turning so fast now, wild lines along the bottom of the company. We'd lost another two months off the life of the shadow network. Two months. In just one week. And even if the stock somehow did rebound soon, Core would still be in competition with Regence. Sales were slowing. Together, the falling stock and falling sales would kill us.

"What about our bonuses?" a voice on the speakerphone asked.

I took a breath, I paused.

"What about grace?" someone whispered from the back of the room.

"Your bonuses are threatened," I said, and paused again. "Grace is moving back."

The looks on the faces, a grayness that crossed over each of them in just one second. But I looked back at each of them, the CEO who had to look them in the eye, who had to show he understood their fear.

Except that I didn't have the same fear. In truth, Regence's Green Boxes were the best possible protection I could have wanted. With Regence attacking us, no real effort could be given to rogue sections or the shadow threads Shimmer might find. Because with Regence attacking us, there was now a reason we could fail.

Once more I was on a path toward my millions. My assets, my cash, ever-increasing amounts tied up in the shadow network. Owned entirely by me.

I was back at my beginning. Once more caught in the perfectly protected trap I had created myself.

Cliff's phone rang and I paused, inadvertently, leaning toward him to see the text message on the screen. I felt somehow proud that Cliff did not stand, or leave. He only put his hand on the seat of his chair, staring now at a message we would all receive over the next few minutes.

The stock had fallen another $15.

Cliff nodded confidently. I nodded too. I made the motions of a man scanning the faces of the people in the room. I bore the expression of a CEO remaining confident despite the storm around us all.

"Make no mistake," I said to the group. "This will be hard. It will be ugly and awful. But we will survive this."

Yesterday, I'd had sex with Whitley.

She was sitting five feet away.

And for a second, no more, I let myself feel that she was beautiful.

And for a second, no more, I let myself wonder what this meant, this sex and touching and time with her.

The phones rang. The heads nodded. The news from outside invaded our world, taking another step with each second that passed.

And for a second, I glanced at her.

COO. Head of SWAT. The only person who ever told me *no*.

And for a second, no more, I let myself feel how I was not afraid of her anymore.

In the morning I laid off two hundred people from the New York office.

I cut programs.

I cut expenses.

I cut people.

Wall Street applauded.

The board sent me notes of thanks and encouragement.

I read each word. Each note. Each positive article in the paper.

I read them, sitting in my office, and, every few moments, I turned to my computer, looking at the security cameras throughout the building, watching as the people left the office. Carrying their boxes, their briefcases, their thick, thick piles of paper.

And by night I'd finish reading each positive article. Each positive note.

By night I'd see that I'd added a few weeks to the shadow network.

By night I turned to a list of who I would fire next.

The shadow network spun in dense, growing circles near his head.

Leonard had called me to the DMZ. He was walking along the raised path at the foot of the main status board, Shimmer's hundred shapes spinning, turning, nearly violent in their motion above and behind him.

And a section of the shadow network spinning—unidentified and undefined—in the corner of the screen.

"We will figure out what they're doing," he said. He was talking about the Budapest thread. And the rogue section that he thought was responsible for it.

I sat down in a chair. "Leonard," I said, "we can't afford to spend time on this."

He was nodding, back turned to me, looking up at the board as he moved left to right. He didn't speak.

It was a full minute before I said to him, "Leonard, do you understand me? I know these rogue sections are a huge danger. But they aren't as important now."

He nodded. Moving slowly. His body, full and wide and spread across the screen, now cast as a near silhouette against Shimmer.

Another minute passed. Only eight other people were in the DMZ, Leonard having cleared out all nonessential personnel before projecting Shimmer on the main status board. The lack of people, the quiet in the room, it was as if somehow our network had begun to shut down, not dying the quick death of the shadow network collapse, instead lost to the slow demise of losing clients to Regence.

"It disappeared, you know," Leonard said now.

"What did?"

"The Budapest thread," he said. "I can't make sense of it. I can't even find it."

"Leonard, please. Look at me. Wait on this rogue section. It doesn't matter."

"They're very smart," he said. "Whoever they are."

"Leonard," I said, but couldn't think of what else I should say. What else I could tell him.

The screen blinked, then changed completely, only a few dense shapes now filling the display. I realized Leonard had a remote control in his hand, able to change the view of Shimmer that appeared on the screen.

"Do you see?" Leonard asked now. "See these lines pulling in on themselves? See these circles collapsing? The company is changing."

And of course I saw it. Saw it in the dense, collapsing shapes. Shimmer was showing a company falling in on itself. People in every group were withdrawing, their communication and interaction with other groups, with each other, all of it disappearing.

The screen blinked again, another view, more of the very slow but steady collapse.

"They turn inward," I heard Leonard say, almost whispering as he spoke.

"And these," I heard Leonard say, pointing absently toward two small, dense squares on the board. "These are new."

He was pointing at the shadow network. Still he didn't know what he was looking at. He pointed them out only because of that very fact—they were mysteries in the system, unidentified anomalies caused, he was worried, by the changes in the company. Or by his suspected rogue section.

The screen blinked and now Leonard was showing Regence, there in the cameras and facilities database.

"Regence just watches," Leonard said.

"How are we doing on toilet-paper updates?" I asked, trying to smile, wishing Leonard would turn to me.

He shrugged.

"Maybe I'll get Perry to agree to those naked pictures Julie suggested," I said.

He spoke very quietly. "It's all lost so much of its joy," he said, and I felt my eyes try to close.

The main board blinked, then returned to its normal view, a map of the world, the positions of our satellites. Leonard put the remote control in his front pocket, carefully, slowly, with an almost exaggerated motion. Like a boy putting his pet mouse into his jeans.

As I left the DMZ, walking now across the eleventh floor, I noticed the concentrations of people dressed in green. Programmers and admins, clustered near workstations, moving toward conference rooms. Weeks ago I'd seen these people in their all-green ensembles, and it had made me happy. The unspoken celebration of the people in this company. A joke maybe even they hadn't understood. Now, though, I couldn't help but see these people as a landmark in the increasingly rapid passage of time. An indecipherable symbol walking freely among the people who most needed to know what they represented.

It's the first of the month. The people are in green. We are thirty days closer to the end.

And I thought about what Leonard had just said.

Joy, he had said. Leonard had called it joy.

I tried to find Perry. But he was not in his office. I sent him an e-mail from my phone.

You've been spending too much time away from your desk.

It was only a minute later that he responded.

Missed you in your office, he wrote.

Leonard isn't doing well, I responded.

I know.

What can I do?

It was another five minutes before Perry responded. I'd thought maybe he wouldn't answer till later that night, maybe the next day. I entered a conference room for another meeting, another talk to another group. My phone clicked as I went to the front of the room, the assembled Core staffers waiting anxiously for what I had to say.

I glanced at the phone. Perry's answer was short.

Nothing.

I could barely keep up with the changes to the model. The falling stock. The drop in sales. I sat at my computer updating the spreadsheet, checking the results of the changes I made. Staring at the projected date of our collapse. A date that moved closer—by hours or days—every time I entered a new number, a new change, a new piece of bad information.

Shimmer so dark, so fast, filled with the motion of so many frantic changes.

Day and night I'd been in meetings with staff from all areas and levels of the company, trying to keep them focused, keep them positive in the face of the fall.

Day and night I'd been holding interviews with any reporter who would speak to me, talking about every positive in the company, every customer we'd held on to, every success I could spell out to them.

Day and night I'd been working with Cliff to juggle the finances of the company, cutting spending, slicing programs, as Cliff, sitting beside me, shook in place, his hands, his head, sometimes his feet.

Day and night I'd been lobbying government officials on the history of abusive actions by Regence, its attempts to monopolize whole market segments, the evidence of price fixing, product dumping, the violation of basic labor laws.

Day and night I'd been stroking, coddling and arguing with every analyst and broker who would listen.

Sex with her again. Every night. Whitley, appearing at my office door at ten. Walking in, sitting down on the windowsill near my desk. Something she'd done a thousand other times in the past three years, looking just the same, so still and focused and calm. But now she talked in a voice slightly different, slightly more quiet than ever before. Saying only a few words. Saying, *Hello.* Saying, *Hi.* Moving with a speed slowed even more. Moving, and she leaned toward me. Now kissing me. Now touching my arm and neck and face.

This was not guilt-ridden or scared. This was not giddy or fun. In those moments, we had safety.

Safety. Safe. Complete.

Please don't let this go.

I held on to Whitley now. Silent in the dim light of my office. Silent here on the couch where I'd spent all these years trying to sleep.

I had nothing to say. She had nothing either. Even though, all day, we had talked to one another—about the stock, Regence, survival. Even though we'd been working together since six A.M. Even though we knew each other so well. We had nothing to say.

Safety.

No one wanted to admit that the party should be canceled. The lobby was full again, the mezzanines crowded with a few hundred people from inside and outside the company. The music rolling upward from the lobby, circling in the darkness above everyone's heads.

But, really, we shouldn't have been here.

It was nine o'clock on a Friday. People arriving through the building's front doors. And people coming down from upstairs. Working late on this Friday like every Friday.

I could not find Perry, like me usually a bystander at these parties. I called him, then e-mailed him from my phone, but there was no response.

I sat with Cliff now, the two of us quiet. Cliff in a chair with his feet against a table, legs bent, arms wrapped tightly around his knees, hands firmly under his arms, captured as he gnawed his lip, tapped his teeth. Clearly grinding numbers in his mind. Unable to stop. Cliff with his own internal model of the finances of the company. A model that, like the shadow network, was changing impossibly fast. The two of us had talked very little tonight. Both of us knew we had to be at the party. But neither of us wanted to talk to anyone. And so we'd been sitting silently, watching the party in motion in front of us.

In some ways it seemed that the people had come to the party because they wanted to watch. To see. Outsiders, I think they came to see if it was true. To see if Core really was threatened. The people who worked here, I think they came to watch people from other departments, to see if they looked different or the same.

But ultimately, everyone came to see if this, this company and everything they'd put into it, was still real.

There were people who drank too much. There were people who cried. There were people who got angry, who argued with friends and coworkers, who yelled at their managers, who left in anger. But most people just stayed. Just stayed at the party. Smiled some, laughed. Stayed close to their friends.

"I'm going to have to give you some more numbers," Cliff said, not looking at me. It was the first time we'd spoken in nearly an hour. When I turned to him, I saw he was still gnawing his lip, still sitting with his arms wrapped around his knees. His position had barely changed all night.

"Numbers," I said.

"More," he said.

In a moment, I realized and said to him, "Okay."

"They'll have to be let go immediately," he said.

"Okay," I said.

"I'm sorry," he said.

"Another two hundred?"

He nodded.

"Okay," I said.

He was still nodding, still tapping his teeth, still gnawing his lip.

The noise in the room was rising, a blurry, wooden sound, louder now, but muffled, distant, tired.

"I'm sorry," he said.

"No," I said carefully. "Don't be."

"I wish," he said, then stopped. Nodding. "I wish I could see another way."

"There isn't one," I said.

"I wish I hadn't let this happen," he said.

I sat forward. Turning to him. Pushing my hand across my face, wanting to sink in my chair, wanting to melt away. Because it was a conversation I'd had with Julie two days earlier, with Whitley that morning. "You didn't cause this," I said. "There was nothing you could have done."

He nodded slowly.

"Cliff," I said, "there's no one to blame but me."

He nodded. And for the first time he moved his arms, his body. Leaning forward. Slowly picking up his drink, a light-brown fluid looking warm and pale. He took a small sip. Nodding again. He sat back, once more finding his familiar position, hunched up and staring, though now with a warm drink in his hand.

"It's not," I said, starting, then stopping. Waiting a moment. "It's not your fault," I said.

He nodded. Slowly. We were quiet for a minute, the party rolling on in front of us. Then he tapped me on the arm. "It'll probably be three hundred," he said.

There were people who drank too much. There were people who cried. But still, a few hundred people were here at midnight. Standing close to one another. Smiling, laughing some. Staying close to their friends.

I found myself standing. Walking along the edges of the group. Cliff still sitting in his chair, still wrapped up tight.

I couldn't find Perry. Hadn't heard from him in days. Hadn't seen him in a few weeks.

Leonard wasn't here. Leonard was still upstairs.

I moved along the edges of the crowd, the noise, the groups of people. People who looked so tired. And worn. And sad.

And I found myself near the door. The main entrance from the street. The street I hadn't been on in so many months.

Whitley was beside me. Saying something that was nothing. Talking briefly, standing next to me, saying words, and I spoke back for a moment, and we stood there, looking toward the door, and what I wanted was for her to hold me.

There was dancing, midnight, then one o'clock, and I was still moving along the edges, from first floor to mezzanine, sometimes finding Whitley, or she would find me, and we'd talk nothing words again, and stay beside each other as long as it would look okay.

And Julie found me now, and pulled my arm, and said only, "Dance." I was with her, and walking into the group now, and not dancing, but Julie smiled, and said, "Dance," and so I followed her. Into the noise. The people. The talking. Motion.

And people touched me now. They touched me on the arm. They touched me on the shoulder. I thought they were joking, some joke orchestrated by Julie, who still pulled me through the crowd. But there was no joking. There was just each touch. Sometimes they said words, things I couldn't hear, the music rising, turning, falling onto it-self again. But I could see what they were saying. They were saying we would make it. They were saying they would not give up.

They were saying they didn't blame me.

I couldn't remember the last time I'd slept.

They said they didn't blame me.

I followed Julie, I saw Cliff in his seat, I felt Whitley next to me for a moment in the crowd, I wished Leonard was not still working. I wished so much that I could find Perry. I wished so much that I could see my cousin, Trevor.

They didn't blame me.

They didn't blame me.

And I circled. I followed Julie. Saw Cliff. Watched Whitley near me again. Felt each person touch me. And wished I could touch each one of them.

They didn't blame me.

They only should have.

"Lie down here," I said.

"Here?"

"Lie down quietly. Next to me."

"Next to you."

Half dressed, next to me. A face I didn't know. A body I'd never touched.

"Don't move," I said. "Don't touch. Just lie there. Still."

"Don't touch."

"Don't move."

"Okay."

Whitley out of town. But, even then, Whitley wasn't this. This was something else.

"Lie here. Still. And pretend."

"Pretend."

In my mind I was thinking just one thing.

"Pretend you're staying."

"How?"

Repeating in my mind.

"Just pretend."

"Okay."

Over and again.

"Quietly. Pretend you're staying. Pretend you live here."

"Okay."

Trying to stop it but it wouldn't.

"Pretend you're staying. Pretend you're happy."

"Okay."

This is what I needed.

This is all I'd had.

This is what had kept me sane.

"Pretend you're happy."

"Are you crying?"

And this could only stop if I were free of Core.

"Pretend you're happy. Pretend you love me."

Repeating it. Over and again.

This can only stop if I am free.

He feels like he has disappeared.

He can't remember when it happened. But now he knows he's disappeared. From the world of the people around him, the rooms he is in, the computers and phones he touches all day.

He moves through it all, watched and watching and not really there.

Not really here.

He thinks it will end, this life. He thinks it all is moving toward an end. But he can't see that end. He can't tell when it will come.

And he doesn't know what it means for it to end.

Why would a company find itself having meaning?

How could work, a job, turn into such a place?

Core is his life.

What a silly thing to realize.

There are moments of slowness in the best parts of his day. A stillness in the fray. Over the phone, in a darkened office, in a conference room. There is stillness.

And there is a waiting, people looking at him and waiting. Waiting for what he will do or say.

And there is arrogance in this. There is.

He's never really cared enough about grace. About what it means to everyone else.

There is arrogance, and presence, and aura, and waiting, and watching, and hoping, hoping that he will have an answer for others

There should be a better way.

In the dark, in the night, awake, looking up.

There should be a better way.

CHAPTER 10

It was hard to take him seriously. Some brightly mysterious man talking circles in my ear.

"You answer your own phone," the man said, his English accent very narrow and distant.

"Who is this?" I asked absently.

"You answer your own phone," the man said again.

"Usually," I said, phone held away from my mouth. "Although sometimes I just let it ring and ring. Who is this?"

I was staring at Shimmer.

"I assume this phone line is secure," the man said.

"Secure enough. Who is this?" I asked, barely paying attention to the call. Not sure why I continued to listen. Yet somehow finding comfort in the annoyance of his overly enigmatic tone.

"A package has just been delivered to your assistant," he said.

I was staring at the spreadsheet. Counting up programs to cut. Efforts to end.

People to fire.

"This package contains a very important gift."

"Gifts are nice. Who is this?"

"What do you think this gift is, Mr. Case?"

"A letter bomb, maybe?"

He did not respond. I thought I could hear him mumble a question, maybe to someone else in the room.

This was a man without any sense of irony.

"Who is this?" I asked, annoyed and absent and yet surprisingly happy to let this call go on forever.

"This package contains a very important item," he said, apparently having decided it was best to ignore my comments, his voice already regaining its lulling rhythm, seeming to return to a predefined script. "It contains an address. A hangar number."

I smiled slightly. "A hangar? You're sending a plane for me? I don't even know you."

I turned back to my computer now, e-mailing my assistant. *Call SWAT. Ask them who this caller is.*

Paranoia or curiosity, I'd never decided which, but for the past two years all of my incoming calls had been traced, even those that tried to be untraceable.

He spoke. "You will fly without your entourage."

"I don't have an entourage," I said.

"You will fly alone."

"I don't have an entourage."

"I am instructed to tell you that you must come alone."

"You're dwelling on that, which is interesting to me," I said, for the first time taking my eyes off my computer. Glancing now toward the windows around me, the sky that seemed to have been there, around me, for days, unbroken. When had it last been night?

"I am instructed to ask that you come with an open mind."

Salaries, benefits, day care.

All would be cut.

"Where am I going?" I asked.

"To a meeting."

"About?"

"I cannot say."

"With whom?"

"I cannot say."

"Where?"

"To a place where all your questions will be answered," he said warmly, simply, and I imagined him shrugging, confident in the finality of his words.

"Who is this?"

"Again, I have been instructed not to say."

"What?"

"Are you able to do this, Mr. Case?"

I kept adding up the savings. Wall Street would be pleased. And weeks would be saved.

My assistant's e-mail arrived. *Regence.* No name or identity on the caller yet. But this was a call from the Regence headquarters.

I heard myself saying, "Is this what you do all day?"

It was a moment before he responded. "Do what, Mr. Case?"

"Call people and make mysterious requests. Is this your job? You arrive at the office at nine, get your coffee in the break room, place a few calls, spread a little intrigue?"

"What?" the man asked.

In some part of my mind, I wondered if I was finally on the verge of a breakdown. In some part of my mind, I wondered if I was maybe imagining this. This circling call. This artificially elusive voice in my ear.

In a way, none of this had ever felt entirely real.

"What do you mean?" the man asked.

"Is it a job that pays well? Is there specific training you go through? Do you have a college degree?"

"I do not see this as relevant, Mr. Case."

"Are you sitting in a very bright, spartanly furnished, windowless room?" I asked him, and in a way it did feel like I was talking to myself.

"Excuse me, Mr. Case?"

"I'm picturing stainless-steel furniture, a glaring and omnipresent overhead light. I'm picturing you, blond, of course, in a gray, generic but highly tailored suit."

"Again I am not sure how this is relevant."

"Still, it's worth discussing," I said.

"Do you want to know how I obtained your direct phone line, Mr. Case?" the man asked now, seeming to change the subject. Or maybe returning to his script.

"I assume you got it from the company directory," I said. "Or maybe off our Web site. Or the phone book."

"Well, no."

"Did you hack into one of our servers, then? That was probably the hard way."

"No," he said somewhat weakly.

"Did you bribe my assistant? Blackmail an intern? Intercept my mail?"

He didn't answer for a moment. Then only said, "No."

"This is Chairman Tor, isn't it?" I said slowly, although I doubted it was actually him. It was only something to say. Some piece of confusion to add.

There was a pause. "Chairman Tor does not place his own calls," the man said.

"Because he travels with an entourage," I said, staring toward New Jersey now, standing now, for the first time noticing a park, a small park, that sat near the waterfront.

Again there was the confused pause. I thought I could even hear papers shuffling but was sure my mind was only supplementing the mildly orchestrated drama of the moment.

"And so?" the voice asked, confidence fading again.

"Yes?"

"And so, are you coming?" he asked.

"Coming to where?"

"To the hangar."

"To fly to Finland?" I asked. "To meet with Chairman Tor?"

He was quiet. Apparently he had only just realized how clear he'd been with me. Another moment passed. "Yes," he said.

I hung up the phone.

I had a second e-mail from my assistant. A direct phone number within Regence.

Staring at that park again. Still not sure how much of this was real.

In another moment, I dialed the number.

It was the elegant voice, somewhat less polished or practiced, speaking now in what I assumed to be Finnish, saying something to the effect of *hello*.

"This is Robbie Case," I said. "Tell him to meet me here. If Tor wants to meet, he'll have to come here."

And I hung up.

I sent a quick e-mail to Cliff, Whitley, Leonard and Julie. Outlining the scope of the next round of cuts.

I stood. I went to the window.

And I wasn't sure why I'd been surprised that Regence had called. After all, I was the one who'd reached out to them first.

I was the one who'd called, days earlier, letting them know Core was available. Core was for sale.

He entered with what, in fact, could only be called an entourage. Chairman Tor, walking into a conference room on the twentieth floor, surrounded by a group of eight vaguely Aryan, remarkably large men and women. Broad-shouldered and tall, full-breasted and dense. There was something very fertile about all of them. Their well-defined faces, their sharply honed jaws, their beautiful hair and mouths. They were made of genes that seemed to call out for reproduction.

I, on the other hand, was meeting with them alone, a thin and tired man leaning against the edge of the windowsill. Pressing one hand against the glass behind me.

The group had been brought up in a freight elevator by my driver, then escorted quietly to this conference room out of the sight of any employees.

Tor shook my hand. He was, like his entourage, a deeply fit, remarkably handsome man. His hand gripped mine as if it were clinging to the edge of some slick Nordic ice shelf. His eyes stared into me, clearly searching for my inner life, my deepest secrets, my sense of self.

I tried, in my way, to give him nothing. A half smile, a firm grip, a nod toward a chair near me.

"I'm glad to meet you, Mr. Case," he said in a voice tinged nicely by an English accent.

I barely registered the next twenty minutes, filled as they were with his stories of starting his company, of launching new products, of hiring and building his empire. They were folksy tales, less the tightly drawn insights of an entrepreneur and his visionary plan than the loosely relayed anecdotes of a simple but strong man who'd one day found himself atop this international machine.

He'd reached the 1980s when I noticed that his entourage had formed a kind of perimeter around the room, two men near the door, two women standing equidistant along the windows, a man and woman at each side of him, two men with laptops sitting close at the end of the room. I thought for a moment that I was being surrounded. But I saw that they were actually surrounding him, monitoring the room, the exits, the windows, some kind of security posture that, probably, they kept up at all times.

I realized I should have met with them in a room with a set of children's chairs.

"I'm an engineer," Tor said to me now. "The rest of this, it is merely a function of the power those fundamental skills did bring me."

I nodded. I smiled some. I was so incredibly tired. The exhaustion in my body, in my eyes, the exhaustion ever present in everything I saw and did and felt, here now amidst this cast of elegant intruders. I blinked, and again, and light shot in streaks across the black surfaces of my vision.

"I could tell you my stories too," I said. "But I really don't have time."

He nodded. He sat back, taking a very careful moment to clasp his hands in his lap, to stare down at them. Studying his motions, preparing his comments for me.

"You and I," he said, "left to battle in the vacuum created by Fadowsky's genius."

"Genius," I said. "Yes."

"You see, our cultures, our people, they have more in common than you and I want to believe."

And it was a moment, a slow, slow moment, but I finally found myself nodding, smiling. Smile.

"Let's end this fighting."

And I kept on nodding, smiling.

"Our two companies should not be at war," he said.

And he was going to say it now.

"I'm talking about the new economy," he said, "a borderless world, the free flow of information between nations and old adversaries."

And I blinked again, looking away, toward the window. Seeing streaks of light still crossing fast across my eyes, and I could see the words as I spoke them, "You want to buy my company."

I turned back to him and he was smiling wide, leaning forward, nodding slowly. "A majority stake," he said in English now perfect, clean, without any accent at all. "At a multiple of, say, one-fifth of your current revenue."

I smiled. I could not help but smile. It was what I'd wanted. An offer to buy this company. But, still, I had to smile.

And I said in a moment, "A price that's a fraction of what your emissary offered me just a few weeks ago."

He smiled. His eyes seemed to sparkle. His lips were so wet. "And just think," he said slowly, "think about what price I will offer you a few days from now."

Next to the pile of letters was a tall stack of legal documents. The offer from Regence.

Just a few days since my meeting with Tor.

No one in the company knew about the offer yet. But soon I would tell them.

I read letters from people who'd been fired.

I read letters from shareholders praising what I'd done.

I read articles in the paper in support of my actions.

I read articles in the paper telling the stories of the people without jobs.

And other letters. A month's worth of letters from my parents. All morning I'd been reading and rereading the story of each person. Picturing each city in which they lived, each neighborhood and home they described. Reliving the details of the decisions they had once made.

Imagining one of these letters might be real.

Core was now just a few months from collapse. Selling to Regence wouldn't stop the collapse. But it would give the company a little life, a few extra months. Enough time to finalize the sale. And enough time that the sale might help cover up some of the reasons for our collapse.

Although the senior staff would be marked by this failure forever.

And I would be done, marked like all the senior staff.

But rich.

Sued. Tied up in lawsuits. But nothing I couldn't settle in time.

I stood up now. Restacking the letters. Then leaving my office. No direction or place in mind. Thinking only that it had been weeks since I'd last walked through the office. Since I'd held a meeting on the fly.

I only had to walk for a few minutes to see it. Hear it most of all. The quiet. It wasn't that people had given up. They weren't silent in their offices, they weren't sitting quietly at their desks, heads lowered, just waiting for some end. They were still in motion, still moving quickly. Still loud in their calls and work.

But I could hear the silence. The quiet that hung between each word that was spoken.

Fear.

And yet, for all the reaction in the market and the press and inside the company, we could see now that we were losing very few clients to Regence. The stock had fallen sixty percent, but our client base had dropped only five. I'd tried to emphasize this to everyone who would listen. And the financial analysts and reporters all agreed with what I said. None saw us in decline because our clients were fleeing, because our services were so dramatically diminished or because our revenue was falling off much at all. What they saw, only, was the stock. Diving. And diving because, with Regence against us, now there was definition to how large we could grow, a cap on how many clients we could get. That cap alone was burying us. Because what had kept the stock so high for so long was the undefined potential of Core Communications. And without definition, our potential had always been limitless.

Now, though, our future had been seen, explained and quantified.

And so what I'd been cutting was our new products. Our new efforts. Our less profitable services.

I'd been cutting our future.

Yet, for a week now, the stock had been stabilizing. Down $75 since Regence had introduced its boxes, but this week there were buyers in our stock.

"Faith in the company?" Julie had asked me that morning, sitting in a chair in my office, staring absently toward the door.

"Cliff says no," I said. "Cliff says it won't last."

And I wasn't sure how much it had helped. Weeks, maybe. Even a month.

But not enough, of course.

Now I stood near a glass conference room. Stood near the tall multipaned windows. Stood near desks and workspaces and chairs and printers and copiers and people.

I'd forgotten, for a moment, what floor I was on.

I thought about heading toward the DMZ. Wanting to pass through that collection of juvenile programmers and game-playing admins. But I knew that wasn't what I would see. Instead the DMZ had become the worst floor in the company, the most tired, the most pained, all of it a reflection of Leonard's anxious, dying state.

I needed to call Trevor. To tell him about Regence. And to tell him what was about to happen.

But I couldn't do it yet.

I wondered if anyone still played putt-putt.

I wondered if anyone still played basketball.

I wondered if anyone could find the energy to form an active rogue section.

The night before, I'd found Cliff in his office at one A.M., staring wide-eyed into a computer screen, typing rapidly on his keyboard. "Looking for a way," he said quietly, not turning to me, his shoulders pulled forward, his office filled with the vaguely bitter scent of vomit.

And I'd only turned away.

The night before, I'd found Julie in her office at two A.M., carefully filing away papers related to every employee program, every community service action the company had ever done. "Never did," she said slowly, "have time to sort through all this." And she stared down at the piles, her hands touching each paper, carefully placing each document in a file, each file in a box, each box in a corner of the room.

The night before, I'd found Whitley alone in my office. And for a long time we'd only sat quietly on the windowsill.

But I hadn't found Perry. Not for weeks. It seemed that he was never in his office. There were rumors he'd gone to Budapest as part of Leonard's investigation. Rumors he'd gone to India to join Frederick Fadowsky in retirement. Rumors he'd killed himself in some forgotten room of our basement. Rumors he'd gone to Russia to live with my father. Rumors he'd hacked into the accounting system and run off with millions of dollars. None of the stories were true, not least because he was well-known to be continually managing his group by phone, e-mail and a periodic live appearance.

Actually, it seemed that mostly he was simply avoiding me.

At night I was making changes to the shadow network without fully understanding every ramification. With the finances of the company under such stress, all I wanted was to save us another day or hour. Which meant I was taking chances. I moved money faster, opened new companies quicker, took fewer precautions as I repointed satellites, as I redirected contract programmers, as I shifted mainframes from one shell company to another.

And I stood now in R&D, near Perry's dark office. Having walked for half an hour. Standing here now, seeing so much abandoned promise in every direction, on every floor.

Standing here now, seeing so much failure.

Seeing so much arrogance.

I needed to tell Trevor about Regence's offer.

How could I feel like I had failed Trevor?

And still, after walking through the office, still when I got back to my desk, the sale documents were waiting. That hadn't changed.

Turning, slowly and slower and turning, in place, with the motion below me, around me. Whitley, like always, but not. The image I'd had for three years, but not. Talking now, but not. Intermittent words forming sentences between motions.

"The stock," she said, so close to me, finding quiet breaths between each word. "It stopped its fall."

And my words too, there between each breath, matched somehow against each motion inside me. "Only for a week," I said. "Only a week."

Turning.

"There are no more games," I said, finding a way to talk, keep talking, keep making words between the motions and breath.

"I know," she said, her breath catching, eyes blinking and again, hands across my neck before she could open them again.

Tomorrow I had to respond to Regence.

Tomorrow I had to say yes.

Tomorrow the board and Wall Street and the markets, all would be so proud of this decision.

"Yes," I said. "Yes," I said.

"Why," she asked, words coming to her again, lips somehow full and dry as they mouthed at the words, "why did you meet with those people from Regence?"

And again I tried to shake my head. Saying only, "Can't say."

"Why did Leonard's thread," she said, blinking her way from one word to the next, tongue moving left as she found each sound, "the Budapest thread, why did it disappear a few hours after he told you about it?"

"I don't know."

"In three years," she said, whispering now, losing all force behind her speaking, moving just faster in the motion between us, "I've never doubted a single thing you've said."

Faster with the motion.

"But, Robbie," she said, eyes only barely open, staring, "this time I don't believe you."

Her lip caught below the edge of her teeth.

"The reports," she said, staring, staring through eyes that blinked with each motion, "SWAT. There's something happening. Something's been happening."

Faster with the motion.

"I think," she started, "I think Leonard is right. Some rogue section. Some rogue section gone wild within this company."

Motion, all motion.

"Nothing adds up. The computers are wrong. The satellites transfer information at incorrect speeds."

And the turning, turning more, it was as if we'd been turning, slowly, still turning. And I heard myself say, "Shimmer." Heard myself say, "How much is left for Shimmer to see?"

"I think it's seen everything," she said. "I think now it's only trying to understand."

Trying to nod. Trying to say words.

"Tell me," she said.

"What?"

"Tell me," she said.

Trying to nod.

"Tell me what Shimmer will see, " she said.

"I don't know," I said.

"Tell me," she said.

"I don't know."

"Someday," she said, "please someday tell me."

Once more, I went to find Perry.

It was morning, and I had to respond to Regence. To the offer Tor had made. There would be due diligence later, board approval, meetings with executives and shareholders and investors. All that would come later. For now, Tor just wanted me to say the words.

It's yours.

I wanted Perry with me for the call. I needed to tell someone what was about to happen. And I needed the comfort Perry gave me. Perry had been here from the beginning.

He wasn't in his office. I looked around a moment, seeing the now suspended construction of the antechamber to his office.

As I had so many times in recent weeks, I asked a few people from his department if they knew where he was. None had seen him in a few days.

I was making my way toward the DMZ when I got an e-mail on my phone.

I'm in your office.

"How did you know I was looking for you?" I asked Perry when I got back to my office. He was sitting at my desk, typing rapidly at my computer. I was too tired to tell him to stop.

He didn't look at me when he responded. Only his fingers were allowed any motion at all. "Spies," he said flatly. "I'm having you watched."

I didn't know whether or not to believe him. And I knew that really all I wanted was to pursue that question with him. To talk in circles with Perry.

I sat in one of the chairs in front of my desk, Perry still typing. He was hard to see, his face so dark against the bright light from the window. And I realized this was how most people saw me when they came to me in my office. Features lost to the light, eyes unseeable, the windows framing me in their mind.

I said to him, "Regence has offered to buy this company."

He didn't look up from the machine. "I know," he said.

I shook my head slowly. "How?"

"An unprecedented exchange of favors."

"But no one here knew," I said.

He shook his head. "I didn't find out from anyone here," he said. "I found out from Regence."

It took me a moment to understand. "SWAT," I said.

"Whitley doesn't know," he said, nodding. "But I managed to find out through SWAT."

The chair I sat in was terribly uncomfortable. I'd had it for three years. I shifted in place. "I have to call Regence now," I said. I glanced out the window. I wanted to touch the glass, very lightly, with my fingers. "I'd like you to be on the phone with me."

For a moment, he seemed to finish what he was typing. He sat back in my chair, turning toward me. He nodded. "I'd like that too."

As I called Finland, I glanced at a daily financial report from Cliff's group. The stock was still stable. There was no clear reason why this had happened. It was being caused by something more than the layoffs and cuts. There were buyers of the stock. A few people or companies intent on purchasing large quantities of Core stock right now, even when it looked like the price would soon fall so much farther.

"Is this you?" I asked Perry absently, nodding toward the financial report.

"The stock?" he asked. "Not me. I already sold what little stock I had. Unloaded it before it was worth even less."

All I could do was shake my head. And smile. I couldn't help but smile.

Tor's entire entourage seemed to answer the phone. They sounded as if they were crowded into a very small office in their Helsinki headquarters, all of them rapidly and loudly firing off a range of opinions and suggestions, each a voice surrounding Chairman Tor as he led Regence through another day.

It was Tor's voice that broke through the noise.

"And what do you have for me today, Robbie?" he asked.

"I think you know," I said.

Across from me, still in my chair, Perry was once more typing rapidly at my computer. As he did, I could see that he was accessing systems with the highest security levels—servers and networking in the heart of the DMZ.

"Actually, I don't know, Robbie," Tor said, his voice echoing out from the phone. "Tell me. Tell me what you have."

I knew I'd have to say it. Knew he wanted to hear the words. *It's yours. I give in. Take it. Take it all.*

And then Shimmer launched itself on the second monitor on my desk. And I saw it immediately. Saw it in the dense circles, the isolated structures, the lines turning back on themselves.

It was the shadow network.

Perry was staring at me. Smiling only slightly. But smiling.

It wasn't my shadow network.

It was someone else's.

And in a moment, I said it. Staring at Perry. "They're lying."

Perry nodded. He reached down slowly and scratched his foot. Bare.

"They've built it on a lie," I said.

And he nodded again.

Perry had managed to connect Shimmer to Regence's systems.

Tor was on the phone. Talking. "Tell me," he was still saying.

"It doesn't work," I said into the phone.

In a moment, Tor asked, "What doesn't work?"

"Your system," I said again. "Your boxes. They don't work."

Perry was absently tracing Shimmer's dark lines with a finger. He tapped on the screen. He slowly turned back to me. Smile.

"You move the work," I said. "Your boxes don't do the work. They just shift the work to some other place. Other servers."

The entourage in Finland had gone quiet.

"I don't," Tor started, then went silent.

"Server farms," I said into the phone.

"I'm not sure," Tor started, then went quiet again.

"Another network," I said.

"What does," Tor said slowly, then stopped.

"You haven't drawn blood from a mainframe," I said. "You've just created a very intricate, carefully crafted lie."

The phone was still silent. Finally Tor said, "I expect your answer tomorrow."

He hung up.

It was a minute before Perry spoke. "Spies," he said quietly. "A few passwords. Favors I'll spend my whole life fulfilling."

"And so we'll be okay," I started to say. "They'll fail and we'll make it," I heard myself say.

So much lying. All I seemed to do was lie.

Perry spoke quietly then, nodding. One word. Sitting in my chair. Shimmer still painting Regence's shadow network across my screen. It was a long, quiet moment, Perry's voice hanging above it. Perry saying only, "Except."

I stared at him. Trying to find a look of confusion. Searching for the right words to say back to him.

"Except," he said again.

I started to stand, hand on the desk to push myself up. Then stopped. Because I couldn't. Could only sit back in this most uncomfortable chair. Leaning back now. Farther. Feeling my head fall slowly back. My eyes moving from my desk to Perry to the windows and the sky.

"Except," I said. "Except that I still have no choice. Except that still my only option is to sell."

And I didn't have to see it. Simply knew it was true. Knew Perry was nodding, very slowly, slightly.

It was just so sad.

We still had to sell. And Perry knew exactly why.

"Which did you look at first?" I asked. "Regence? Or Core?"

It was a moment before he answered. "Regence."

"And seeing what Regence was doing," I said slowly, pausing, voice fading, and all I wanted was to sleep. "Seeing it there."

"It made me realize."

"There's more," I said. "More than you could have seen. Even with Shimmer."

"I can imagine," he said.

In a moment, I said quietly, "I don't know what to do."

"When will everything collapse?" he asked.

I started to say it, words I'd lived with for all these horrible weeks but hadn't spoken aloud. I started to speak again. Lowering my head. Looking at him as I spoke. "Two months. Less if the stock starts falling again."

He blinked. Still staring.

"All we can do is sell," I said. "Even though Regence is just living the same lie. Selling will buy us a few months. Then it will collapse. Under their watch. Not Whitley's, not Julie's, not Cliff's or Leonard's."

He nodded.

"I don't," I started to say, but stopped. When I did speak, it was quiet and empty and the words seemed to come from someone else. "I'm not sure how to explain."

In a moment, he nodded.

And the words were not mine, so distant and quiet and if only I could sleep. "I'm so sorry," I heard myself say.

"I know," Perry said.

"I thought," I heard, then it was gone, then back, "I thought I'd find a way to make it work."

"I know," Perry said.

"I always thought I'd find a way," I said, and my eyes were closed.

"I know," I heard Perry say. "I know."

I stood in my office, midnight and staring at the window, and I realized for the first time that I was nearing a different kind of an end. My end. All along I'd known there was an end to the company. But now I was faced with an end for me. Finally I would break. Finally I would give in to my exhaustion and my fears and my sadness and my regrets. Finally I would just give up.

I looked at my desk.

The papers in tall piles.

I had signed the Regence documents. They were ready to be sent.

And I was ready to leave.

I am ready to leave.

So I did.

I picked up my laptop and headed through my door. I rode down a silent elevator, here in the quiet of midnight at Core. I walked past the guards in the lobby of the building.

And then I went outside.

It was cold, and there was wind, blowing lightly at my bare hands and up the sleeves of my jacket and against my lips and nose and eyes. I looked up, past the streetlights, the sky a brightened black with the reflection of the city against it.

All of it was much quieter than I'd remembered.

I was leaving the building. But I would have to manage the company through the sale to Regence, the transition to Tor and his people. I could do that from somewhere else, though. Somewhere with a phone and computer.

A car passed. A truck sat idling near the end of the street. A man walked his dog two blocks away. An old man in a tightly fitting gray suit moved past me, looking at me.

"Robbie," someone said. I turned, and it was the old man I'd just passed in the street. I'd thought maybe he was a homeless man. He was staring at me, smiling only slightly, looking deeply into my eyes. He was not a homeless man. He was yet another father, come now to reveal the truth to me.

"I don't have time," I said, turning away. "I'm tired of you. Of all the people like you."

He pulled back some, surprised, and I'd already turned away.

I found a cab. Climbed into the backseat with my laptop in my hands. Told the driver to take me to 125th Street, the farthest address I could think of, then would tell him when I got there to take me somewhere else. What I wanted was to drive. The city was so still, few cars, fewer people, but so many lights. The shifting brightness of streetlights and buildings, of car lights and stores, all turning across my eyes, shadows in the car, light that struck my hands, then disappeared, and it was so nice to drive. The motion, the speed, the drift of changing lanes, the hard lifting bumps at the intersections, near the curbs. I opened my window and there was air, cold air, hard against my face and wrapping now around my whole body, reaching into my shirt and around my ankles, and so thick and full against my hands.

I hadn't been out of the building in six months.

I closed my eyes.

I would hold together the shadow network until the acquisition was in motion. Until Regence had clearly taken control of the company. Which would not take long. A few weeks, and Core would little resemble the place it had been. And once Core was theirs, then the shadow network would collapse. Collapse with some cover for Core's management, its employees.

These people had given so much time. So much of their lives had been centered on the company.

How does that happen? What did they want? Will they ever get what they wanted to find?

I would manage the demise from somewhere else. From a hotel room. An apartment. Here in New York. Then someplace back in California.

I would manage it from anywhere but that building. My home of three years.

The stock was still stable. For some reason the decline had leveled off, nearly halted. This had bought us a full month now. An extra month to let Regence get that much more involved.

Tomorrow I will sell my company.

I still hadn't managed to call Trevor. I hadn't even sent him a message. Every day, I'd started to do it. But every time, I'd stopped. I told myself I didn't want to hear his anger, didn't want to listen as Trevor launched into some attack on me, my choices, the people around me, everyone. I'd had a lifetime of that from him, I told myself. I didn't need it anymore.

But even then I knew why I didn't call. I simply couldn't face it. Couldn't hear it. Couldn't hear his disappointment.

Each time I'd started to call, I felt like I was calling my father. Calling to tell him. *Finally I have failed.*

From the very beginning, I'd been hiding from that moment of facing my father. Facing him even in my mind.

Telling him I had failed.

I pressed my hands along the edges of the laptop. Slowly pulling it closer to me.

And if I closed my eyes now, here in the flashing darkness of New York at night, if I did that I would see my father. Staring at me. From his chair. Watching me from his office, behind his desk, seeing me now and the look would only be sadness. Sad that I'd done this. Sad that I'd set all of this in motion. Sad that I had brought so many people along. And sad, most of all, that I had done this to myself.

He would think that. *Why,* he would say, *why did you do this to yourself?*

He would pick up each piece for me, each part of the world I had created in these three years, and he would take each moment and each decision and each person and life and company and place, and he would fold each one up and put them away. And tell me, *It's over. That's it, Robbie. It's over.*

Unqualified. Unending. Without judgment. Without anger. Without disappointment. Complete.

It's over. I don't know what will happen, Robbie. But it's over.

I didn't have the ability to say this myself. I never had. I'd only ever been able to push forward. To try. To think that I was capable of finding a solution. To think my failure came from within. To think I'd never found a solution that was, for someone else, most certainly possible.

Make this work.

For three years, for thirty years, always I'd believed I had the ability to do it. *It is there,* I'd believed. *The solution is there, inside you. Right there.*

But it wasn't.

And that was okay. I should have realized. That was okay.

Don't worry, Robbie. Don't. Because it will be okay.

I missed him. I missed him so much.

The cab crossed a steel plate at high speed, lifting for a moment into the air, gliding for that second above the plate and the street, my stomach going empty, and there was Cliff, in my mind, so sick these last months.

An image of the mailroom on four, one of a hundred meetings I'd held there with Julie.

The edge of my laptop so square and rigid and at right angles in my hands, and a memory of Leonard.

The vision of Whitley standing at the edge of some workgroup on seventeen, her SWAT team ready to bust a rogue section, Whitley smiling eagerly, childish and driven and watching all at once, Whitley chasing a shadow network she knew nothing about, trailing it half blind through the depths and reaches of the company, in the end coming to me, both of us together, in sex and in safety, hiding out from the world.

I rode through the streets. I saw and heard and felt each memory. All I wanted was to smile.

All I wanted was to cry.

All I wanted was to sleep.

My phone rang. I looked down at the screen. It was Perry.

I didn't answer.

He called again. Then again. The fifth time, I finally answered.

"Was that you I saw leaving the building?" he asked.

And I had to smile.

"I need to see you," Perry said.

It was a moment before I answered. "Maybe tomorrow," I said quietly, the air still pushing through the windows, across my face.

"I need to see you now," Perry said.

"I signed the documents," I said.

"That's why I need to see you now," he said.

"To talk me out of it?" I asked slowly, eyes half closed, the light from the city still crossing, turning, spinning around me.

"Someone's here," Perry said. "You need to talk to him."

I couldn't answer. Actually, I was only barely finding a way to speak at all. I saw the words, pictured my talking, but couldn't find a way to say anything, the wind instead pushing across my mouth and across my face and across my eyes, too strong even for me to push back against it.

"He's here," Perry said. "Here. Talk to him."

And I saw myself hanging up. Saw myself moving the phone from my ear. But still, in the air, there was no way to move my hand or arm.

"Hello," a new voice said. The voice of an old man.

"Robbie," the voice said.

I was trying to lean away from the window, but couldn't.

"We need to talk," the voice said.

I was trying to push back against the air.

"My name is Frederick," it said.

I thought maybe, maybe I could reach the seat in front of me.

"Frederick Fadowsky," it said.

I wanted so much to reach the seat in front of me.

"You and I," it said, "you and I very much need to talk."

The car hit another steel plate in the road, lifting once more, pushing me forward, and now I did float toward the seat in front of me, hand touching it easily, and the air now not pushing against me. Not pushing at all.

"We should talk," I heard myself saying. "Yes, you're right, we should talk now."

I hung up. I pressed my back into the seat. I wished somehow I could sleep, sleep for days, sleep ten days right now in the back of a cab.

But I only asked the driver to turn around. To head downtown. To take me back to my building.

Frederick Fadowsky had been on the phone.

And it's not as if I had anywhere to go.

I was sitting with Fadowsky in the children's chairs in Perry's office, Perry in his small chair at the end of the low conference table. Lines along the wall, twelve inches above the floor, the markings for Perry's raised floor and antechamber.

Fadowsky was the old man from the street, of course. The man I'd mistaken for another wayward father. He was old and gray-haired and slow-moving. But as he sat with us now, he began to smile. Very slightly. Very small. But he began to smile.

"Finally," he said, "finally I have figured it out."

It took a moment for me to respond. To realize what he was saying. "The formula," I said. "Your system. You never understood. You never knew how the formula worked."

He nodded. "It was a mistake," he said. "Simple luck. There was no solution to the formula. Instead the formula worked without my understanding it."

"And so you hid," I said.

He nodded. "In embarrassment. In shame. Sure that, if I didn't, I would be forced to admit that I did not understand how my formula and my boxes worked."

Perry, just barely, had begun to smile.

Fadowsky shrugged now, a full and slow motion that seemed to command all the energy in his body. "I hid. From my lie. An unintended lie. A lie of circumstance. But a lie. I didn't understand what I'd done. And I hid from it."

"But you've figured it out," I said slowly.

"Yes," he said. "And I plan to give the solution to you."

My head was tilting now, slowly, to the left. I said, in a moment, "To me."

Perry had slowly begun to sit forward, staring at me. "To us," Perry said. "But to others also."

"I'm giving it to everyone," Fadowsky said. "I'm giving it to the world."

And I had to smile. Fadowsky, even in this moment, full of grandness and self-importance. Talking as if he were giving some gift to the world, not a mere software program meant simply to pass information at high speed.

What this meant was that Core Communications was about to become worthless. Because now anyone could draw blood from a mainframe. Regence might still want to buy us. But only for scrap. For the equipment, the clients, maybe a few of our people. But otherwise we offered Regence—anyone—nothing unique, nothing special.

And so we would collapse.

"Why did you surface now?" I asked.

He stared at me, confused, his lined, small face pulling inward slightly. "Why now?"

"Yes."

He shook his head. "I'd have never done it," he finally said, "if not for Perry. Your friend Perry here. He found me a few months ago. We talked. Shared ideas. And then he called me a few weeks ago. With a new idea. About the formula."

"An idea," I said.

"He mentioned a program. Some software. Shimmer. He said Shimmer gave him an idea."

Perry was watching Fadowsky. Still smiling just slightly.

"Shimmer solved the formula," Fadowsky said. "Perry gives me the credit. But Shimmer solved the problem."

Perry was watching. Smiling.

"Hiding is an embarrassment in and of itself," Fadowsky said. "For thirty years I've wished I had faced my lie." He stood. He was small. He towered over us in our low chairs. "And now I will."

Perry and I walked Fadowsky downstairs. Watched him wander out into the street.

And somehow that was the moment when I felt most empty. An end so unexpected was being imposed. This company was worthless, the work was done, it was over.

"It's nothing now," I said to Perry, standing in the lobby. Staring up at the mezzanines, toward chairs he and I had sat in just a few months earlier. Where we'd sat and watched this company in motion, in happiness, having restored the network, having done the best work we could do.

Perry nodded. Nodding. But smiling. In a moment, he said, "Maybe."

And he started walking.

And, of course, I followed him.

Into an elevator. Along a hall. Into the DMZ.

He brought up Shimmer. Painted it on the wall.

And there it was.

I saw it immediately.

Saw it in the dense, bottomless funnels and cones.

Saw the answer.

The solution.

Now that Fadowsky would give everyone his formula.

Now there was a solution.

Possible only because Fadowsky would give his formula to the world.

An answer.

So clear and so obvious that I wondered if Perry had made it up. How could the answer be so easy?

So simple.

So real.

Perry was standing a few feet away from me. Staring at the screen. He spoke quietly. "It means giving up everything," he said.

"Yes," I said.

"Satellites," he said. "Servers, mainframes, networking."

"Yes," I said.

"All of the shadow network. And all of your stock," he said. "Everything you have."

"Yes," I said.

"But if you do it," he said, "I think it will work."

And I followed Shimmer as it moved, drifting, building images on the screen. All the pieces, every piece of my shadow network. Each being folded into Core's main systems. The shadow network brought in, no longer separate, now made part of the company. We would expand the capacity of Core Communications twenty to thirty times over. We would bring in the Fadowsky Formula, using it to speed up everything we did. And no one else in the world would have so many satellites, so many mainframes, so many facilities. No one else would be able to work with as many customers as Core. Even Regence would have just a fraction of our abilities.

And it could all be done in just a few weeks.

"Everything," Perry said. "Every machine, every person, every dollar. You give up everything."

I watched Shimmer, tunneling down, seeing farther into each piece, each place, each connection I'd built. I closed my eyes. For that moment it seemed that I was actually asleep. A full and rested and wonderful sleep. I said it again. "Yes."

"I can help you do it," he said.

I felt myself nodding. Eyes open again. But still in that place, a place like sleep, like rest, so quiet and warm and simple and real. "Thank you," I said.

"Is there anything more?" he asked. "Anything that Shimmer has not seen?"

I shook my head. I was smiling now, and I reached my hand out to Perry, held his shoulder, staring at the screen. "There's nothing else. Just this. And all of it, all of it can be given to the company."

He was nodding now, smiling just slightly. But looking at me. "Are you okay?" he asked.

I said it and heard it and saw the words like they were painting themselves across the screen, joining the images of the shadow network as they folded back into Core, Shimmer bringing together these systems and plans and hidden lies and secret places and all of it going back, given up, pulled away from me, and the words I'd said or was about to say or had thought and only now realized hadn't been said aloud, the words circled through me and through Perry and across the screen holding the answer. My answer. My end.

The way to make it work.

"I am wonderful."

There is the annual meeting then. Held in the tall lobby of our building. Two thousand people jammed into every space. A meeting where the rehiring of all our former employees is announced. A meeting where the senior staff honors everyone in the company for incorporating the now public Fadowsky Formula in just a few weeks. A meeting where we welcome our new sales team from a recently purchased company in Omaha.

A meeting where I announce my resignation.

Without the shadow network, there was no reason for me to stay. That had been my job. And my job was done.

Whitley, of course, the new CEO.

There is a party, then, in that same lobby, these people once more happy, once more focused, once more finding a silly joy in it all.

Fadowsky's revelation of a solution to his formula had assured that the stock would be worth much less than ever before. But the company was profitable, sales were good, our client base grew. Because of the shadow network now folded back into the company. Because of

Shimmer now looking at everything we did. Because of the people who'd been here for so long.

But those aren't criteria for a rapidly growing stock.

Grace is reached. But it amounts to far less than had been anticipated.

No one seems to complain much, though.

The people still dancing, turning, shooting toothpicks through the lobby of Core Communications.

I play putt-putt each day during my final month.

I hold transition meetings in the walkways of the building, moving from floor to floor as I pass off everything I know.

I sleep, every night, from ten till morning. Unbroken and full. Sleeping. Sleep.

And so, in the end, I do walk away from Core Communications. Just as my model, my spreadsheets and plans and Shimmer had all foretold.

But I don't walk away with millions. Instead I walk away with nothing.

Nothing except two years of bills to a New York City escort service. A not inconsiderable sum.

Regence continues to compete against Core. But given that its speeds are no different than ours, few companies are interested in signing up with Regence. Says one financial analyst, "No one much likes them, so customers seem to be saying, 'Why work with them if you don't have to?'"

Hardly anyone has claimed to be my mother or father in weeks. Those letters that do straggle in are clearly from people who just aren't in the know.

And yet even those that do come, I throw them away. Unread. These images of a life other than mine. These images of a father who would know what I had done. Some way to believe that maybe this— this work and this life and this lie I'd made for myself—maybe it was all just some small and temporary mistake.

It wasn't small. But it is over.

The last of my stock sold to increase the shadow network even more. The shadow network all moved back into the company. All as Perry had described. All done under the cover of Shimmer. The secrets I had always kept track of within Shimmer were now revealed. More capacity, more equipment, than had ever been made clear.

"It makes sense now," Leonard said.

And Cliff said.

And Julie said it too.

Only Whitley simply stared at me. Smiling slightly. Saying nothing.

And days after I announce my resignation, I start to tell the senior staff the truth. Sitting at a table, Monday morning in what is about to become Whitley's office. All of us pulled up to the new low table she's moved into the room, all of us sitting near the ground in our children's chairs, and I want to tell them the truth. Tell them about the shadow network. My lies. Tell them I am broke. Tell them all the lying is, now, over.

But I don't.

I've taken three years of their lives already. Telling them that all of it had been built on a lie, that would only make them feel like the three years were simply stolen from them.

Really, I'd only have told them to ease my conscience. To receive forgiveness.

And that's not fair to them.

Leonard can look at me for the first time in months. Cliff looks lighter and still and not ready to vomit. Julie no longer seems ready to crush every item within her reach. And Whitley doesn't smoke those invisible cigarettes.

And all of that makes me feel good.

Leonard can look at me again. I shake his hand. I say good-bye. I hold him for just a moment.

Cliff tells me he is going home. At five. Going home, to sleep and eat and play with his kids.

Julie just smiles. She is the shy one, really. And so she just smiles.

And Whitley, she has moved to a new apartment. Has left her marriage. I see her on a weekend. Dinner, and a movie, and what else we do not know.

Except we know we will see each other soon.

She will need to know the truth, I realize. I'll tell her. Not for forgiveness. Or to ease my conscience.

But because I love her.

In those last days before I leave, I try to find Perry. But of course I can't. His office is cleared out. The lights on, brightness flooding his once darkened chamber, and it seems for a second that maybe he hasn't ever been there at all. Sunlight shining through four large windows along the wall.

I'd never known his office even had windows.

And as I walk into the street in front of the Core building on that last day, I hear it and know it before I even look. *Trevor,* on my phone, calling me now from I don't know where. But calling me.

The phone rings again. The letters blink on the screen, then blink again.

Trevor.

I haven't spoken to him in months.

I finally answer.

I have to answer.

"I have an idea," he says.

"Why more ideas?" I ask. I look up, toward the sky, far up above the buildings. "You're a rich man."

"Not really," he said. "All I have left is some shares of Core Communications stock."

"I thought you sold it all."

"I did," he says. "But then I had to buy it back. Buy it, sell it, and keep the stock price up."

And I was smiling.

"It seemed," he says, "like you probably needed a little more time."

And I am smiling, shaking my head, smiling because Trevor has given up everything too.

"And so I have an idea," I hear him saying.

"No ideas," I remember saying.

"But do you want to hear it?" he asks.

"No lies," I remember saying.

"Can I tell you about it?" he asks.

"I don't even have a place to live," I say.

"It's a very simple idea," he says.

"But I'm asking you," I say, "can you do anything without lies?"

"So you will listen to the idea?"

And I can only shake my head, saying again, "No lies."

"I'll try," he says.

"Please," I say.

"No lies," he says.

"Are you sure?"

"Actually," he says slowly, easily, voice near the phone, "actually, I am."

"Where are you?" I ask him.

His voice goes distant, then close as he speaks, somehow circling through the phone, and I picture him walking through an airport, then sitting in a hotel, then entering an office building, then leaving a conference room, then another building, then another plane, and his voice is quiet now, and I smile some as I replay his words.

"I don't know, Robbie," he says. "I don't even know what country I'm in."

"Maybe I can try to find Perry," I say.

"I already did. He's already there. Down the street. There's a building. And we're waiting for you."